The Custard Corpses

A delicious 1940s mystery

M J Porter

M J Publishing

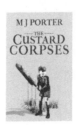

Cover design by Flintlock Covers

Ebook ISBN: 978-1-914332-89-0
Paperback ISBN: 978-1-914332-90-6
Hardback ISBN: 978-1-914332-88-3

This book is dedicated to my forebears who made
Erdington their home and who I never knew.

CONTENTS

PROLOGUE

He looked at the man through narrowed eyes, noting the fine weave on his suit, his knee-high brown riding boots with wry amusement. Really, he thought Lord Fitzpatrick was quite mad.

"I'll pay you handsomely for this. I know of no other with the skills to bring to life the painting and pose as I require it." Fitzpatrick spoke with the condescension due to one of his class when talking to someone they deemed inferior and yet from whom they still wanted something.

He licked his lips in anticipation. Yes, it was a strange and bizarre request, but was that a good enough reason to turn down work that could ensure he never had to slave away as a book-keeper again? That he'd no longer be under the command of Mr Ashley and his stringent and ridiculous demands; that he could live his life as he wanted, as he'd always dreamed.

The temptation was huge, but could he? The client said he had the required talent, but did he? He'd never been allowed to apply the hours to practise his art in the past. His doodles, as his father had always named them derisively, had never achieved any great acclaim.

At least not until now.

And how did Lord Fitzpatrick even know of his skills? It wasn't as though he exhibited his work to more than the few people whose judgements he could tolerate. It was a strange request and yet, still appealing. Perhaps the fewer questions he asked, the better it would be in the long run.

For just the time it took to blink, he considered the legality of what he was doing. Would it get him in trouble with the local constabulary? He shrugged the thought aside. It was little different to those macabre Victorian photographs he'd seen proudly on display in the houses of his father's friends and enemies, so why not?

"I'll do it," he confirmed, detecting the other man's impatience in the way he rubbed his hand over his face, and paced around the small space of his front room. He imagined such circumstances would make any man wary, uneasy, and that was even before the grief was considered.

A sly grin lit the other's face, delight at accomplishing what he wanted in the snap of his sharp eyes. Lord Fitzpatrick's arrogance shone from his eyes as he raked in the small dwelling that was his home. The disdain was evident in the sneer of Fitzpatrick's tight lips. Once more, he felt a slither of unease, but the deed was done now, the agreement made. He'd always been a man of his word. Always.

"Come, tonight. I'll have the car pick you up. Bring everything that you might need. Everything. You'll need to complete the work in one sitting. I'll ensure there are food and drink laid on for you."

"Until tonight." He only just stopped himself from bowing to Fitzpatrick. But no, he didn't need to show that level of respect, not knowing what he knew. Neither, he realised, did he appreciate being spoken to as though he was little more than a beast of burden there to carry out a duty and then to be dismissed to a warm barn.

Again, another thread of fear. He should have been going to the police, reporting what he'd been asked to do, but the thought of such a considerable amount of money was too great a temptation.

Instead, he took the time to prepare what he needed; the brushes, the colours, the canvasses and other items, his sketchbook as well. He didn't know how long the task would take him, but he did know he wouldn't be leaving until it was complete.

Belatedly, he turned to grab a few items of clothing, his razor and his toothbrush. He would need them.

He turned to look around his small home. It was tiny and cramped, the scent of dampness impossible to completely drive away, no matter that he kept the fire burning brightly even in the summer months. It cost him a vast amount of his meagre salary earned from being a bookkeeper. But no more. Once his task was completed, he need never come here again.

He found a smile tugging at his tight lips at the thought of his suddenly much brighter future, at the idea of accomplishing so much more than his doubting father had ever believed him capable.

He would turn his back on this house and this life, and he need never look back. Never. It would be as though these thirty years of his life had never existed.

Freedom from the drudgery of day to day work, that's all he'd ever wanted, and now it was to be his.

From outside, he heard the unusual sound of a rumbling motor engine, and he quickly scanned the front room, just to check he had everything he needed ready and waiting. Content that he did, as his eyes swept over the three bags he'd prepared, one full of paints and brushes, he collected his possessions and opened the door wide.

It was dark outside, with nothing more than the chink of light through curtains to show him a final glance of his home. The cold weather ensured everyone stayed inside no matter the unusual arrival of a car on the quiet street. No one wished to find trouble when they could ignore it inside their snug front rooms. The fire kept the cold at bay until they needed to use the outdoor toilet or make their way up to their freezing bedroom, blankets piled high on hard beds, the floor cold to a naked foot.

He nodded to the chauffeur, noting his smart clothing, neat hairstyle and unshaven face. This man had freedom of sorts, but still, he was in the employ of his master and must run to follow his wishes, no matter the time of day. There was no expression on his face, just cool efficiency in concise movements.

Soon, well soon, he'd have the same expensive clothes, made to last and to look smart. Perhaps, he considered, he might even invest in an expensive motor car. How he'd love to drive along the lanes at high speeds, scaring those consigned to the verges, carts and horses, as he flew passed.

He slammed the door sharply behind him, only belatedly thinking to lock it. His thoughts were already on the future and not the past. He looked down at the keys in his hand, considering what he should do with them. But despite his dreams for the following days and all those after them, he knew better than to count the money before he had it in his hand.

He pocketed the keys in his ancient overcoat. If Fitzpatrick stinted him, or if he was caught, he would need somewhere to hide away. He would need the house at his back.

But, he hoped, as the rumble of the engine thrummed through his body, that he'd never see this street again, never endure the knowing looks of the matriarchs at his unmarried state at such an age, never shudder to see the grey of his white washing when he'd made a mistake with it, never have to endure the snide remarks from the children who all repeated what their parents said in private, only in front of him.

No, he'd not miss this place. Not at all.

CHAPTER 1

ERDINGTON, OCTOBER 1943

S am bit back the cry of pain, coming to an abrupt stop. The pavement was shaded with the colour of the advancing night, but even so, he knew where the uneven step was. He really shouldn't have kicked it. Not again. Would he never learn?

He blinked the tears from his eye and lifted his right hand to rub it over the ache of his lower back. All these years, and still it hurt. It would never stop. He knew it, and yet sometimes, he forgot, all the same, only to be rudely reminded when he over-balanced or attempted to take a step that was just too wide.

There was a reason he was here and not on one of the many front lines of this terrible war, the second in his lifetime. There was a reason he was here while his son, John, fought in his place.

His breath rasped through his suddenly tight chest, and yet the thin shard of light from behind the tightly closed curtains encouraged him on. Inside, there was companionship, and it drove him onwards, made him quest to be a better man. Despite the fact he knew it wasn't true.

"Come on," he urged himself, and although it was going to ache, he forced his legs to move, left, then right, then left, and his hand reached up to push the welcoming door open.

Appetising smells greeted him, and he dredged a smile to his face, turning to hang his hat on the waiting peg and to shrug the overcoat from his thin shoulders, revealing his policeman's uniform beneath. The blue so dark; it was almost black. He hooked his gas mask above his overcoat. There in case he should require it. But no bombs had fallen for half a year now. He hoped none ever would again. No voice was raised in greeting to his noisy arrival. It never was.

With the door closed and locked behind him, he slipped his feet from his black shoes, using one foot to force down the ankle and then doing the same in his socked-feet. It was better than being forced to bend when his back was so painful, even if it was destroying the back of his shoes, as his wife complained whenever she witnessed it. He'd taken to hiding his work shoes behind the boots he wore to the allotment. Better that Annie did not see them.

Opening the door that led into the heart of his home, he paused, just watching her for a heartbeat.

"Evening, love." He bent to place a kiss on his wife's head, refusing to notice the thinning brown hair, the streaks of grey making up more and more of it as the years passed. A skeletal hand reached up to grip his, and he squeezed tightly, settling beside her at the table.

A single lamp afforded the only light in the small kitchen, a warm fire burning in the hearth in the sitting room as he settled beside her. His wife didn't so much as look at him, and he considered that she didn't want to see the ruin of her husband.

Time hadn't been kind to either of them and yet he couldn't help but be grateful for the years they'd had together. It could have been so different. So many of his brothers-in-arms lost fighting over two decades ago. They would have loved to live long enough to see the ravages of time etched into their skin and their characters, to grow weary with aches and pains, to learn the experiences that only time could afford.

A flurry of movement from Annie, and a plate was placed on the table before him, the lid swept aside. The steam took only a moment to clear, and he suppressed his rumbling stomach. It was a meal as any other day, not particularly appetising, and yet, food all the same. He was grateful for the potatoes, harvested from their garden, and the gleaming orange carrots, if not for the small sausages. Gravy pooled around the meat, and he closed his eyes, imagining a feast fit for a king, before meticulously cutting, eating and savouring every mouthful.

His wife didn't speak, and neither did he. No doubt, she was as caught up in her thoughts as he was in his.

He considered reaching for his newspaper, but instead, his eyes were fixed by the bright image that lay open on the magazine discarded on the table before him. The Picture Post. Was there ever a magazine more filled with stories that titillated while offering little or no actual facts?

Not that he ever complained. Not anymore. If she enjoyed the stories and bright images of the adverts, then why should he? Anything that distracted her from the constant worry about their son. Anything.

Now, he found a smile tugging on his lips, and his mind cast him back to when his son had been a small boy. John had delighted in such simple antics as that on display. The custard advert enticed all parents to part with their hard-earned ration coupons. He couldn't see that a liberal dollop of the sugary, creamy mixture would help any child become an athlete, professional cricket player or ballerina, but what did he know? He was just an old man, with a job that kept him busy and an ache in his heart where his youth had once been.

Sam reached for the folded newspaper, the smirk still playing on his lips.

"Don't." His wife's voice shocked him, sounding more formidable than he'd heard for the last few years, ever since their son had left to fight Britain's fresh battles against the might of Hitler and Germany.

He lifted his eyes to find hers boring into his.

"Don't," and now there was more softness, but it was too late. His eyes had alighted on what she'd been trying to keep from him.

Once more, he felt an unbidden tear form in the corner of his eye as he gazed at the hazy black and white photograph. Not that he didn't know it intimately. He did. He'd stared at that image, and others besides, until they were emblazoned on his very soul, overriding even the final images of his lost comrades from the Great War, the war to end all wars. How wrong they'd been.

He swallowed, the burn making it feel as though it were cardboard and not the remnants of his dinner that he evacuated from his mouth.

"Again?" he felt the need to say something.

"Again," she replied, and there was understanding and sorrow in that look, and he didn't want any of it. He didn't want to add to her fears and worries with his own.

"It was a long time ago," he tried to reassure, reaching for her hand and encasing it within his. It was no longer soft but instead forged in iron, the wiry strength surprising him, even though it shouldn't, not after all this time.

"It rolls around too quickly, these days," a hint of a smile on her thin lips, blue eyes glistening with sorrow, and he realised that she was trying to reassure him. He hated it that she felt the necessity.

"And still, there's no closure for the family."

"No. But they're not alone in that. Not anymore." Her voice trailed off as she spoke, and he turned to gaze into the glow from the table lamp, allowing it to haze in front of him. She was right in that, as well. Many would never hold the knowledge of what exactly happened to their loved ones. Yet, there was a world of difference between adults and children. It was the fact he'd been a child that cut the deepest.

His mind returned to that terrible day. How could it not? He'd been a young man, wounded and broken after his time at The Front, but at least he'd still breathed. Not like the splayed body found in the undergrowth close to the church hall, eyes forever staring. Somehow, the rigour mortis of a smile on that cherubic face, so that anyone could be forgiven for thinking the boy was merely caught in the act of playing hide and seek.

But the face had been blue and white, the eyeballs rimmed with the grey haze of death that he'd come to know so well during his time in the trenches before his injury had ensured he need never revisit the place.

In the faded light of the lamp, he watched the scene, as though he'd been a bird, able to watch from above. His eyes alighted, not on the corpse, but rather on his Chief Inspector, the man who'd made him who he was today, and yet who'd been broken by the failure to solve the death of the boy.

Sam found a soft smile playing around his lips. Fullerton had been a meticulous man, with his long mackintosh and tightly wedged police hat covering the tendrils of greying hair showing beneath it and in the sideburns that snaked down to meet the dark moustache quivering over his lips. Many would have been forgiven for thinking he had no compassion for the corpse. But no, he'd had more than most, but he had desired to solve the case, to bring the perpetrator to justice. It was a source of unending disquiet that it had never been possible.

It had marked him from that day he'd found Robert's body to the day of his death.

It hadn't been Sam's first case, far from it, but it had felt like it. He'd learned so much, and yet it had never been enough. Not for young Robert McFarlane and his family.

He swallowed once more, his keen memory fastening on the scene. Or rather, on the way that the body had been presented. The murderer hadn't killed young Robert beside the church hall behind the High Street. In fact, they'd never found the place the murder had truly taken place, only where the body had been found.

Sam thought of Mrs McFarlane, her tear-streaked face, her shaking shoulders. Her oldest son, taken from her, just as her husband had been by the enemy's bullets during the Great War. There'd been so much grief and loss in the years during and after the war, if not dead on some far-flung battlefield, then carried away by the terrible Spanish influenza. It had all seemed never-ending. And then, the spark of an untainted future when all had seemed calmer, taken between one breath and the next.

Sam had never seen grief festoon someone so entirely. As Chief Inspector Fullerton had told her the news, she'd aged before their eyes. It had taken his quick reflexes to ensure she didn't collapse to the floor on the bright red doorstep, her young daughters, wide-eyed and sobbing as they watched their mother, hands clasped tightly together, as though they could hold their mother up with such an act.

There'd been a time when Sam had wished Chief Inspector Fullerton hadn't told Mrs McFarlane in such a way, his words hard and unfeeling, and yet, he'd come to appreciate that there was no right and wrong way to impart such terrible news. It was almost a kindness to say the words, 'your son is dead,' as quickly as possible. There was no need to use superfluous words, to offer sympathy, to say anything but the facts.

Her accusing eyes had followed him through the years. Why they'd said that day and many days since, is my son dead, while yours yet lives?

It was not Mrs McFarlane who'd marked the anniversary of her son's death, each and every year for the last twenty years, but rather, her daughter. The older one, Rebecca, had taken on the responsibility for ensuring that no one ever forgot her brother when her mother sadly passed away, worn down by grief and loss, by the need to survive in a world turned upside down, with nothing but a war pension to ease the burdens.

It was Rebecca who routinely sent letters asking for updates on the case. It was Rebecca that he tried to avoid at all costs when he saw her at church, on the tram or along the High Street. It was Rebecca who'd broken Chief Inspector Fullerton, in a rare show of emotion that shocked him to recall, even now. He'd never seen Fullerton like that. He'd never imagined Fullerton could be so very emotional that tears would run from his brown eyes, that he'd tear at what remained of his hair in frustration.

Chief Inspector Fullerton had retired a few years ago, but he'd not lived long enough to enjoy it. Sam shook his head. One murder and so many lives destroyed, and still, the murderer was out there, perhaps hiding, perhaps luxuriating in what he'd managed to get away with, or maybe, he was dead as well, getting away with his crime for all time. Twenty years was a long time.

Sam was snapped from his reveries by a bowl appearing before him. Somehow, he'd become so lost in the past; he'd not even heard his wife stand at the stove for the last many minutes.

A cheeky smile from her, driving away the wrinkles and the grey streaks in her hair, making her look twenty years younger, and he looked down at the bowl before him.

"Custard?" he asked, enjoying the unusual light-hearted look on her face.

"I know it's your favourite. There's even some apple in there, somewhere, and some blackberries, picked from the country lane on my walk yesterday afternoon to Pype Hayes Park."

"How did you get it?" he asked, eagerly spooning the sweet mixture into his mouth.

"I've been saving my packets. I didn't tell you. I knew you wouldn't be able to wait."

"Then you have my thanks," he grinned, fully returning to the present. He couldn't do anything about the past. No matter how much he wished he could.

"This is delicious," he complimented his wife, leaning back, hand on his full belly.

"Well, now you just need to wait another year, and then you can have more." But there was a lightness to her voice when she spoke, and the flash of joy in her eyes cheered him. There was so much wrong with the world at the moment, and yet here, beside his wife, in their cosy front room, everything was well. Even if only for now.

CHAPTER 2

Sam Mason settled into the uncomfortable hard-backed chair with a grimace that only intensified when he realised that someone had been kind enough to leave him a copy of yesterday's Birmingham Mail on his immaculately tidy desk. He didn't like anything to be out of place. Neither did he appreciate the reminder, not after the convivial evening he'd enjoyed with his wife.

He glanced around the room, considering who it might be, only for his eyes to settle on Sergeant Jones' stubborn back. It would be him. He was sure of it. Jones had been around back then. His resentment at never advancing beyond the role of sergeant was matched only by his maliciousness towards Sam, especially considering the McFarlane case. Jones had always believed he could solve it. The fact that all of his leads had been useless and had never amounted to anything didn't seem to concern Jones. He was sure he'd been right, and that was all that mattered.

Yet, he didn't want to give Jones the satisfaction of knowing that the paper upset him. Instead, he unfolded it and once more peered at the black and white image of young Robert, taken from a school photograph, the rest of his classmates removed.

Robert had been a lively child, a little bit cheeky because his mother had allowed him far more leeway than his younger sisters. And yet, for all that, there didn't seem to be anything malicious about Robert. He'd been a good lad, bright at school. His teacher, the strict and unbending, Mr Williamson, had condescended to admit that, even while looking down his nose at the Chief Inspector. And Robert had been a firm friend of John's. That had accounted for more in Sam's eyes than anything anyone could have said about him.

Sam had liked Robert. He'd made him smile with his bright humour.

Jones had been convinced that Mr Williamson, Robert's teacher, had known more than he'd ever said, but Sam had never agreed. Mr Williamson had been as scarred as the rest of them by the events of the Great War. Jones had simply refused to see it and still did, even though he'd not been recalled with the outbreak of the new war. Sam found it ironic that Jones claimed to understand so much when he couldn't even determine his personal motivations.

Robert hadn't deserved such a death. There might well have been a smile on the boy's face when he was found, but he knew it would have been a terrifying and painful death.

"Mason," Sam found his eyes rising from the newspaper to fasten on Constable Williams. He was young, filled with enthusiasm, his uniform smart and bright, the numbers on his collar easy to read. His blue eyes offered the hint of an apology from beneath his smartly cut brown hair.

"What is it?" there was exhaustion in Sam's voice, and he cursed Jones for it when the day had only just begun.

"Sorry, Chief Inspector, but she's here." There was no need to explain who 'she' was. Williams had managed to lower his voice, knowing not to alert Jones.

"Bring her in, and make her a cup of tea. A decent cup of tea," he commanded with a caution, moving to fold the newspaper once more and place it in the top drawer of his desk. There'd be no need for Rebecca to see it. She would have reminded the newspaper of the anniversary; he was sure of it.

"Miss McFarlane," he stood to greet her, noting her carefully styled hair, the figure-hugging coat and the smart leather shoes on her feet. Rebecca smiled shyly at him, pulling her gloves from her long fingers, and he felt a flicker of delight as he saw the sparkling band around her ring finger.

"Not for much longer," she exclaimed, her voice high and bright, as she delicately touched his hand with her own and settled onto the seat on the far side of his desk. Her voice was filled with excitement, very different to the young woman who'd sat there last year and in all the years since her mother had died.

Rebecca had grown into a careful young woman, minding her words, warding her emotions; Sam had considered how scared she must be, all the time, that those she loved could just be taken from her, without any warning. Now, it seemed, something had changed that.

"Congratulations," he complimented her, hoping her beau was not off fighting in the damn war.

"Thank you. We'll be married when Frank is next back for his leave." He nodded, keeping the smile on his face, even though his heart sank at the news. She was an attractive young woman, blessed with a fuzz of curly blond hair and bright blue eyes. But her mobile face and slim build masked the turmoil she'd felt ever since that terrible day when Fullerton had knocked on her door.

A brief silence filled the space between them, and then they both opened their mouths to speak simultaneously, and he indicated she should go first.

"Thank you," she muttered. "I just came because I always do. I know you won't have discovered anything new. I trust you to tell me, even amid this horrible war. But, I didn't know what else to do with myself, not today." Her hands twisted one inside the other, speaking of her unease.

Such a terrible day to try and skip over every year. He knew how hard it was. He could try and forget, but he always remembered, no matter what. In the years immediately after Robert's murder, it had been his son's confused face that had begged him to remember, had forced him to pick over once more the notes of the case on the anniversary, see if there was something new to investigate.

With every one of John's birthdays, Sam had thought of Robert. And he knew his wife did the same, as did John. He'd failed his son, or so it had always felt. John, so proud that his father was a policeman, and had fought in the Great War to protect them all, had never understood why he'd not been able to protect his friend, Robert.

As Rebecca spoke, Williams placed an ungainly mug of muddy looking tea before her and even a plate with four dry biscuits on it. Rebecca turned and thanked him with a smile that flashed bright teeth behind her red lipstick. Williams flushed with pleasure. Sam didn't have the heart to demand where his mug of tea was. Perhaps he'd not been clear enough. These recruits didn't have the sense with which they were born.

"I saw the paper last night," Sam confirmed. "I was expecting you. And no, I've nothing new to offer. It's been many years now, and while I would hope one day to catch the perpetrator, I just don't know if that's possible. Not now."

Rebecca nodded, almost too eagerly, her hand hovering over the mug of tea, waiting to pick it up until the movement had stopped. Her cheeks were flushed, and he wondered what else she'd come to tell him.

"I don't truly know what I'd do if we ever found who murdered my brother. I like to think I wouldn't spit in their face, but I can't make such a promise. He'd have been a man now, probably off fighting in the war and maybe with children of his own. He certainly wouldn't be the brother I remember when I think about him, the one who used to pull my hair and laugh at my squint."

He nodded. Rebecca was wise beyond her years. She always had been.

"And how is your sister?"

Rebecca lifted the mug to her lips to cover her feelings, but he knew that the younger sister had struggled through the death of her brother and mother. It was unlikely that she'd ever marry.

"Patricia lives with my Aunt now, in Weston. They, well, it pains me to say it, but they're good for each other. Both of them live firmly in the past. My Aunt lost her husband in the Great War as well and her only son in the air raids a few years ago on Weston. She married a wealthy man, though, and has enough money to support them both without either needing to work. It's just better this way, although I do miss her."

There was both regret and relief in Rebecca's voice, and he well understood it. Living with the embodiment of what had happened was a draining experience. It seemed right that at least one of Robert's sisters were able to live a full life, as untainted as it could be, by what had befallen him.

"That's why I'm here, actually," Rebecca's sudden change of tack startled him, and he realised she was fumbling in her petite blue handbag, the shade perfectly matching her coat. He almost groaned when she pulled a crumpled newspaper from its reaches and passed it across the desk, over the plate of untouched biscuits. He was just about to say that he already had one when his eyes focused on the headline.

"The Weston Mercury," and then he scanned down, and he couldn't help himself. His hand snaked the newspaper towards him, his eyes focused on the grainy image of the smiling boy who looked so much like Robert. He checked the date, a month old, and then he read the headline.

"Murder victim would have turned twenty-four today. Family still seeking answers."

He glanced at Rebecca.

"What is this?"

"I found it on the train, on the way home. It reminded me of what happened to Robert."

Sam was already nodding, his mind trying to filter through the possibilities. It was all too familiar.

"But we asked other forces, and none of them ever said they'd had anything similar."

"This was after Robert's death," and her red-polished nail pointed out the date when the young lad had disappeared and been found murdered. There were few enough details, not so long after the fact, yet he could immediately see why Rebecca had brought him the newspaper.

"I'll look into this," he promised, already feeling a strange stirring of anticipation. After all this time, was it truly possible that their murderer had struck again? Had Robert's death not been an isolated occurrence?

"I thought you might," Rebecca nodded, relief on her young face. He had the feeling she'd been torn about whether to share the information or not.

"You've done the right thing, thank you. I'll get in touch with the police force in Weston and see what they can tell me."

"It was a long time ago," she breathed, as though already resigned to failure.

"It was, yes. But it could make it easier, perhaps. It might not, and it could all be happenstance, but it feels like too much of a coincidence to me. I've always wanted to solve this, as did the Chief Inspector before me. I'll do what I can, and I'll keep you informed. Are you still at the same address?"

Rebecca was already shaking her head.

"No, when my sister moved away, I decided to make a fresh start as well. You can find me at 56 Bracken Road now. I should have made the change years ago, but well, something kept me at the old address, some half-hope that he might come home one day. I know it's ridiculous, but well, I can't deny that I didn't think it might all be a nightmare that I might wake from one day. I didn't want him to come home and find no one he knew at the old house."

Wisely, Sam held his tongue, allowing the flurry of emotions to calm on her reddened face. When he thought she was in control of herself once more, he changed the conversation, even as he pulled the newspaper to one side and placed it with the more local edition that showed her brother's photograph.

"Tell me, what does your beau do?"

"He's a mechanic in the air force."

"A clever man, then?" The news cheered him. A mechanic was more valuable than a pilot. There was hope that he wouldn't be sent into the fray anytime soon, provided he wasn't in the firing line of the air raids.

Rebecca's face glowed again, and she nodded rather than speak.

He stood, and she followed him, as he'd hoped.

"I'll see you out. But, I'll follow this up, and thank you for bringing it to me." He couldn't deny that even the glance he'd had of the boy and the details of his murder had sent a spurt of energy into his tired, broken body. Could this be it? After all this time, could there be the possibility of solving the crime that had driven his old Chief Inspector into an early grave? He certainly hoped there was.

CHAPTER 3

"**W**hat do you think of this?" Sam slid the newspaper toward his new superintendent. The man was younger than him and had only come to the station after the furore of the unsolved murder had long since settled down. Smythe knew of it without being stained by the failure of it. It was a position Sam thought he might have enjoyed.

"What?" He might have been younger, but the superintendent's eyesight was poor. Sam took pity on the superintendent and thrust the newspaper even closer over the old wooden desk, pitted and marked by years of action, but serviceable all the same.

It took only moments for Superintendent Smythe to absorb the details from the Weston Mercury. And he was a quick-thinking man. Immediately, a flicker of understanding spread around his scrunched-up eyes.

"Who brought this in?"

"Rebecca McFarlane. She saw it and thought it might be relevant."

"Might be relevant!" Smythe exclaimed, sitting back in his chair and meeting Sam's eyes with a hint of reproach in them. "Didn't the station inform every district of what had happened here, Sam?" The accusation stung; he couldn't deny it. He paused to allow himself the time needed to remove the outrage from his voice. He was always amazed by how raw the experience remained.

"Of course, they did. But nothing ever came back to us. I'm not surprised. This is dated after the death of Robert. They'd probably forgotten about it by then or never known about it in the first place."

"Bloody hell. This could be it. You need to get in touch with them and see if it's worth travelling down to look at all the evidence. Just think about it, if we managed to solve the case, after all these years!" Sam couldn't deny that he shared Smythe's enthusiasm, but he didn't want to look too keen, not without official sanction. He'd heard of the chief inspectors who became obsessed with long-unsolved cases. He didn't want to be thought of in the same way as those other 'crackpots,' laughed about by their fellow officers and derided by the superintendents who'd risen above the scandal. Sam was only too aware of what others had said about Fullerton.

"So, you think it might be important?"

"It can't hurt to find out more. You know the case well. You know the questions to ask. See if you can speak to the Chief Inspector who investigated the case. And if not, then have them hunt out the case file."

Sam nodded.

"I'll get on with it now." And he turned to leave, only for Smythe to call him back.

"Shut the door, would you," he cautioned, and Sam did as asked before turning an arched eyebrow to look at his superior. Smythe was a fit man. He wore his old army wound lightly and had never let it stop him from accomplishing a great many achievements. Yet, in the wrong light, it was still possible to see the puckered skin that ran down the left side of his face and beneath the neckline of his police tunic. That it made his eye useless, even while it looked normal, often fooled anyone who didn't know him.

"Sam, I know you're closely tied to this case. But equally, it was over two decades ago. If you don't want to follow up, I'll understand, I really will, but I can't give it to Jones. He couldn't find a grain of sand on a beach at low tide."

Sam grunted. Smythe wasn't one to share confidences such as this.

"I appreciate that, but yes, I want to do this. I owe it to the old Chief Inspector."

"Good, that's settled then, and try and keep Jones away from it all. Daft old git will only try and interfere, and he's lethal enough with a pencil and the sugar jar without him trying to catch a murderer. It would be good if we could catch the bastard and bring some closure for the family. With all that's going on now, even something as old as this being solved would cheer people. No one should get away with murder. No one."

"I'll let you know how I get on," Sam assured before opening the door and returning to his desk.

Not that he immediately contacted the police station in Weston. No, Jones seemed to have realised that something was amiss. He kept casting narrow-eyed glances towards Sam all morning, even as he got on with the tedium of filing and signing reports on anything from petty theft of milk bottles to the more heinous crime of counterfeiting ration books. Sam shook his head. Didn't these people realise there was a war on and that they should all be acting as one for the greater good? Evidently not.

Eventually, Jones was called away or went out for his lunch. Sam put down his pencil and made his way to the single telephone at the front desk.

O'Rourke was on duty, a bright young woman, with her hair tightly braided close to her head, visible beneath the smart hat she wore, whenever anyone walked into the police station. The rest of the time, she kept it close but didn't wear it. Sam didn't blame her. With such a hair design, he'd have wanted to show it off as well. He smiled at her as she moved out of his way quickly, her brown eyes intelligent in a chestnut face. He liked what he'd seen of O'Rourke. She was undoubtedly far more sensible than Williams.

"The Chief Inspector knows about this call, but no one else. I know I can trust you," Sam commented, and she nodded, her cheeks darkening at the compliment. It was no secret that Jones meddled in everything. It was in everyone's best interests to keep as much from him as possible. When he'd drunk more than his fill in the local public house, Jones was likely to regale any unfortunate soul with even the most secret details obtained during police work. He'd been hauled over the coals more than once about it, and yet, Jones would never learn, and the complaints would routinely arrive when he said too much and upset the locals.

"Weston Police, please," he spoke into the receiver, and in no time at all, he heard the elongated ring of the call being placed. It always surprised him, the telephone. It was so quick and also so impersonal. He much preferred being able to watch the facial expressions of the person with whom he was talking.

"Weston," the accent rolled, and Sam almost repeated the word, just to confirm, but he didn't.

"This is Chief Inspector Mason, from Erdington Police Station. Do you still have a Chief Inspector Allan there? I'd like to speak to them about an old case."

"Allan?" The voice sounded perplexed for a moment.

"Ah, you mean old Bill. Sorry, he retired seven years ago. He's living in the countryside now, milking cows or growing grapes. I can't quite remember."

"Is there anyone else who could help me? It's about the McGovern murder."

"McGovern?" The man seemed unaware of the case.

"Hang on, I'll get Superintendent Hatly. He might know what you're talking about." The receiver's sound being placed down on the desk jolted Sam, and he held the telephone away from his ear, listening to the distant tread of footsteps and people speaking, the words indecipherable over the crackling handset. It seemed to take at least five minutes, but then the receiver was gathered together again.

"Hatly here. Who is this?"

"I'm Chief Inspector Mason, from Erdington. I have a few questions about the McGovern case."

"Gods man, that's nearly two decades old. Why would you be asking now?"

"We have an older case. There might be a connection. Another young boy murdered. Possibly in similar circumstances, but I only have a newspaper cutting from the Weston Mercury to go on."

"What, after all this time? Why didn't you ask before?" The flicker of temper brought a tight smile to Sam's face. He recognised the feeling all too well.

"Well." Couldn't the Superintendent decipher it for himself? "Your case happened three years after ours. It should really have been the other way round." A resounding silence greeted his words, and he could hear the other man breathing heavily. Not the most pleasant of sounds, even with the crackling line.

"I think you should probably come down, take a look at our case notes, bring your own as well. There's no one left in the department who worked that case, but we've lived with the legacy of it. Can you come tomorrow?" There was a flicker of hope, mingled with resignation in the request.

Sam wasn't entirely sure if he could make it the following day but then realised that O'Rourke was sliding a train timetable along the chest-high workstation. He noted the details on the cover, smiling at her in thanks because it was the correct timetable for the trains that ran from Birmingham to Weston. He hadn't even realised they had such information to hand. It was even in date. Quickly, he ran his eyes over the list of times, nodding as he did so.

"Yes, yes, I think I can do that. I'll arrive at about 12 pm. Will that be okay with you?"

"Yes, we'll send a car to meet the train. It can be a bit of a trek if you don't know where you're going."

"Until tomorrow then," Sam agreed and replaced the handset when Hatly said his farewells.

"Thank you," he said to O'Rourke, his mind busy mulling over everything he'd learned.

"Sounds like you're off on a nice trip," O'Rourke offered, her words lyrical, no doubt because tomorrow would find her doing what she always did, taking reports of missing items, consoling mothers who'd lost their small children and small children who'd lost their mothers. It wasn't as though there was a great deal going on in the sleepy settlement.

The terrible reports of air raids were few and far between now —a welcome change, but one that made the day to day tasks even more tedious. But, better tedium than the horrors of broken homes, businesses, and worst of all, bodies.

"Maybe. But I've never really enjoyed a train ride. It makes me feel a bit ill."

"Sit facing forwards," O'Rourke offered eagerly. "It helps me. My brother can only travel backwards, but I prefer forwards. Not that you can see where you're going, but watching the scenery slip by in front of you is better than watching it after you've gone through it, all mingled with the smoke from the train." Her words rolled with her accent, the hint of warmth oozing from them. It almost made him shiver, especially when the door whipped open, caught by a stray gust of wind that brought a small trail of wrinkled and brown leaves inside the door.

"Thanks for the advice. Now, I need to find those case notes."

O'Rourke nodded. "Leave it with me. I'll cross-reference them and bring them to you, discreetly," she assured. The front door opened again, and Jones walked inside jauntily. His small eyes flickered between O'Rourke and Sam, but he said nothing, even though he must have been curious. He was always inquisitive. And still, he was remarkably ineffective. Sam laughed softly to himself at the thought.

"Thank you. Now, do you want your lunch, and I'll stay out here for the next half an hour. It'll give Jones long enough to forget his questions."

"Right you are," O'Rourke eagerly agreed, a rumbling stomach assuring Sam that he'd done the right thing. He could ponder what he might find tomorrow just as easily on front desk duty as he could sitting at his desk.

CHAPTER 4

T he landscape flashed before his eyes quickly, stray puffs of smoke occasionally obscuring his view, and he felt the familiar unease in his stomach. Still, he had to confess, O'Rourke was right; just changing his position in the carriage was making it less severe than expected.

He was settled in a carriage. There could have been another three people with him, but he was alone, and he relished the quiet, and the mechanical clanking of the wheels over the train line, the scent of smoke and coal in the air. There was an order in the sound that he could appreciate, like the ticking of a clock.

In his hand, he held not his old notebook, or indeed his current one, but rather Chief Inspector Fullerton's notebook. He'd found it in the case files for Robert McFarlane, and rather than bring the bulky file; he carried just the notebook. It contained all the information he felt was relevant. Fullerton had been a fastidious man.

Not that it was easy reading, or at least, it wasn't, unless you held the notebook, with its stained and yellowing pages, at a slight angle. Only then did the spiralling scrawl of Fullerton become legible. The man hadn't so much written, as disgorged all relevant pieces of information in a system that started orderly and quickly became a myriad assortment of random facts and even stranger observations.

But the information was extremely valuable, and it reminded Sam of just how much he was missing without the steadying presence of Fullerton at his side. The man had been old and tired, a chief inspector for decades, not just years, and yet he'd known his stuff. He'd never failed before, not until the case of young Robert.

Now, Sam concentrated on the pen drawing that Fullerton had made of the boy's body. He'd flicked through the black and white crime photographs, the yellow edges speaking of their age, the starkness of those staring eyes seeming to reach out to him over the years since the boy's death. It had been unsettling. It was easier to look at the drawing to distance himself from the extinguished life. After everything he'd seen and endured in the trenches, still, the splayed body of that boy haunted him.

While some still woke to hear the guns and the sound of bombs falling, it was the white, marbled face of Robert that had plagued Sam's dreams for nearly a decade until he'd managed to banish it. But, he was sure that Robert would be back, soon, if this new but old case proved to be at all relevant.

Sam focused on the drawing of the body Fullerton had sketched in the notebook. It had always felt unnatural, even more so than just any dead body. In death, Robert's eyes had remained open, his clothes apparently undisturbed, his school uniform seemingly as clean as when he'd first donned it, three days before he'd been found, his cap still on his head.

Even his long, white sock had been devoid of all stains and had stayed up firmly, close to his knee, his polished shoes showing not so much as a scuff mark. The only mystery had been where his other sock had gone because he wore both shoes. For all that, Sam had thought the corpse looked as though it moved. It was still, and yet not still. It had always perplexed him, and Fullerton had shared his concerns.

It was the single-most horrific murder scene he'd ever been forced to visit, and not because Robert had been so young. It wasn't as though he'd not solved other child murders, unfortunately. He'd never understood the desire to kill the coming generation.

Sam closed his eyes, focused on the memories he had, which didn't involve looking. The smell of the undergrowth, the richness of the soil on which the body had been placed. The use of the word forced his eyes open. Placed. He didn't think he'd ever managed to find a name for what he'd seen, but now he felt that was it. His murderer had arranged Robert. Whoever had killed the boy, ostensibly without touching him, although the doctor asserted that he'd been drowned, had been making a statement. The corpse hadn't been left like that by chance.

Sam flicked through the notebook again. Had Fullerton realised but never done anything about it?

Pages and pages of scrawl greeted his eyes. There were names, addresses, some telephone numbers, details of where people had been during the period Robert had been missing, even little maps showing the road layouts of the surrounding area, the school, and the church hall where the body had been found, separated by a quiet road, an expanse of fields stretching out behind it, the idea of space impossible to ignore.

What had always perplexed Fullerton was the lack of evidence found on or near to the body. They'd searched those fields stretching out behind the church hall; they'd searched the church hall, even closing the road and checking the thick undergrowth on hands and knees, finding all sorts of objects that didn't need mentioning. People would cast off all kinds of rubbish while walking along. There had been some sweet wrappers, but they'd proven to be nothing more than one of the local children, notorious for discarding his wrappers when he walked to and from school.

They'd hoped to find some sort of tire tread, or even horses hooves, anything that might have shown where the body had come from because it had quickly become evident that Robert had been murdered somewhere other than beneath the reaching branches of the oak tree. The place had been far too clean for a child to have died there, even without the problem of the lack of water in which a child could drown.

Surely Robert would have fought? But if so, where was the evidence for it? Even his nails had been clean, a fact that had upset his mother, for she'd been adamant that he'd not cleaned his hands the last morning she'd seen him. She'd sobbed at the news, wondering why Robert had cleaned his nails when he'd never done so for her before.

The train rumbled to a stop in a shriek of brakes and wheels, distracting Sam from his reverie as it pulled into Bristol. He gathered his things together and changed from the Bristol train to the one heading for Weston. It all went surprisingly well. He'd been concerned there might be a problem, after the delay in Birmingham first thing, when they'd been forced to wait for a freight train to rumble through; of course, it was the priority, not where police inspectors needed to go to solve decades-old cases.

Sam settled into yet another empty carriage, still thinking of the old case. So much of what had happened to Robert didn't make sense. Was it possible that he might finally be able to answer the questions? He both hoped it would, even while guilt made him wish that they'd done more to solve the case when it had happened. Perhaps then the other child would have lived.

Sam found his head dropping back; the early morning started having an effect, so he folded the notebook and placed it in his inner pocket. The number 64 tram had left Erdington High Street while it had still been dark, taking him to Steelhouse Lane, where he'd had to walk to New Street Station. He'd shivered into his thick coat, a slither of worry for the coming harshness of winter—another winter, and who knew what it might bring. Yes, there seemed to have been a let-up in the night raids, no bombs had fallen since April of that year, but he knew better than to think it was all over. Still, he felt he could risk a nap now.

When he woke, the train was pulling into another station, and blearily, he realised it had arrived at Weston.

He stepped from the carriage, patting his coat pockets to make sure he had everything he needed, and then slammed the heavy door closed as the station master moved up and down the quiet platform while the engine groaned and huffed. The station master tipped his hat as he ensured all the doors had been correctly closed. Sam joined the small trickle of people making their way towards the exit signs. It was a bright day, with a sharp sea scent in the air, and it invigorated him after the long journey.

He could have driven, but even the police didn't have enough petrol to make such a long journey worthy of squandering it all.

"Chief Inspector?" A young sergeant stepped in front of him, fresh-faced, and with keen eyes, uniform gleaming, skirt reaching well beyond her knees, shoes shiny enough to please even the most pedantic of superintendents.

"Yes."

"I'm Sergeant Pat Higham. They sent me to pick you up." She struck out her hand, and Sam took it, surprised by the wiry strength there, for she was much shorter than him, hair neatly tied back beneath her plain, peaked cap.

"Thank you."

"Not a problem. Come on; the car's over here." She directed him to the side of the railway station, where a thin line of cars waited, the black Wolseley prominent at the front, with the white letter proclaiming who owned it. He could feel curious eyes on him, but Higham didn't seem to notice.

As she settled behind the huge steering wheel, she grinned at him.

"They don't often let me drive this, but I assure you, I know what I'm doing."

Sam was yet to be convinced, but he perched in the car easily enough, pleased that the window was open and he was free from the confines of the train carriage and the unsettling motion.

Abruptly, he was thrust back against his seat, and he gripped for the door handle as the car sprang to life and rushed from the car park. He didn't need to look at Higham to know a huge smile covered her face. Sam suppressed a grimace. He remembered how much he'd enjoyed being allowed to drive the big old car that had served Erdington when he'd been newly qualified. Back then, it had felt like one of the best perks of his job.

Now he rarely drove but gave the job to one of his subordinates. Not that he couldn't have driven if he'd wanted.

"It's not far, but it's tricky to find," Higham trilled, her eyes flashing from side to side, busy in the mirrors, as she man-oeuvred through the slight congestion close to the railway station.

Sam found himself watching the people on the street as they passed the butcher's, the baker's and then the general grocers. It seemed similar to Erdington, although his eyes alighted on the boards proclaiming the news of the day. It was never good. Not anymore.

The scars of air raids marked the area as well, evident in the ruins of houses. Had nowhere escaped the German bombs?

"Do you know anything about the case?" He asked, keen to distract himself from the current problems, but Higham was already shaking her head.

"Before my time, sir. Sorry. I'd never even heard of it until they asked me to come and get you and explained why you were interested. Such a shame. Poor boy. They said you might have something similar?"

"Potentially yes, I've no idea until I examine the file."

Her forehead wrinkled in consternation.

"Then how did you know about it?"

"A sister of our murder victim saw the anniversary article in your local newspaper."

"Ah, okay. That makes more sense. No one could work out why you suddenly called."

Abruptly, she stamped on the brakes, and the colossal car lurched to a stop.

"Here it is, nothing pretty about the building, but it's serviceable, and at least, we get some sun through the windows."

"You hop inside. I think the Superintendent is waiting for you. I'll just park the car."

"Thank you," Sam offered, opening the door and looking at the building. He couldn't have hopped inside, but he appreciated the sentiment.

Although he could see what Higham meant about the windows, it was little different to his police station. The double doors were glass as well, and even now, a warm glow suffused the desk behind which he could see the curious gaze of another young police officer.

"You must be the Chief Inspector from Erdington, Mason, was it?"

The young face was welcoming enough, and at least he was expected. That always made these sorts of things go far more smoothly.

"I'm Constable Hughes. Come on through."

Higham opened the desk hatch to allow him entry, and Sam followed the constable's shining boots. The man walked with a slight limp, and Sam deduced that accounted for the fact he wasn't away, fighting on one of the many active fronts of the war effort. It had become the norm to look for the disability in those who remained. For those with an obvious infirmity, it was somewhat more straightforward than those who carried it unseen. Far better to walk with a limp or carry a burn to the face than appear whole.

"Here you go." And Hughes tapped on the door and showed him into a pleasant office, where an older man wallowed behind his desk. Although a large beard and moustache covered the lower half of his long face, he was entirely bald.

Keen eyes looked up and then nodded to dismiss Hughes.

"Can you bring us some tea, please," and then the man turned to Sam.

"You must be Chief Inspector Mason. Welcome to Weston. I'm Superintendent Hatly. I've had the old case notes found. I tell you, it was a bit of a bugger. Our storage area needs a good sorting out. Someone's managed to get the alphabet inside out and upside down." Hatly laughed as he spoke, the sound cheerful despite the complaint.

Sam shrugged out of his coat and folded it carefully over the back of the wooden chair. The chair legs scrapped on the tiled floor as he sat, and he winced at the discordant sound. But Hatly didn't even seem to notice. Perhaps it was a regular occurrence. Hatly's hands rested on a bulky paper file, and to the side, Sam could see a box, festooned with cobwebs and grime. It seemed apparent that this was the rest of the file.

"Now, it says here that Allan was the man in charge. He retired some years ago. A funny fellow. Picky some days and others, almost not seeming to care at all. It's reflected in his case notes, that's for sure."

The tea arrived, and Sam almost smiled to see the dark shade of it. It seemed they liked their tea strong here. Or maybe it was just the lot of the young to over stew everything. There was no finesse. His wife would disapprove.

"Did you ever work with him?" Sam asked Hatly while the biscuits were distributed, and he sipped the steaming brew.

Sam couldn't help leaning forward to try and get a look at the case file, but Hatly held it open in such a way that he could see little but the yellowed edges of old paper, the scent of dust permeating the air.

"No, I came here six years ago, and he'd been gone for a while, but, well, the others liked to moan about him. Not an easy chap to work for, so they say. I'd have sorted him out, quick time, but he and the superintendent were golfing friends, so it never happened."

"Now, I have no problem in handing this over to you, none at all, but can you tell me about your case?"

"Young boy, seven, Robert McFarlane. Found dead close to Erdington church hall. The body didn't look as though it had been touched, but he'd certainly been placed there and drowned elsewhere. We never found where he'd actually been killed. There was some suspicion it might have been the school teacher, but it wasn't. I was young and new to the job when it happened. My chief inspector was a meticulous man. I've found his notebook. The fact the crime was never solved tormented him, and he routinely tried to have the case reopened, but he died without ever discovering the perpetrator."

Hatly was nodding along.

"And why do you think it might be related?"

"The age of the child and the way he was discovered. It was the victim's sister who brought me the article from the Weston

Mercury. I feel I owe it to the family to see if there's anything relevant."

"Um, well. I don't know. But, anyway, you're welcome to hunt through the case notes, see if there's anything that stands out for you. I'd like to see the nasty business solved. It's not good to have an unsolved murder on our books. That damn newspaper reminds everyone every year, and I get a flurry of complaints and requests to look into it, and even people coming forward, even now, who think they might recall something. But it's been nearly two decades. I don't hold out much hope for you. The damn brute's got away with it. I don't like it. Not at all."

Sam nodded.

"I feel the same. I resent the feeling that something's unsettled. What can you tell me about the family?"

"I've asked around and had a look through what we know. It seems they were a good family. The lad was bright; everyone said it. He was one of seven children. I believe the older boys are fighting for our country now, well not the oldest one, they lost him in 1939, but I'm not sure about the girls. No doubt they're equally doing their bit, nurses, or perhaps working in the munition factories. Both parents are still alive. They carry their grief well, if heavily if such a thing can be done. Very Victorian."

"He's buried in the churchyard at St Paul's. You might want to take a look if you have the time. It's a monument to the lost soul. A very Victorian monument."

Hatly seemed determined to press the point, and Sam leaned back in his chair and eyed the older man carefully.

"What are you trying not to tell me?" He asked, determined to find out if he was wasting his time before he began.

For a moment, it appeared as though Hatly wasn't going to say anything, but then he leaned even further forward and fixed Sam squarely with his penetrating stare.

"It seems that there was some suspicion about the father. He could be violent. The mother said nothing, but others weren't as restrained."

"And was there any proof?"

"Nothing and he had an alibi, but the rumours persisted. The monument at the graveyard was always, I believe, an attempt to dispel the whispers. I can't say it worked. It's always made me suspicious, but then, I'm suspicious by nature. I think all good coppers are."

"Well, if it were familial, that would make it very different. Certainly, my victim couldn't have been killed by his father because the poor man was long dead. But, if you will, I'll have a good look through. I searched our files yesterday, and I've brought my chief inspector's old notebook because it's more portable. A clever man. I can't believe all the detail in here," and Sam brandished the notebook but kept his hand tightly on it.

One of them would have to relinquish their treasures, or this would have been for nothing, and yet Sam felt strangely reticent.

A heavy silence filled the room, and then Hatly reached for his tea and simultaneously thrust the file towards Sam.

"Here you, good man. I've set a desk aside for you, in the main room. Go and have a look, and perhaps we could chat in a few hours, if or when you find something or don't find something. I have to leave at five tonight. What time's your train?"

"There's one at six or seven. I'll see how I get on and thank you."

Sam stood and pulled the file beneath his arm before turning to step into the larger room behind him. He was aware of eyes watching him, and then Higham appeared to scoop up the dusty, web festooned box as well, as though she'd been waiting to be summoned.

"Sir, I've set you up over here," Higham offered, leading the way towards a far corner, where sunlight streamed through a window set at head height.

"I'll bring you some more tea and biscuits, and you can crack on with it. Just shout me if you need anything. Oh, and the lavatory is outside and to the left. You can't miss it."

"Thanks," Sam offered, but he was already settling himself and turning the dirty cardboard cover of the case notes.

His eyes scanned the case's details, the number, the date, the chief inspector involved, and the details of the crime committed. He nibbled on a biscuit, enjoying the sweetness and trying not to consider his rumbling stomach. He really should have eaten his sandwiches first, but he'd come this far; he wanted an idea of whether he was wasting his time or not.

The next page showed a pencil drawing of the place where the body had been found. He gazed at it, immediately noticing small details that made his heart beat a little faster. Surely, surely, it had to be related? The body had been as carefully placed, or so it seemed. He pulled the box closer to him and stood to riffle through the contents, searching for photographs. He felt sure that if he could see the scene as it had been found, his suspicions, or rather, Rebecca's, would be justified.

Yet, a cursory exam found no crime scene packet of photographs, and he bit his lip, flicking through the pages of the case file to see if they'd been appended to it. He found no black and white images, but he did find more pencil drawings. He cursed softly. Surely, they'd taken photographs of the scene? But it seemed not. Stifling his frustration, he settled once more, turning to the small drawings and finding the ones that Chief Inspector Fullerton had drawn as well.

Sam's eyes flashed between the two, and he expelled his pent-up breath. It seemed he'd been too quick to find similarities. The bodies hadn't even been placed in the same way. Robert had his feet close together, his hands as well, and was slightly bent over. Anthony might well have been posed, but it wasn't in the same position if he had. His right arm was flung to the side of his body, and both legs had been bent at the knee.

Sam sat back, looking from one to the other, already considering giving up. Only then he thought of something else, and he paged through the report from the Weston police until he found what he wanted.

The words were typed, but haphazardly, as though the paper had kept moving under the impact of the typewriter's heavy keys on the form. For a moment, his eyes seemed to blur, the words making no sense, and then, just like Fullerton's scrawling script, he managed to make sense of them.

"*Young male child found by the Women's Institute, on Walliscote Road, at 7.03 am by a Mr Harrap out walking his dog, a Dalmatian called Bobby.*" Sam smiled at the attention to detail and continued reading.

"*Mr Harrap didn't touch the body. It was apparent the child was dead. Instead, he walked to the police station on Walliscote Grove Road and informed Sergeant Cook of what he'd found. Chief Inspector Allan attended the scene, along with Cook, Smith, McDougal and Singh. On arrival, a body was found. Young, male, evidently dead for some time. Dr Hastings was summoned immediately to examine the corpse.*

The body was fully clothed, clean and tidy, in what seemed to be school uniform, stripy socks, knitted blue jumper, white shirt, and a blue tie. Black shoes were on the feet, and they showed no scuff marks. There was no sign of violence on the body.

Dr Hastings arrived promptly and examined the body but was unable to determine the cause of death at that time. Detailed drawings were made, and measurements were taken. The body was promptly removed and taken to the morgue for further examination.

Allan instigated a full search of the scene, and unable to find any identifying marks on the body, could not inform the deceased youngster's family at that time. No one had been reported missing in recent days; records were checked.

The child measured four foot four inches long.

Cook and Smith door knocked local inhabitants for any information they might have. See their reports for details of who they spoke to and the information offered.

It had been a cold night, the first frost on the ground, and an ambient temperature of thirty seven degrees Fahrenheit as a point of note. There were no footprints or tyre tracks to show how the body had been transported."

Sam was nodding as he read. It all sounded too familiar. He quickly scanned the rest of the brief report, looking for details from the mortuary examination. The fact the body was clean and tidy made him sure the two murders must be related, but he wanted to know if there had been any signs of violence on the boy, especially under his nails, or if they'd been clean, like Robert's.

But, for all he examined the case file more than once, he could not find the report that Dr Hastings must have prepared for the police and the coroner.

He stood again and pulled the discarded box closer to him. Perhaps, the report had come loose. As he did so, his eyes fastened on a tightly wrapped packet, and he felt it.

It seemed they'd not taken photographs, but they had kept the victim's clothes, if not his shoes, for there was no sign of them. Sam unravelled a knitted blue jumper, a white shirt, and a blue tie, smelling damp. They told him nothing, and so he refolded them and moved to place them back in the box. As he did so, Sam spotted a pile of papers, rolled with age and yellowing. The smell of dust and old paper assaulted his nostrils as he unfurled them, using both hands to hold them flat on the table

Not the mortuary report, but instead details on the mother's statement of her son's disappearance. He looked at the time of the report and realised that even as they were finding her son's body, Mrs McGovern was reporting Anthony as missing to the desk sergeant.

How easy it was sometimes to forget the human element of such terrible crimes.

Sam knew a moment of sorrow for her as he read the description of when she'd last seen her son and the clothes he'd been wearing, which mirrored those detailed in Allan's report, and which he'd just seen.

He read on, curious as to how her son could already have been lying dead when she was only just informing the police.

Sam scanned the page, picking out the pertinent details. He was last seen on 3rd October 1926 walking to school along Windwhistle Road, alone. He'd been running late, and his older brothers had already left without him because they didn't want the wrath of the schoolmaster. Mrs McGovern had offered to walk with her son, the mile to school, but he'd said he was happy to go alone, and Mrs McGovern had let him because she was feeling unwell herself.

It was obvious that Mrs McGovern blamed herself, but it wasn't that which intrigued Sam, but rather why two additional days had gone by without her reporting her child missing.

There didn't seem to be any reason for it, and he tried to read between the lines. She'd cited an illness; perhaps it had kept her in bed for those two days? But he remembered what Hatly had said about the father. Maybe it hadn't been an illness at all. The thought consumed him. Could she have been suffering her husband's ill-temper while her son was missing and ultimately murdered? It was far from a pleasant scenario.

Sam returned to the typed report and found the page which listed the details of the body being identified by Mr McGovern. There was no description of the man's appearance, yet Sam could envision him as stooped and greyed by the task assigned to him. Perhaps he'd believed it some sort of retribution for his fists. Or maybe he'd not considered it at all. Sam shook his head, dismissed his idle wonderings and delved deeper into the case file.

The rest of the details were just a comprehensive account of the murder investigation. As with Robert McFarlane, the chief inspector had initially suspected the schoolmaster, and then the leader of the local cubs' group, and someone who assisted at the Sunday school, but they'd all been able to explain their whereabouts for those crucial few days of Anthony's disappearance. Not that Sam couldn't see through some of the alibis; after all, it had been days, not just hours that the boy had been missing, but he could also appreciate why Allan had dismissed them.

And then the case had gone quiet, with nothing but the report of the coroner's hearing added to the file. Sam smiled to see the haphazard typing on the coroner's report, just as bad as that on the initial investigation. They'd needed some new typewriters.

After that, there were only sporadic entries throughout the beginning of the following year, until a year to the date of the body being found, the file had been marked as archived with an official stamp. Sam sighed as he closed the back of the case file. It was more a hunch than anything else, and yet, he couldn't help but think there was a connection between the two murders.

Higham caught his eye as he glanced around the room.

"Alright, Sir?" she asked.

"Yes, thank you. Well, yes, but also no. There's something here, I know there is, but I can't quite say more than that. It's similar, and yet, perhaps I just see a connection where there isn't one."

"Would you like to see the place the boy was found?" she asked, almost hopefully. And he nodded.

"Yes, I think I would. For the time being, can you have the case file returned to the stores? I've written down the pertinent details, and I'm going to ask my Superintendent if I can send out the information again, as we did all those years ago. I might be completely wrong, but if the murderer struck somewhere else, maybe it wasn't an isolated occurrence. It's got to be worth the effort."

Higham nodded, her eyes focused on something inside the box.

"What have you found?" he asked.

"Just this," and she pulled out a frayed newspaper.

"What's this doing in here?" she asked, and Sam shook his head as she unravelled it, and they both glanced at the date, and Sam gave a cry of surprise.

It was the Weston Mercury once more; only the cover showed an image of what must have been where Anthony's body was found. It was grainy, and no matter how closely he held it to his face, Sam still couldn't quite make out all the details on the old, dry paper. He could see a group of three police officers standing smartly to attention, with a tree behind them, the domed hats they wore making him appreciate the new directive to wear peaked caps instead. The words above the picture were stark. *'Seven-year-old child murdered in Weston. Suspects sought."* The newspaper hadn't used an image of Anthony's body but rather the location. Still, it set Sam thinking.

"If they have this image, maybe they have more photographs because there aren't any official police ones here."

"No photos? How strange." Higham exclaimed. "The newspaper does have an archive. We could go and ask them."

Sam nodded. "And on the way, you can show me the Women's Institute as well."

"Right, I'll just put this back in the storage room, and then we can go." Once more, her voice was filled with enthusiasm, but Sam relinquished the newspaper only slowly.

He wanted there to be a connection, a breakthrough after all these years. But either way, these revelations had reinvigorated him. He would, as he'd said, send out information once more to all the police forces the length and breadth of Great Britain. Only then would he know for sure.

CHAPTER 5

Outside, the day had moved on while he'd been research-
ing Anthony's murder, and he pulled his coat tight as
the wind rustled the undergrowth, bringing with it the
promise of rain.

"We'll take the car unless you prefer to walk." Sam considered
his answer but found he couldn't deny Higham and her enthusiasm.

"Come on then. Just a bit slower this time."

"Sir," she responded smartly, but there was a grin on her
youthful face, and even Sam found himself caught up in her excitement. For a moment, he forgot all about the niggling pain in
his back from sitting on the train for too long. No doubt, he'd be
unable to move the following day.

Higham drove him along quiet streets, and Sam appreciated it
was the end of the school day as children ran hither and thither,
some of the boys and girls stopping to play games on corners,
while older girls gossiped or shared treats if they had some. It
all seemed so routine it almost brought a pang of sorrow to
his face. All so common, and yet who knew where their fathers
were, their brothers, or even mothers and sisters. This war took
its toll on everyone, even on the buildings, and Weston was no
exception.

"Here it is," and Higham pulled the car close to the kerb and
pointed to the same tree that Sam had just seen in the old newspaper article.

"Is it still the Women's Institute?"

"Yes, but they don't use it much, not at the moment, and not really since then. Too many memories."

The building before him was typical of the others in the street. Quite grand, with a large enclosed front door, a bit too fancy for his eyes. He couldn't help but think that the building looked cold, despite the stack of chimneys on the tiled roof. Perhaps it was always cold inside.

"I think the body was found here." Higham had taken herself to the enormous oak tree and looked around as though the corpse might still be there.

Sam twirled to take in the view before him. There was the scent of rich earth and an overwhelming salty smell from the sea, even though he couldn't see it through the press of houses on the other side of the road. It was very different from Erdington and yet also the same. Even now, the street was quiet, the building silent and foreboding but offering the illusion of privacy.

"I think there used to be a cut through to the park, behind the building. That's why the dog-walker found the body."

Sam smirked. He'd just been considering why anyone would be hovering in what seemed to be an abandoned garden, screened off from the main street by a tall stone wall and a thick cover of trees.

"But, I think much of this has been planted since."

"You seem well informed?" he offered. Higham grinned.

"I live over there," and she pointed to one of the large Victorian houses on the other side of the tree-lined road, with a bright red door. "I've watched this place change throughout my lifetime. It used to be popular, but not anymore. I don't think it's because of the murder. It's just a bit out of the way now that everyone goes into the busy shopping area. I would think the Women's Institute might sell it. They mainly use the Town Hall for meetings now. There's more parking for those well-to-do women who have access to a motor vehicle and it's much warmer than this cold, old building."

"So, you're what? Twenty-two?"

"Twenty-four, sir. We moved here seventeen years ago, just after the murder. I think my parents managed to get the house cheaply because of what had happened. The other family just wanted to move away."

Higham paused, and Sam waited, curious to see what she'd say.

"It's always been a bit strange around here. It's not as though people avoid the place, but I've seen people of a certain generation cross over when they get close to the Women's Institute. The memories of what happened here are long for people who lived in Weston at the time. New arrivals know nothing about it, and so they're not at all bothered. They don't cross the road or avoid coming here."

"It's similar where my victim was found. It's a church hall still, but no one uses it other than for necessities. Certainly, parties and fétes are held elsewhere."

Higham nodded, a flicker of relief on her intense face.

"Right, do you still want to go to the newspaper office?"

"Yes, I do," he confirmed, and they returned to the car, but not before he cast a long-lingering glance at the area surrounding the Women's Institute. It was all far too familiar to him.

Higham drove far more carefully as they followed the road back into the centre of town and then onto the seafront, where the sand gleamed darkly. The beach was thronged with families at the end of the day. Sam watched them, but he didn't see them, too caught up with the thoughts shifting through his mind. It had been years since Robert's murder, and yet the possibility of finally solving it filled him with renewed vigour. Maybe he wasn't just another dried up old copper, after all.

The sea looked cold and uninviting, and the people on the beach were bent over, straining to walk against the force of the wind. He was pleased to be inside the car, even if Higham was driving.

The car came to a stop, and only belatedly did Sam realise that Higham was once more opening the door. He peered through the window and saw a stately building with the newspaper's name, in gold letters, proudly proclaiming what it was, over the door. It looked big enough that he hoped the archive would be stored inside as well. No doubt there was a basement, mouldering and carrying that unique scent of neglect, that infected any space left abandoned for long enough.

Higham preceded him inside, and she was already engaging the receptionist when he joined them. The woman was probably about his age, glasses perched precariously on the edge of her nose, greying hair neatly tied back so that it didn't keep falling into her face. He decided she was a likeable woman, just from the welcoming smile as she listened to Higham's elaborate description.

"Ah, that poor boy," she consoled. "I remember it well. It would be Cyril Rothbotham who took the photos. He doesn't work for the newspaper anymore; rumour has it he's doing some work for the government. It's supposed to be a secret, but of course, he never could keep his mouth closed. Come on through. I'll show you where the archive is, and if you're lucky, I might even be able to find the images straight away. I'm Beatrice, by the way."

She smiled at Sam, her examination starting at his feet and ended at his eyes. He nodded in greeting all the same. It was always a relief to find someone efficient who knew what was what. It was seldom the case these days. Everything was up in the air, with people in new positions. He was only grateful that it hadn't happened in his station. Not yet.

"Sandy, will you mind the front desk," Beatrice called to a younger woman who was busy making tea. The girl watched Higham and him walk by, her mouth open in an 'o' of surprise, and only then went to fulfil the request, her patterned calf-length skirt sashaying with every step she took, her shoes a little higher heeled than Sam was used to seeing. He suppressed a smile of amusement. The young never changed, always out to catch the eye of a potential suitor. Perhaps, he considered, he didn't look quite as old and grey as he believed.

Beatrice walked through the office confidently skirting between the haphazard arrangement of desks. Sam was once more surprised by how disorderly every newspaper office he'd ever visited was. There were always files lying around, seemingly discarded, random items, perhaps prizes for competitions, and the clack of typewriter keys, and of course, a thick haze of smoke, and an equally telling array of filthy and discarded tea and coffee mugs left on any clear piece of desk

Few even raised their eyes to look at the small procession, perhaps too caught up in their story or so used to the police appearing; they were no longer wary. Sam hoped it was the former and not the latter.

"Here we are," Beatrice led them through a glass-fronted door, flicking on the light switch to illuminate the vast space. "We're lucky that our archive is here. I know in many places that it ends up in the damp basement, but here we have enough space. The newspaper has been running for over a century, well, just over a century. The centennial was in April. A pity more fuss couldn't be made, but that's to be expected. We do have copies of every single issue, apart from one or two. But I keep saying we're susceptible to fire. We need fire doors. Maybe it would be better if we were in the damp basement, after all."

Sam looked around. At least in here, there was order. Lines of open, wooden shelving ran from the door to the far end, still shrouded in darkness. He had the idea there should be a window there, but perhaps the blinds were never swung open. He was well aware of the damage too much light could do to old papers.

Beatrice had pulled out a chair before a small filing cabinet and was expertly flicking through small white cards in one of the drawers.

"I'll just find the location for you. It doesn't run by date order, because," and here, a smile touched her cheeks as she peered over the rim of her glasses at them both, "where would the logic in that be?" Higham grinned. This must be an on-going complaint from the supremely efficient Beatrice.

"I'm searching for the location of that edition of the newspaper, and when I find that, I'll hunt out Cyril's archive. Of course, they're not kept together either." Yet Sam was sure she'd find what they were after anyway. She just had that aura about her.

"Ah-ha," here we go, and she pulled out a card and quickly wrote something down on a pad of paper to the side of the small wooden cabinet. "Here you go, this is where the edition of the newspaper is. Sometimes they're stored with the notes of the reporters. It's worth a look. The shelving runs from A-Z, starting from that end," and she pointed to the shelves furthest from the door. "There's a light switch half-way along the wall when the glow from these diminishes. I'll look for Cyril's archive."

Sam took the offered piece of paper and noted the details, Higham trying to read it upside down.

"Row F," he read aloud, already moving away. Each row of wooden shelving had a small cardboard overhang proclaiming its position in the alphabet, but as they strolled from N onwards, the lighting noticeably dimmed.

"We need to find the light switch," he mused.

"Ah, here it is." He'd not been aware that Higham had moved away, but the distinctive 'tink' of the overhead lights flickering to life assured him that she'd been thinking ahead of him. He blinked in the brief flash of bright light before it dimmed to a more pleasant shade.

"Here it is," he called, looking up at 'F' row. It stretched away in front of him, boxes and files in some semblance of order. He glanced once more at the piece of paper Beatrice had handed to him. "Section 137," he mused to himself, moving along the row, running his hand along the shelves. They were divided into more and more sections, although not all equal sizes and lengths, and neither did the numbers seem to run in any sort of order.

"They go up and down, and then across, and then up, and then across and then down," Beatrice called, as though expecting the question.

"Right, keep your eyes out," Sam said to Higham. "This makes no sense at all."

"I think it's supposed to be like a snake, in snakes and ladders," Higham didn't seem at all fazed by the strange filing system. It probably wasn't the first time she'd delved into the archive. And then she sneezed, the sound loud and shocking.

"Bless you," he offered, and she smiled.

"All the damn dust," and she ran her hand along the shelf that rested at waist height. "I've never been good with dust. Here it is," she immediately exclaimed.

Sam glanced where she pointed and saw a motley collection of sturdy looking boxes, all with dates meticulously written on the front in a bold, black pen.

"This one," he rested his hand on the bottommost box. "I'll move the other ones." There were three boxes on top of it, all haphazard, as though they'd been disturbed recently. And he considered that they probably had been. After all, they'd have needed the old photograph to run it on the anniversary of what should have been the boy's birthday. Why, he considered, had they not left the box on top of all the others?

Plumes of dust filled the air, and Higham sneezed twice more, every time apologising, but he wasn't far from it either. With the three boxes on the floor, all of varying weights, he finally reached the one he was after. Pulling the lid aside, he peered in to see an indiscriminate array of old newspapers and, as Beatrice had warned, notebooks and other odd items.

"Let's take this back to the main desk," he confirmed, bending to heft the box into his hands. It was damn heavy.

"There's a trolley. I'll go and get it," Higham offered brightly, but Sam gritted his teeth.

"No, it's fine. I'll carry it. Can you put the other boxes back, so I don't fall over them when we bring it back?"

She leapt to do so as he made his way down the row. Once there, he peered at the desk, where Beatrice sat, and wished he'd not been quite so stubborn. Already he could feel sweat on his forehead and running down his back, the uncomfortable twinge of pain making itself felt. But he wasn't about to back down now, despite the knowledge that he'd regret such determination tomorrow.

"Ah, you found it," Beatrice announced as he thumped the box onto the table, a cloud of dust filling the air and making them both cough. "I wish I was having as much luck with Cyril's photographs. I know they're here somewhere. Honestly, the person who put this system in place had no idea about setting up a serviceable archive. They clearly didn't ever want anything found." The complaint spoke of years of experience with the system.

Again, he lifted the box lid and looked inside the foot-high box.

"Well, it looks like there's quite a bit in there," Beatrice offered. "Maybe you'll find what you need anyway, but I'll keep looking."

Sandy appeared then, a silver tray in her hands, steaming mugs of tea and a small plate of biscuits wedged onto the small space.

"Thank you," Beatrice offered, surprise in her voice.

"No problem," Sandy all but curtseyed and then made to leave.

"You don't know where Cyril's archive is, do you? The photographer."

"I think it's all on Z," Sandy replied easily. "I think it's there because James makes so much use of the old photos. If he doesn't need to take an up to date photo, he won't. Lazy sod," she offered breezily. Beatrice sighed as Sandy opened the door and exited into the busy newsroom itself.

"She's not wrong. I'll go and look. I can't find anything. I might give James the job of sorting it all out if he's messed it up, or rather, put it into an order he can use, and so can I."

Sam heard her words, but his gaze was focused on the contents of the box. He could see, rammed down the side that there was a thick bundle of photographs, some of the edges crimped, and he eagerly reached for them. Higham, once more beside him, sneezed and made to apologise.

"No need to apologise again. It's all the dust. It's making my nose itch as well. Have a cup of tea. It might help," he offered. The photographs were bound together by a piece of string that ran all around them, and he levelled them onto the table and quickly undid the string. The pictures stayed neatly stacked, one on top of the other, more than a hint that they might be slightly stuck together. They were all the same size, about eight inches by ten, large enough to see details, but also not because the photographs were old and faded in places.

The first photograph was of the beach, the promise of an enticing sea view lost because of the angry-looking clouds overhead; the threat only intensified because they were black and white. The second ripped in the top right corner was of a church with a bride and groom gazing at the camera, a small bouquet in her hands, a lace veil pulled back from her face. They didn't look thrilled. The third was of a football game, one team wearing vertical stripes, the other horizontal.

Sam sighed. Of course. He didn't know the views or the places in the photographs.

He turned the first photo over, relieved to find the date written onto the back of the photograph.

"This one is from 1926, so we're in the right year."

"Here, split the photos. It'll be quicker if we both look," Higham offered, placing her tea mug back onto the tray.

"Okay, here you go. So what was the date again? September?"

"No, it was October," Higham replied. Sam hid his grin of delight. It had been a test, just to make sure she knew for what to look. Higham was bright and paid attention. He would have been content to have her as his constable in Erdington. Not everyone was so intuitively inquisitive.

He reached for the tea and savoured the warmth as he picked up another photograph, this one of some sort of farming event, glanced at the date on the back, and then carefully placed it on top of the other pictures. He and Higham worked quietly and quickly, and he snagged a biscuit and hoped it would settle his increasingly hungry stomach. Even with his sandwiches in his pocket, he couldn't be distracted from his task for long enough to savour them. There would be time for that when he was on the way home.

Sam shuffled through all sorts of photographs, so often found in local newspapers, people and dignitaries he didn't know, places and events that were alien to him. He was convinced that he'd find nothing of help and was already cursing the plan when recognition struck.

"Is this the Women's Institute?" he asked Higham. She glanced up, biscuit crumbs on her lips and nodded.

"Yes, yes, it is. What's the date on it?"

He turned the photograph but cursed.

"September 1926."

"Well, you're nearly there," she encouraged before letting out a cry of victory.

"Here we are," and she spread seven photographs out, like a fan.

Sam fastened his eyes on the familiar building. He was looking for a photograph of the body and quickly picked up one of the many images that Cyril had taken on that fateful day. It showed Anthony as he must have been found, only surrounded by police tape and other people, probably Allan and the other police officers, as they examined the body. One bent low, and Sam imagined it was Allan. Two stood close by, one with a notebook in hand, perhaps Cook and Singh. And others stood further away, no doubt ensuring no one looked, who shouldn't.

He couldn't quite see all of Anthony. His head was hidden behind Allan's kneeling shape. But it was the rest of him that intrigued Sam.

"This is it," he confirmed, a spurt of triumph in his voice. Again, the image was grainy, but it felt much more immediate than the pencil drawings he'd found earlier. They'd shown things, given the hint of what Sam had hoped to find. But now he had it confirmed.

"What does this look like to you?" He turned the image toward Higham, and her eyebrows knit together as she concentrated. He wanted her to see it but didn't want to tell her. He wanted someone to confirm his suspicions.

Time stretched between them, and still, she looked confused, and Sam felt all of his enthusiasm draining away. He was seeing things that weren't there. He was convinced of it.

"Well, with those stripy socks, and his feet spread like that, it almost looks like he's playing football, only he's lying on the ground."

"He does, doesn't he?" Sam asked, a broad grin on his face.

"He does, yes, but I don't understand."

"Neither do I, neither do I, but my victim, if you study the way the body lay, looked as though he was playing cricket, it's just come to me, here and now. I knew the body had been placed, but now I realise it was placed in a very particular way, to give a particular image."

"Well, that's a strange coincidence," Higham offered, her words slow, picking up the other photographs to gaze at them carefully, considering what he was telling her.

Sam's attention was caught by Beatrice returning to his side, carting a wooden trolley behind her. There was a large box on the cart.

"Here it is. Honestly, I'll be having words with James when I next see him—messing with the system when it's already a pig's ear. Now, this box says 1926. Ah," only then did her eyes fall on what they'd found.

"Oh, you've found them," her disappointment was palpable.

"Well, we've found seven images. Do you think there might be more in there?"

"Oh, I would think so. Seven isn't many. Even for a crime scene, where he always tried to be a bit more restrained. What was the date again?"

"3rd October 1926."

"This box contains all the negatives for 1926. Let's hope they're not all mixed up."

Without moving the box, Beatrice removed the lid and began to take out neat little boxes.

"See, they have the months on. Here's October. At least Cyril kept these in order."

Beatrice picked the long, thin box up and placed it on the table.

It'll be fiddly." So speaking, she pulled the first image toward her, squinting at it.

"Oh, I can hardly tell what it is. Here, you look." She directed the comment to Higham, but Sam stepped in first. He didn't want either upset if the images were unintentionally graphic.

The first image, all highlighted with shadows and white lines, seemed to be the Women's Institute. He picked up the second and immediately noticed a foot in the foreground. The rest of the body was more difficult to decipher.

"These are them," he confirmed. Picking up the next and the next. All in all, there were twenty-five images, including the ones he'd seen already.

"Would it be possible to get them developed?" he asked Beatrice.

"Hum. We'd need James, and I'm not sure he's even in the office today."

Sam was immediately torn, but there was no huge rush to solve a nearly twenty-year-old murder in all honesty.

"Would you be able to get them done when he's next in? And send them on, or get Higham here to collect them for me. She knows how to find me?"

"Of course, that won't be a problem. Shall I leave everything here in case you need something else?"

"I think now we know where everything is; it would be a good idea to keep everything together. If that's okay with you." Beatrice nodded, her lips pursing.

"It shouldn't be a problem. But, let me know if you decide you're not going to need anything else. I don't like the mess; I'm sure you can understand."

For a moment, Sam wavered, thinking that he didn't want to upset Beatrice. But it was either leave it here or try and get it back to the police station, and it might well get lost there. No, it was better where it was.

"Thank you for your help," Sam offered, and Beatrice looked him square in the eye.

"If you can solve this, it would be a weight off the mind. That poor family, every year, coming in to place their memorial. It breaks my heart."

"I'll do my best," he felt compelled to offer, and then he handed the negatives over to Beatrice, watched her place them in an envelope, with James' name written on the front, as well as Higham's and his own, and only then did they say their farewells.

"Now, show me the graveyard at St Paul's," Sam asked Higham.

"Absolutely, but explain to me about the football."

"I can't," he quickly confirmed, "I can only tell you what I see when I look at it."

"Well, it's extraordinary," Higham muttered uneasily, opening the car door and starting the engine, which rumbled to life quickly.

"I'd never even considered it. But something was niggling away in my mind, and the photographs have confirmed it."

"Why would they do such a thing if indeed the perpetrator did do it?" Higham was evidently curious.

"I don't know the answer to that either, but it resolves the conundrum as to why Anthony was found away from where his life was taken from him."

Higham drove in silence then, slower than before, and Sam hid a smile. He could almost hear her thinking as he risked a glance at her serious face. Her amusement in the task had disappeared.

"It's just up here," she broke the silence. "It's vast, but I know where to look."

Sam saw a sign up ahead, a wooden one, with the church's name carefully depicted on it in a golden shade. It reminded him of his local church.

"We'll have to park here and walk the rest of the way."

Sam glanced upwards, suppressing a groan at the steepness of the path. His back was starting to ache once more, but he wanted to see the grave. It seemed important, even if he merely bowed his head and offered words of apology.

"It's not that far," she assured him, interpreting some of his look, but offered nothing else. Sam worried that she was already too preoccupied with the long-unsolved murder.

"I think we need to check what the report said about the victim's socks." Sam startled at her words, and she shrugged, even as she pointed to the left.

"It's just down here."

"What do you mean?"

"Well, I'm sure the report mentions plain, white socks, not football socks. I might have misremembered."

They'd walked beneath an elaborate iron gate and were now in the graveyard proper. It was peaceful, tranquil, as they so often were. Sam noted some of the names and the dates on the gravestones, and he was aware when they were drawing closer to the McGovern family plot, just by ticking down the intervening years. But even so, he was unprepared for the sight before him.

The plot was a large one, probably a triple, and not a double, and a black marble gravestone covered most of the area, a stone garden covering the plot itself. But, it was the words, again, in a golden script, that were most unsettling.

"Here lies Anthony McGovern, 18th August 1919-6th October 1926. Taken from this life too soon. Here too, will lie his family in good time. Together once more."

Just below those words, more had been recently added. "Here too lies Harold McGovern, his brother, 14th February 1912-28th December 1939. Taken from this life too soon."

Sam shivered. Just once.

"It's weird, isn't it?" Higham stated some verve back in her voice. "I think it caused a lot of problems when the stone was put in place."

"I'm sure it did," Sam responded honestly. There were fresh cut late-blooming flowers in a small vase, their colours starkly red. It was apparent that the site was routinely visited and well-maintained.

The gravestones that surrounded it looked diminutive in comparison, the words on them much more challenging to read, where they'd been chiselled into the stone and left to the elements. Some of them even had green moss and other creeping growths over them, but Anthony's grave had none of those things. It almost seemed to glimmer in the waning light of the day.

"Well," but he could think of nothing further to say.

"Can you take me to the railway station," he said instead, glancing at his watch and realising that it was nearly 6 pm. Too late to speak to Hatly.

"I want to report back to my Superintendent and decide what to do next. If you could send on the photographs when they're developed, it would be a huge help and will solve the mystery about what sort of socks they were."

"Yes, I'll do that. Will you let me know if you find out anything else?"

"Yes, I will. You've been a huge help and confirmed my suspicions. Thank you."

Higham's face transformed with a bright smile, which only dimmed when her eyeline flicked over the gravesite before coming to rest on a woman coming towards them.

"As Beatrice said, it would be good to have the murder solved. Even now," she finished. "Especially for his mother. This is her now. If you want to speak to her."

Sam paused, watching the slow progress of the woman. She was so bent; it was almost as though her nose scrapped the ground. He swallowed heavily, but perhaps this was too good an opportunity to miss. Especially as an upright man followed behind, his steps slow, but his eyes focused on Sam and Higham. It was evident he'd noticed their interest in the monument.

"Good day," Sam took the initiative, startling the woman, if not the man.

"Who are you?" the man's accent was rough, the sound like a stone being pulled over cobbles.

"My name's Chief Inspector Mason, from Erdington Police Station."

Two sets of tired eyes settled on him, and he knew whatever he said next might spark hope in them. Could he be so cruel when so much was as yet unknown?

Mrs McGovern puffed through her cheeks, and he noticed the fine hairs above her lip in an unwelcome flash of late sunlight. Her lip quivered, and in her hand, she clutched yet more bright red flowers for the graveside.

"I'm visiting Weston because I may have an old murder to solve from Erdington, that could, and I must stress, could, have some connection to your son. My sympathies for your loss." He held his peaked cap in his hand, aware that Higham had managed to step behind him so that Anthony's mother and father didn't seem to notice her at all.

"What?" Mr McGovern startled, his eyes fierce. "After all this time?"

"Potentially, yes. I must warn you; this is only a preliminary investigation. I came to see if there were any similarities between my victim and your son. I believe there might be. I plan on investigating further, provided my Superintendent allows me to do so."

The words settled on Mr McGovern like a thunder cloud, his eyes flashing with fury, before he turned aside, evidently done with the conversation. Sam couldn't quite hear the words he muttered beneath his breath.

But then there was a claw-like hand on his right arm, and he focused on Mrs McGovern's pain-hazed eyes. Despite her infirmity, they held the promise of ice, their gaze piercing.

"You must find out the truth, even after all this time. I would like to sleep in peace for the first time in seventeen years. I should like to wake with the answers instead of the questions that run through my mind throughout my every waking moment. Even now. Even now, it would bring me peace. My oldest son lost his life fighting for our country, but at least I know what happened to him. I can honour him and mourn him. But not poor Anthony. Even now, I still sometimes open my eyes and think he stands before me, ready for school, as he was that day."

Sam held his hand over Mrs McGovern's. The grief she carried had stooped her.

"I would make my peace with my God for what happened to Anthony. But I can't. Not until I know everything."

Sam nodded his lips a tight line.

"I'll do what I can. For now, can you tell me if you can recall if there was anything strange about Anthony the last time you saw him? Or anything that happened before he disappeared that has since made you consider if it was all connected."

A single tear trickled from Mrs McGovern's eye at the question.

"I believed my son had gone to school. I was too ill to rise from my bed for a day or two. The older girls looked after the children for me. Somehow, we all managed to lose sight of Anthony. So no, I can offer you nothing, other than it was not my husband who did this. I know people have whispered about him over the years, but he wouldn't hurt the children, only ever me." Mrs McGovern spoke with surprising candour, and Sam only understood it when he looked away from her gaze and realised that Mr McGovern was making his way into the church, deep in conversation with the vicar.

"He comes every day," Mrs McGovern offered, noting her husband's movements. "He comes to pray for forgiveness for his sins. It doesn't matter that I tell him it wasn't his fault, that he wasn't to blame; he's carried that grief all these years. And I tell you, he's never laid a hand on me again. Not in all that time." Her voice trembled as she spoke, and Sam bit back his flurry of emotions. So often in his profession, he only saw people at their worst. It wasn't for him to see how they sought restitution with themselves or how they came to forgive themselves.

"Anthony was my youngest child, my last baby. And he was the first to die. If you can bring me some satisfaction, I would thank you. It would make it easier if we only understood."

"I understand, and I'll do what I can. I assume the police at Weston know where to find you?"

"They do, yes. They always have. But tell me, why only now?"

"The newspaper ran an article on Anthony. A family member of my victim saw it and brought it to me." A pleased smile touched her lips.

"Then, it was not a waste to keep reminding the newspaper people. Not at all. Thank you, Chief Inspector Mason. I offer you my best wishes, and I hope to hear from you soon."

With that, she placed the new flowers before the grave, her movements surprisingly smooth, and hobbled after her husband. Sam and Higham watched her in silence.

"So, the railway station," Higham eventually prodded him.

"Yes, the station. Thank you." And he turned aside, vowing to do all he could for the family of Anthony McGovern.

CHAPTER 6

"**H**ow did it go?" Sam looked up, surprised to find Smythe out of his back office.

"I didn't hear you come in, apologies."

"You seemed focused on something. It's not a problem,' Smythe mollified, surprising Sam, both with his interest and understanding.

"I think they must be related. It's all very strange. I was going to speak with you about it when you came in. I believe we should send a nationwide appeal to all the police forces. I can't help but think that there must be more than just these two cases."

"But why would one occur here, and one so far away, and three years later?"

"I can't answer that. But perhaps the perpetrator realised they couldn't keep murdering young victims in the same place. It's worked for them. Twenty years and I'm only now convinced there's a pattern and that these two sad cases are connected."

"You make a good point. Do what you think needs to be done. You have my agreement. If anyone else gets back to us, you'll have to go and investigate as well. Decide as to whether they're related or not."

"I will, and I'm waiting for some more photographs from Weston. They didn't have a police photographer, or if they did, the photos have been lost in the intervening years. There were only pencil drawings. Luckily, the local photographer for the Weston Mercury took quite a few shots. But they only had the negatives to hand for most of them. I want to see as much detail as I can."

"I can't believe they didn't have a photographer. I thought everyone had someone who could point a camera and record all the facts for later use. It sounds like a cock-up to me."

"Hum, maybe. Anyway, I'll see what these other photos can show me. In the meantime, I'm going to write a detailed report containing all my suspicions and questions. I'll let you read it when I'm done."

"Very good, and let me see the bulletin you want to send out. Just to be doubly sure. You know how some of these stations can be. They'll pick you up on the smallest details. You'd have thought they had more important things to worry about these days."

Smythe's eyes scanned the information that Sam had been pondering on the desk before him. He had the copy of the Weston Mercury, the McFarlane case file, and the notes he'd taken in Weston. The more Sam looked, the more he was sure that the same perpetrator had been involved. It was just too bizarre that two murders should look the same without being carried out by the same person.

"Similar ages and similar looks," Smythe confirmed, reading the description of Anthony.

"Very similar, indeed. They could perhaps have been twins. Although I've not yet managed to get a good photo of Anthony when he was alive."

"Poor lads. They'd have been fighting for their country had they lived. A damn shame," and Smythe took himself off to his office. Sam watched him go, thoughtfully. Smythe was right. Perhaps, in some strange way, the boys had been spared. But no, it should have been their decision, and no one else's, as to how they risked their lives. No matter the state of the world right now that needed to be remembered.

Sam had been to search through the case file again for Robert McFarlane, and he'd found the original alert that had been sent out to other police stations. He suppressed a smirk at the state of it. It had been typed, but perhaps not by someone best skilled in the art of the typewriter. While the words were all correctly spelt, there were strange gaps. At some point, it appeared that the paper had been taken out of the machine and then fed back into it, only too close to the lines above. The person hadn't considered starting again but had forged on all the same.

Sam couldn't quite place the name of the receptionist they'd had back then. In all his years, he'd noticed that people did tend to fade and merge, one into another. That was how he knew Robert's case had deeply affected him because he could remember even the smallest details of finding the body, from the smell in the air to the scent of petrol fumes that had accompanied the doctor's arrival with his huge car.

"Alert," he reread the paper, just to see if the same wording would suffice this time around.

"Erdington Police Station, the murder of a child, boy, aged seven years old, on 30th September 1923. Found with no identifiable wounds, although later confirmed as death by drowning. Victim missing for three days, as reported by his mother, before being found. Please be alert, and contact me if you have any information or experience of a similar situation. Contact Chief Inspector Fullerton on Erdington 3299."

Sam admitted it wasn't a great deal of information, but even so, he would have expected any superintendent or chief inspector with a child murder to have made contact, but no one ever had. No one. He remembered the days after the alert had first been sent. The chief inspector hadn't daren't move far from his desk, confident that someone would have some information to help him solve the case. The ring of the phone had occasioned a rush to answer it, but no answers had ever come that way. Eventually, they'd stopped thinking that Robert's death had been anything but a singular occurrence.

Sam glanced to the piece of paper attached to the warning. It listed where it was to be sent, and he startled when he realised that it had only been sent to English police stations and not to the Welsh, Scottish or Northern Irish ones. He suppressed a sigh of irritation at the oversight and pulled the typewriter towards him. He wasn't the best at it, but he could get by with the right level of determination.

This time, Sam determined to be more expansive, aware that the alert would be sent to the local printers and only then sent on to the relevant places.

"Request for information." He couldn't call it an alert, not after all these years.

"Information request for any similar crimes committed in the last twenty years. Two child murders, in 1923 and 1926, with striking similarities, both unsolved. Both victims, seven years old at the time of the offence, found with no identifiable wounds but subsequently believed to have been drowned, although found on dry land, dressed in school clothes. 1923 murder in Erdington, 1926 murder in Weston. Suspicion that there might be more, later, victims. Please contact Chief Inspector Mason at Erdington Police Station on 3299."

He would have liked to include much more information, but the idea was always to speak to any officer who suspected a link to an unsolved case. He cursed the fact that there was no central records office, but it was hardly anyone's priority, not at the moment. In fact, he doubted he'd get any response at all. Most would wonder why his superintendent had even permitted him to pursue such an old case when there were war crimes to investigate.

"O'Rourke," he called her to his side, and she came quickly, eyes alight with curiosity.

"Run this by Smythe, and then can you have it taken to the printers for me. I know it's not urgent, but I'd still like it organised as quickly as possible."

O'Rourke scanned the words, biting her lip as she went. He'd not had the opportunity to speak to her yet about his findings in Weston. He'd been at his desk since 7 am.

"A link then, even after all this time. Amazing," O'Rourke mused, a spark of pleasure in the quirk of her lips and went on her way. He watched her go, surprised to find he was relieved by her enthusiasm. Perhaps he wasn't the only person haunted by these unsolved crimes.

Then he turned to the next task, a summary of what he'd discovered. Quickly, he drew two lines down a sheet of paper, and above the columns wrote, not Anthony and Robert, but rather Erdington and Weston, keen to make it feel impersonal.

In the first column, he wrote the pertinent facts; age, seven for both of them; the date the bodies were found; 30th September 1923 and 6th October 1926. Next, he wrote how the bodies had been placed; Robert in Erdington with his legs and hands together, Anthony in Weston, with his right arm flung to the side, and both legs bent at the knee. Then Sam wrote a possible list of suspects. He grimaced, noting how few suspects there had been in the end.

For Erdington, they'd suspected the schoolmaster but only for a short amount of time. In Weston, there had been four people who might have been involved if he included Anthony's father. There really wasn't a lot to go on, and he found himself looking at the pencil drawings once more. It was all in the photographic images that the similarities became apparent, and it was all but impossible to convey that in his tallying. Sighing with frustration, he placed the items in a box he'd set aside for the case notes and moved it beneath his desk.

When Smythe asked, he'd show him what he had so far, but really, it would depend on whether they heard from other police forces or not.

Sam resolved to be patient, and after twenty years, he thought it should be easy, but it wasn't. Not at all.

CHAPTER 7

Two weeks went by, and Sam felt his hopes fading. He spent what time he could on the two old cases, but there were more pressing matters. A spate of burglaries, a suspicion of counterfeit ration books to be investigated, an accident between a bus and a car that, luckily, wasn't fatal but needed careful management. He began to worry that Robert and Anthony's cases would be one-offs, unconnected, and never to be solved despite his initial hopes.

"Chief Inspector?" he glanced up to see O'Rourke calling him from the front desk, her voice high with excitement, her cheeks flushed a ruddy colour.

"A phone call for you about the alert that we sent."

"Really?" but Sam was already on his feet, hand reaching for his notebook, aware his heart was beating loudly in his ears. Was it possible? Could it be true?

"It's a Constable Dougall from Inverness." He looked blankly at O'Rourke, for a moment unable to reconcile the words with a place.

"Scotland," she said slowly. "Nessie, Loch Ness." She looked at Sam as though waiting for him to comprehend.

"Yes, yes, I understand now. You just took me by surprise."

"He has a strong accent, but you just need to concentrate," she encouraged him all the same as he scooped up the black receiver from the well-worn front desk. He heard the crackle of the long-distance call.

"Chief Inspector Mason speaking."

Ah, you's the man I need. You's the name on the bit of paper." The voice was just a bit too loud, the Scottish accent strong but not impossible to untangle. For a moment, Sam considered whether Dougall would be able to decipher his accent. It was thick Black Country combined with a hint of Birmingham. It was not the clearest for those not used to it. People from London he'd encountered in the past had looked aghast at him when he'd spoken, as though their accents were any better. Every sound a Londoner made was harsh and edged, and half the words were some sort of rhyming slang only they seemed to understand.

"Is this Constable Dougall?"

"Aye, it is. Hamish." the man confirmed, and Sam could hear what he took to be the paper of the alert shaking over the connection. Sam couldn't determine how old the man was. Certainly, old enough to no longer be a constable.

"I'm responding to your alert. I think we might have something here. I've hunted out the old files. 1919 it was," Dougall stated. "It wasn't me. It was me Pa, who handled the case. The only difference, it was a young girl, not a boy. But I always remember me old Pa saying the body looked odd. He could never explain quite what he meant, but she was drowned, on dry land, I remember that. Some thought it had to be ol'Nessie," and he chuckled at the ridiculous statement. "People will believe the strangest of things when there's no rational reason."

"When in 1919?" Mason asked, O'Rourke standing so close to him, she could hear as well. She picked up her pencil to make notes because he couldn't hold open his notebook and write while clutching the large telephone receiver at the same time. It wasn't possible to wedge it between his neck and his shoulder.

"Just a moment, I'll find the details." Sam could hear more rustling from the other end of the crackling receiver again, this time more pages, and then Dougall was back.

"April 4th 1919. Here, I'll read the report to you," Hamish offered, and Sam remained quiet.

"April 4th 1919, called to school playing fields behind the new school." Here Hamish paused. "We had a new school built, and

the old one was abandoned for a time before being redeveloped. My Pa complained about it all his life. Built too close to the river, and the houses keep flooding. Poor sods."

"But to return to the report," he seemed to recall himself. Sam could tell that Hamish was what people called a 'chatterer.'

"Body discovered at 7.04 am by a dog walker, a Mrs Elsie Stone, and immediately reported to Sergeant Green at the station. Chief Inspector McTavish responded, alongside Inspector Dougall."

"That Dougall was me Pa, not me. It's confusing. I'm always getting asked about stuff I've never seen. Daft beggars. Nay sense"

"Suspicion of murder confirmed by Dr Jones, who later diagnosed death by drowning."

"But of course, that's not what's interesting. I've been looking at the old photographs, and me Pa was right. Poor wee lass has her long socks on, and short gym skirt, and her hands outstretched, bent forward to the floor. I know the thing upset my Pa, but no one would listen to him. He went to his grave worrying about the wee lass and the fact no one was ever held accountable."

Sam felt his eyes close with distress at the sparse details. The murder had occurred before poor Robert's and was so, so similar.

"Does it sound like what you're after?" Hamish asked, hopefully.

"It does, yes. Absolutely. But you say the site where the body was found has been built on?"

"Aye, there's about fifty houses there now. The whole place is barely recognisable."

"Not worth me coming up then to look at the scene. A blow, really. Would you be able to send me the details from the file? Perhaps copies of the photos?"

"I can do better than that. I can bring them to you. I've got family in the area close to you, and I'm visiting next week if you can wait. My sister married an RAF officer. They're based down there at the moment, at Castle Bromwich Aerodrome."

"That would be extremely helpful," Sam confirmed hastily,

thinking that Hamish's sister had been lucky, or at least her husband had, not to be injured by the bomb that had fallen on the aerodrome earlier in the year. As much as the children loved watching the aircraft take to the skies, Sam was uneasy that there were so many potential targets close by for the German bombers. He thought of the Jimmy Fry killed on 9th August 1940 when eight bombs had fallen from the enemy planes for a brief moment. He'd never forget the terror of that first night of bombing over his home.

"Then, I'll find you at Erdington in about seven days. Glad to be o'assistance," Hamish exclaimed and then ended the call.

O'Rourke looked at Sam with round eyes, her pencil poised over his notebook.

"A girl, and before the McFarlane murder?"

"Aye, and did you see that the original alert was only ever sent to the English stations? If more of these crimes appear in Scotland, Northern Ireland or Wales, there's going to be a real stink." And then he paused.

"Can you hunt out a big map? I think we need to start looking at this more logically."

"Yes, I'll get it set up in one of the back rooms, the biggest one."

"Thank you. I'm going to move everything I've got into there, and then I can look at it when I have the time."

"But what's the connection?" O'Rourke asked, her face furrowed in thought. Sam shook his head. He'd been thinking the same.

"I don't know yet. But there must be one. Three young children murdered, all drowned but found out of the water, all the bodies strangely placed on the ground. I'm going to inform Smythe. It's going to be impossible to keep Jones out of this. I'll let Smythe handle Jones. The fool doesn't listen to me at the best of times."

But before either of them could move, the phone rang once more, the loud sound making Sam wince because of his proximity to the device. He didn't know how O'Rourke put up with it ringing all the time. However, it was much quieter since the last bomb had fallen in April.

"Erdington Station," O'Rourke answered quickly, reaching to claim the receiver so that Sam didn't have to answer. Her eyes widened in surprise at whatever the other person was saying in response to her greeting.

"Really?" she offered when she was able to get a word in edgeways. Sam could hear a quick voice, but not the details of what was being said. "Just hold on for me. I'll get Chief Inspector Mason."

"Another one," she gasped, handing him the receiver.

"Not in Scotland?" He was already shaking his head, hand trembling as he reached to take back the receiver.

"No, it's not, Berwick upon Tweed this time."

"Isn't that in Scotland?" Sam asked, sure it was, wishing his knowledge of geography was much better than it was.

"They like to think they are, but no, it's firmly this side of the border, still in England. Didn't you study Geography at school?" she mused, but Sam merely shook his head.

"Chief Inspector Mason speaking," he stated as he held the receiver to his ear, trying to speak clearly, despite the strange excitement thrumming through him.

"Chief Inspector Quaker here, from Berwick upon Tweed. I might have one of interest for you." The voice was strong, flavoured with the Scottish accent that Dougall had spoken with, only not as rich.

"Go ahead," Sam informed him, trying to determine his age just from his voice, giving up because it was impossible when he couldn't see Quaker.

"It's not as old as yours, only ten years, so that would make it in 1933. It might be too recent for you. But another young boy, eight, not seven. Again, found on dry land, but determination was drowning. The body was found close to the cricket ground, on a grim January day, certainly not a day for cricket." Quaker almost chuckled but sobered before it could genuinely be laughter. "Poor family," he quickly stated to cover-up his inappropriate comment.

"We had no luck even finding where the murder took place, and in the end, there was pressure on the police surgeon, and they had it ruled as death by misadventure. As if you could drown on the cricket square in the middle of winter! I never liked it, never. But they wouldn't listen to me. I was just an inspector back then."

"So, it wasn't processed as a murder scene then?"

"It was to start. It was just changed at the behest of the coroner. A bad business."

"Do you have photographs?"

"Of course. I'm looking at them now. And the more I look at them, the more I can see the care taken to place the body, as though it's been posed. I think that's the right word. Some nasty piece of work committed the murder and enjoyed themselves while they were doing it. I still can't believe they wouldn't accept it was a murder. It seems all the more obvious now."

"Posed," Sam murmured. It was a good word to use, better than his 'placed.'

"I've just had a call from Inverness; they had a female victim from 1919."

"Hum," Quaker sighed. "It's beginning to look as though the sicko got away with a great deal if it was the same person."

"Yes. It's not looking good. Not at all. But, could you have copies of the photos you have sent to me and any other details you think are relevant."

"I will, yes. I'll get them down in the next week. But, keep me informed. I'd like this one solved. I've never forgiven the coroner or my superintendent at the time for what happened. I'd like to take it to them when it's shown that I was right, and they were wrong."

"I will, yes, and if I think of more questions, I'll get in touch with you. What's the number there?"

"It's Berwick 899, and good luck with the old cases. They're never easy to solve."

"Thank you." Sam replaced the receiver and, for a moment, gazed down at the notes O'Rourke had written down while she'd been standing close enough to him to hear the conversation.

She looked at Sam with wide eyes, consternation evident in the way she gripped the pencil so tightly, he feared it might snap in two.

"This is going to be huge. I just know it. We need to find the connection, because there's going to be one, and quickly."

She nodded, and he could tell that she was just as curious as he was.

"Right, I'm off to speak to Smythe. Can you sort the map out, as we talked about?"

"Yes, straight away." She turned aside, and he forged a path into the back office, determined not to meet Jones' curious eyes. It was impossible he'd not heard the telephone ring twice.

He knocked on the door and listened to Smythe's command to 'come in."

"I heard the phone," Smythe stated quickly. "Is there another one?"

"No, two. The phone rang twice straight after the first call. They must have received the alerts today. I don't believe the original was ever sent to Scotland or Wales, and certainly not Northern Ireland."

"Damn fools," Smythe all but exploded. "So, we fight together as a country throughout the Great War, with all that rhetoric about 'Britons, your country needs you,' and then as soon as it's over, we up and forget about three-quarters of it. Bloody disgusting." Sam felt both relieved by Smyth's reaction and also a little contrite. After all, he'd been a constable back then. Maybe it had been his fault. Yet, he had no recollection of being involved with the sending out of the alert. No doubt, it had been an administrative error, but it didn't stop his flicker of guilt. Children had died, potentially for no reason.

"So, what next?" Smythe asked him as he finally ran out of steam.

"I'm setting up a map in the back room. I'm going to start working on what we have, looking for some sort of pattern. There must be one. We just need to decipher it. The reports and photos from Berwick and Inverness will take time to come through, and I need to get started with something. O'Rourke will help me."

"Yes, yes, a good plan. I'll inform my superior. He needs to know that we've opened a whole can of worms here. It can't but be for the good, but there's sure to be some recriminations. That's not our worry. That's why we have these bods who are the public face of the police force. I give you leave to do whatever needs to be done. Jones can field whatever local cases come up. Let me know as soon as you have a breakthrough."

Sam knew he was being dismissed and turned to leave the room; only then he paused.

"What do you think the motive must be?"

"I've no idea. I'm not good at deciphering my thoughts, let alone someone else's. But you, Mason, you're the right sort of chap for such a task. I know you'll work it out. But, it might take time. And, I'd expect more cases yet. This is rotten, and the scandal is far from done. Mark my words."

The statement was far from reassuring, and yet Sam had already been thinking the same. Keeping his head down, he walked through the busy room, minding where he stepped so as not to wrench his back, only to be approached by Jones.

The other man was almost the same age as Sam, but he wore his years far more lightly than Sam. There was hardly a slither of grey amongst his mop of dark hair, and his eyes were almost clear of all wrinkles. Sam might have felt jealous once, but he'd rather wear his age than try and mask it.

"What's going on?"

"The McGovern murder. It's been reopened."

"Why?" For a moment, Sam paused but then made a decision he'd probably come to regret.

"Come and see."

Sam pointed to where O'Rourke could be heard cursing to herself in the backroom, and Jones followed, confusion on his broad face.

Inside, O'Rourke struggled to pin a six-foot map of the United

Kingdom onto one of the walls.

"Here, I'll help you," Jones immediately offered, but O'Rourke shook her head, a nail between her teeth and hammer in hand, as she stood on a table, one leg slightly raised, on her tiptoes.

"Just hold it steady," she asked, and Sam looked away from her where her legs were on display. He knew that was what had caught Jones' attention, and already he was regretting his attempt to include the other man. But, he couldn't help but think that Jones might remember something. Two memories were better than one, and there was only he and Jones who'd been in the force back in 1923.

With a sharp tap, the map hung remarkably straight down the wall, while O'Rourke jumped down to the floor to eye it critically, straightening her skirt and tunic.

"Where did you find this?" Sam asked. He was surprised by its size.

"In the archive. It's been there ever since I started here. I opened it one day. I've always been too curious, but for once, it's come in handy." She smiled with delight.

"I think it was used for some promotion about the police being everywhere," Jones offered, but again, Sam had no recollection of ever having seen it before.

"Well, it's just about perfect for what we need. Even from here, I can see the roadways and cities quite clearly."

"What do you need it for?" Jones asked.

"We've been informed of other murders; they might be similar to McFarlane's. Certainly, I've been to Weston and examined the case file there. Now I'm getting information from two possible cases, one before ours and one after. Smythe has permitted me to look into it in detail."

"Where were the other cases?"

"Inverness and Berwick upon Tweed."

"Well, there's no connection there." Jones' desire to dismiss the matter immediately surprised Sam. "Not with the other one taking place in the west, and ours here, in the centre of the country." Jones pointed as he spoke, but rather than dissuading Sam;

it merely made him think that he was right to pursue the matter.

"Well, you asked what we were doing, and that's what we're doing," Sam offered, hopefully, already turning his back on Jones. If the other man was so dismissive, he was going to be no help. None at all.

"I always knew you'd not forgotten about this. You and your precious Chief Inspector Fullerton, trying to right all the bloody wrongs in the world. What a waste when you could be doing something useful." The fury in Jones' voice astounded Sam, but evidently not as much as O'Rourke, who looked about to launch a tirade against the sergeant.

"Well, Smythe has given his permission. So, it's what we're going to be doing. You can get back to doing something useful,'" Sam stated flatly.

"Suit yourself. I'm fine with you wasting your time."

When Jones had left the room, Sam closed the door and turned to O'Rourke, a wince on his face.

"Sorry. He asked, and I thought he probably needed to know. I didn't think he'd get so angry about it."

"You don't need to apologise to me," O'Rourke offered brightly, shaking her braids from side to side. "He's never happy unless he's right about something, and he's not right about this. Now, where do you want to start?"

"You're helping me, then?" he asked, pleased with her initiative.

"Yes, well, unless Smythe calls me away. I think you'll need some help if that's not too impertinent."

"Not at all. I need someone with a young mind to keep me right. Now, to start with, I think we should mark the places on that map. It's not a lot to go on, but I prefer to visualise such things. Are you alright to hop up beside it again?"

"Oh yes, not a problem. What shall we use?"

"Here," and he passed a rectangular piece of card to her. "Actually, no, I'll write some details on first. The date, the place, and the name of the victim."

"Then maybe add one piece of information to three cards.

That way, we'll still be able to read it from down here."

"Good idea," he agreed and hastened to do just that, the pen lid in his mouth as he carefully wrote April 4th 1919, and then Inverness in his large and slightly lopsided handwriting. He printed the details, making it as easy as possible to read from a distance.

"Ah, I didn't find out her name."

"We'll add that later," O'Rourke stated. "Perhaps just put female for now. I think it's relevant."

"Right, here you go. I'll do the ones for Berwick while you attach those."

"Right-o."

For a few minutes, silence rang through the room, broken only by the brush of his pen against the card, and then he looked up to examine their results. O'Rourke was back on the ground by now, having reached Weston already, the details for Berwick and Erdington added to the large map, although there were more gaps for Berwick than Inverness. Sam squinted at it, hopeful something would become apparent just from those actions.

"Well, nothing jumps out at me just yet," Sam confirmed, his voice reflecting his disappointment.

"Nor me, but we're only just beginning, and we don't have all the details yet."

"No, we don't. Right, I think we should set up tables with information on for each victim."

"I'll do that while you get on with other things," O'Rourke offered, but Sam shook his head.

"No, we should do it together. Make sure we're familiar with all the information we have. I know the McFarlane case well, so you can do that one, and I'll start on the McGovern one. Have those photos arrived yet?" Sam suddenly asked, aware it had been well over two weeks since he'd visited Weston.

"I don't know," O'Rourke muttered, her voice muffled from where she was hanging over the old, cardboard box that Sam had brought from underneath his desk.

"I'll go and see," he offered, turning aside. As he did so, his eyes caught on the map, and for a minute, he was lost in thought.

It was so bizarre. Why would someone, and he would assume it was a man until he learned otherwise, murder children in these far-flung places? And why was he murdering children in the first place? It made no sense to Sam, but as O'Rourke insisted, there would be a connection, potentially only tenuous, but there, when they finally discovered it.

Sam searched for some sort of pattern, but there was nothing. It all seemed random, just like the dates of the murders. Perhaps, he'd bitten off more than he could chew this time.

At the front desk, he found both Williams and a pile of unopened post. Williams should have sorted the post, but he was busy chatting to a young woman, wearing bright red lipstick, while her hand almost touched the constable's which was placed beside hers. They both jumped on seeing him, but he merely scanned through salutation on the envelopes, noting the king's bust on the stamps with detachment. Most of the envelopes were for Superintendent Smythe, but he found two letters with his name on them and was hopeful that one of them was large enough to be the photos from Weston.

Turning aside, he slit open the smaller envelope addressed to him and became so engrossed in the words that he didn't even realise he'd stopped walking on his way back to join O'Rourke until Jones barked at him to 'bloody well move.'

"Sorry," Sam mumbled, moving on and quickly returning to O'Rourke. He settled into a chair without so much as making sure she was alright.

The words shouldn't have shocked him, not after what had happened in the last few weeks, and yet he still couldn't quite believe it.

"*Chief Inspector Mason,*" the letter began, the letters short and stubby, no hint of a flourish in them. Perhaps someone who didn't write very often, and when they did, they wanted to ensure the letters were the right ones and well-formed.

"*I am writing to you as I caught sight of your alert while visiting old friends at the station. I'm no longer on active duty, but your re-*

quest for information sparked an old memory from many years ago. Forgive me if I don't quite remember all of the details. I believe the year might have been 1918, or perhaps the one before, or the one after. I was a lowly constable at Cambridge police station, having been unable to fight in the war due to my flat feet. I was trying to do my bit for the country.

There was a murder, but not a child, a teenager, I think seventeen or even eighteen. What reminded me was not the child's age but because the victim was found in his school uniform sprawled between the rugby posts, with a ball in his left hand.

It was a murder that was solved, the boy's Uncle was implicated, but he always vowed his innocence. I was always inclined to believe him. Although, what do I know? I was barely older than the murder victim and knew nothing of life and death back then. How different it all is now.

Now, I moved from Cambridge to Llandudno only a few years later, and it was there that I happened to come upon your advisory. I would suggest you might want to look into the old case. I'm sure the case file must be available somewhere, although there might not be much to it. I'm sure the Uncle was given the death sentence for his part in it. As an older man now, I would like to know if they sent the right man to his death or not.

Yours, Chief Inspector Willows (retired)." The signature was again neatly printed, and the address was given in the top right-hand corner. It confirmed what Willows was saying about no longer being in Cambridge.

"Oh, did they come?" O'Rourke piped up, a smidge of dust on her nose as her head appeared from behind the McGovern case box.

"Pardon?" Sam asked, for a moment, forgetting what he'd been searching for in the post because he couldn't believe the contents of the letter he was reading. Evidently, the alert hadn't been received today, but some time ago. He supposed it wasn't a surprise that the war effort had disrupted the smooth postage service.

"The photos? Did they come? What's that?" O'Rourke caught

sight of the letter he was reading, the paper, thin, and light-weight, the heavy-handed writer forced to use separate sheets of paper for the two pages. Sam could feel the shape of the letters through the paper.

"Here, have a read," and Sam handed her the letter while he opened the other, larger envelope. It was almost anticlimactic to have the photographs from Weston and the newspaper photographer spool into his hand.

"Goodness me," O'Rourke trilled, shaking the letter in her hand, meeting his eyes. "Shall I add this one to the map?"

"Yes, I suggest you do," Sam confirmed, his gaze sliding between the map on the wall and the photographs in his hand. He almost couldn't stand to look, and yet he made himself, all the same.

There were thirty of them in all. They weren't crime scene photographs, far from it, and yet they made it clear what had been found in the aftermath of Anthony's death. He could almost imagine himself being there, the sensation helped by the fact he'd visited the Women's Institute while in Weston.

The body had been lying on the ground, posed, as Sam was now starting to think of it, in a very specific and defined way, as though he'd been playing football. He found his eyes drawn to the photographs which showed Anthony's feet. Yes, the initial police report had been right to list the items Anthony wore in death, but the stark words covered so much.

Yes, the shoes had been un-scuffed, and yes, his sock had appeared clean, but it hadn't stated that his feet were drawn up tight to his knees, the stripes clear to see.

Sam leaned back, looking once more at the map and then at the photographs, closing his eyes to see Robert's body as it had been found. Then he thought of the body in Berwick, which had been found on the cricket green and the one in Cambridge between the rugby posts.

"There'll be a sports connection to the murder in Inverness as well as the four we already know about. We must find out who did this, even if we never find out why they did it."

O'Rourke didn't respond, but Sam watched her nod violently, braids covering her face. It seemed he wasn't the only one filled with fierce resolve. But, he knew only too well that tenacity didn't solve a crime or a series of crimes. No, he needed to be intelligent in his approach, consider all possibilities. Sam couldn't help but dread the cases about which he remained ignorant.

CHAPTER 8

"**M**ason, this man says he's here to see you." It was Jones who spoke, his eyes looking anywhere but at Sam and certainly refusing to notice the quantity of information that he and O'Rourke had been collating in the backroom regarding the potential victims to date.

Sam nodded, distracted from his job of cross-referencing the cases which had, unsurprisingly, grown to nine in the last few days.

His eyes alighted on a youngish man, well, certainly younger than him, with wild dark hair, crushed down where he'd been wearing a hat. He was about the same height as Sam, so not the tallest, and his boots showed the unmistakable shine of someone who knew the way to keep his Superintendent quiet. Sam didn't like to jump to a conclusion, but he knew who the man was, even without seeing the case file clutched tightly in his hand.

"Hamish," the man said, "Constable Hamish Dougall from Inverness. We spoke on the telephone."

Sam ignored the twisted look on Jones' face at the accent and stood to greet the man, rubbing his dusty hands down his trousers. Hamish had a broad face, free from a beard or moustache, and he was younger than Sam had thought he sounded, no more than late twenties. Perhaps he wasn't too old to be a Constable after all.

"Welcome to Erdington," he shook Hamish's hand, relieved to find he had a firm grasp.

Hamish's narrowed eyes were busy looking at the map, where cases now showed in London, Cardiff, Conway, Glasgow, Berwick upon Tweed, Cambridge, as well as the initial Erdington, Weston and Inverness ones.

"All those?" Hamish swept his hand toward the map, his accent a counter to those flatter ones Sam was used to hearing.

"Yes, and to be honest, there's almost one a day at the moment, suspected cases, we can't say for sure that they're all related."

"But with similarities?"

Hamish was fumbling for a chair, and Sam realised then that while he and O'Rourke came to work each and every day, spending time trying to solve the old cases, it would be a shock for anyone who wasn't aware of the scale of the task they'd set themselves. Sam supposed he was becoming immune to it, and yet he knew he wasn't. Each detail he read about these children's lives upset him. His wife had noticed his moroseness, but she understood too well to do anything but be supportive.

"Yes, a mix of girls and boys, but all could be construed as being 'placed' in death."

"But why?" Hamish asked heavily. Sam appreciated that it was raw emotion.

"If we knew that, the cases would probably be solved by now," Sam offered softly.

"What are you working on?" Hamish asked as O'Rourke slid out the door, no doubt off to make tea because Jones certainly wouldn't after he'd marched from the room, shoulders rigid with displeasure. And it was her turn. Sam had made the last lot, at elevenses. It gave them both an excuse to get away from the scale of the task.

"Right now, we're trying to find something that makes sense of all the different places where the murders took place. We began with the road system, but of course, you can get almost anywhere these days if you're lucky enough to own a car and can afford the petrol. But it makes me consider that maybe it was a tradesperson, or a salesperson, perhaps even an owner of a business who needed to go out and tempt people to buy the products."

"Or someone who just likes to travel, or who has the money to move as they see fit."

"Yes, or that. Perhaps even someone in the army, navy or the air-force. Not that there are bases at all the places, but there are at some of them. There's the airfield in Castle Bromwich, close to Erdington. They test Spitfires there now, but it was built in 1915. "

"There were Americans in Inverness at the time. From a military base. I know because I asked my father, and he told me that the murder didn't get the coverage it should have done because there was a big fight in Inverness on the night the body was found. One of the constables was attacked by the Americans. It was in the newspaper for weeks afterwards."

"So a brawl was in the paper, but not a murder?"

"The murder was given some mention, but not enough. People wanted the Americans brought to justice more than they wanted the murderer found. Strange days," Hamish sighed with regret. "My Dad remembered it far too well."

Sam held his tongue. He recognised the look of someone thinking hard.

"I think there was an airfield at Cottenham, close to Cambridge, but that was just after the Great War. It's not there anymore. In fact, it only lasted a year or two. Actually, there was one at Duxford as well, and that still exists, so forget what I said about Cottenham. Sorry, I have quite an interest in aircraft. I'm quite pleased my sister married into the RAF. There's a base at Hendon, which could be thought of as close to Watford, as well. Oh, and at West Ruislip as well."

Sam nodded. He'd not known that. It had been on his list of facts to check. He considered what else Hamish might have to offer. But Hamish had already changed tack.

"It's a strange spread of dates," Hamish mused, slowly relinquishing his hold on the file he carried, as he shrugged out of his coat and left it hanging over the back of the chair. Sam suppressed a smirk. It seemed he'd found someone as fascinated by the conundrum as he was.

"Yes, but the earliest is 1918, as far as we can tell. In Cambridge. We're still waiting for more details, but the victim was at least a decade older than later fatalities."

"So why change to younger children if it was the same person?"

"I can only imagine it might be something to do with the ease with which the child could be manipulated in life and death. Imagine trying to move the body of a young man like Geoffrey Swinton. It would have taken a strong man, and I don't think our killer is a strong man. If he were, his victims wouldn't be small children."

"Oh, yes, of course," Hamish all but shuddered as he deciphered what Sam was implying.

By then, O'Rourke had returned and seamlessly slid a mug of dark tea into Hamish's hands. He gripped it without noticing her, no doubt appreciating the warmth. It was bitter outside.

"Thank you," Sam offered as he reached for his mug. She leaned close, ensuring only he could hear her.

"It's the shock. I'd not considered it, but we're looking at the ruin of nine lives. It is terribly distressing."

Sam nodded, sipping his tea and reaching for the case file Hamish had brought with him.

"There's no logic to the dates," Hamish continued. "1918, and then 1919 and then a gap of four years to 1923, and then another lull to 1926. Then, one a year for 1927, 1928, 1929, and 1930, before another interlude and then nothing since 1933. Do you think the murderer is dead?"

"It's a possibility that we can't ignore, although we might just be waiting for more details to be sent through."

"Well, if nothing else, the insatiable need would account for the constant moving around. Someone like that couldn't risk committing two crimes in the same location. It would be far too easy to track them down then. See, they've caused chaos with such haphazard cases. Over twenty years, and no one has ever put two and two together."

"No, they haven't, not until now."

"Hum," Hamish startled.

"I believe we've made some connection to the murders. They've all been placed in positions as though they might have been playing some sort of sport or close to a sports venue; rugby posts, a cricket green, that sort of thing."

"Really, then who are we trying to find? An unhappy physical education teacher?" But while it sounded light-hearted, the other man's face was furrowed with unhappiness as he sipped tea and lapsed into silence. And it made Sam startle. He also heard O'Rourke's head swivel.

"There's the physical training college, on Chester Road, in Erdington," Sam stated slowly. Hamish's eyes gleamed at the news.

"Really?"

"Yes, but, well, it's for women. And, of course, the Erdington murder was the third case so far, not the first. Do you think a woman would have done this?"

"I don't suppose we can rule it out, but the fact that it's not the first case speaks to it being unrelated."

"Perhaps we should go and ask some questions," O'Rourke asked hopefully, but Sam shook his head.

"Not yet, but we shouldn't rule it out," he confirmed. He just couldn't see it. Not yet.

"I've brought you everything that I could," Hamish spoke sometime later when the room was filled only with the sound of Sam working his way through the file Hamish had brought from Inverness. He was busy summarising the notes while O'Rourke attempted to set up some sort of system to cross-reference pertinent facts. It was proving difficult. The time of year was often different, the places varied, and in every case, the potential for a different sport or ball game. Yet, that didn't detract from the overriding similarities.

"It's very detailed," Sam mused, pausing to glance at the other man. Hamish had begun to make his way around the room slowly. There was a separate table with all they had on each case. Some of them were little more than a letter or details of a phone call, but from Weston, there were the photographs and Sam's initial notes, and the Cambridge police had been very robust in sending through the case file that Detective Chief Inspector Willows (retired) had written to Sam about. It had only arrived two days before. Sam still hadn't allotted the time to read through everything, even though it wasn't the thickest of files.

Sam was beginning to realise how much had changed in the last twenty years in terms of crime reporting and the robustness of police procedures. And also, how much hadn't.

He'd scanned the initial report and found it contained similar details to those he already knew. It had confirmed the date, which had been 1st July 1918. That didn't rule out it being someone in the military, but it made it highly unlikely if the uncle hadn't been guilty, which was becoming increasingly likely. The Great War had still been dragging on in July 1918. It unsettled him. Had it been the perpetrator practising for later murders, or had it been a spur of the moment thing, the catalyst, that had led the murderer to begin their trail of murders?

Not that Sam doubted the way the case had been investigated. It had been robust, for the time, and yet, the assumption had been made early on that the perpetrator had been the victim's uncle. From then on, all of the focus had been on proving the guilt, as opposed to exploring other possibilities.

"No official police photographs from Weston?" Hamish mused to himself, and Sam nodded, even though the man looked at the images and not at him.

"It seems not," O'Rourke offered in his stead, her voice lilting from where she pored over one of the other files.

"But there are photos for the others, although most of them are grainy and the details not as easy to make out as you might think. It would have helped if they'd all taken the same set of photographs, from the same angle and distance. But of course, some forces allow the inspectors to take the photographs. Not many employ photographers trained to high standards." She spoke with new confidence. O'Rourke was going to make a fine inspector one day. Sam was sure of it. She'd taken the time to acquaint herself with all the details, and her memory was much better than Sam's. He tended to confuse any of the cases other than Robert and Anthony's.

"So, what's the plan?" Hamish asked, sometime later, as Sam was once more disturbed from his perusal of the Inverness file.

"We keep looking until we find something. I like your idea of a physical education teacher, but I've no idea how we'd find out if someone were teaching at all these places."

"We could start by determining if the same teacher was ever in post in the schools in these places. I know the headteacher at the school in Inverness. I'm sure I could ask the question, and they wouldn't think it too strange." His eyebrows shot into his head as he spoke, an admission that it might be an odd question, all the same.

"Make the call then, and I'll see if they have records at the school in Erdington."

"So, we're asking for the name of the physical education teacher at that time, so in 1919?"

"Yes, 1919, and I'll telephone Weston as well because I'm sure Beatrice, who works at the Weston Mercury, will know off the top of her head, or she'll know who to ask."

Hamish nodded. "But first, I need to eat. Is there somewhere I can get a sandwich around here?"

"Yes, there's a decent baker on the high street. I recommend their meat pies," Sam offered. "It's just down the street. You can't miss it."

"I'll return shortly," Hamish promised. "I need to stretch my legs a bit. I'm used to spending my days walking the beat, not sitting in an office," but he laughed, taking the sting from his words.

As the door closed behind him, Sam closed the Inverness file he was working from and stretched as well.

"He's got the right of it. We should remember to take regular breaks." As he turned, he heard O'Rourke stifle a yawn and smiled.

"Come on, outside. You need some air. I'm going to call Beatrice at the Weston Mercury, and then I'm taking a break."

For a moment, Sam thought that O'Rourke was going to argue, but she didn't.

"I'm starving," she admitted, and they both laughed as an angry growl from her stomach backed up her assertion.

Sam followed her outside, locking the door behind him, and made his way to the phone at the front desk. As he walked through the station's main room, he glanced quickly at what was happening, and content that all seemed peaceful, he continued on his way. Hopefully, Jones was out following up on the ration book counterfeit case. It was just the sort of problem that he was good at solving.

"Weston, 392," he spoke into the receiver and listened to the crackling on the line as he was connected. It rang a few times, and he was beginning to think about hanging up when a voice he recognised answered.

"Weston Mercury," Beatrice stated succinctly.

"Beatrice, it's Chief Inspector Mason from Erdington. We met a few weeks ago. I was hoping you might be able to answer a quick question for me."

"Ah, Chief Inspector. I hope the photos arrived?"

"They did thank you, yes. Much appreciated."

"Always pleased to help. Now, what was it you wanted to ask me?"

"Well, it sounds strange, but I was hoping you might remember the name of the physical education teacher at the school at the time of the murder."

There was a slight pause in her reply, and Sam worried that he'd asked an inappropriate question.

"Mr Roberts, I think," Beatrice said slowly, and he could almost hear her thinking. "Now, wait a moment, was it Mr Roberts or was it, Mr Thomas. I seem to remember he had one of those difficult names to get the right way round. It was either Thomas Roberts or Robert Thomas. I'm sure of it. He was there for years and years. He only retired a few years ago. He was always in the paper, encouraging the students to enter all sorts of competitions."

Sam felt slightly deflated by her response, but then he rallied. It would have been strange if their first idea had resulted in some progress. That wasn't how these old cases worked.

"But, now I think about it, there was sometimes a second teacher, and I think they changed fairly frequently. I wouldn't be able to tell you who they were, but the school should have a record. I could telephone them and find out for you. They're used to me asking odd questions," she laughed, and Sam could picture her leaning over the counter as she did so.

"It would be helpful, but I can contact them if you don't want to have to explain."

"It's not a problem. My niece works in the school office, and while she won't know the answer, she will be able to ask around for me if there's no written record, that is. I take it; this is about the case?"

"It is, yes, but it's just an avenue we're pursuing. We've found more than just the McGovern case that has similarities to the McFarlane one, and we're looking for a connection, if there even is one."

"Don't tell me anything more," Beatrice stated quickly. "I don't want to inadvertently say something that I shouldn't," but again, she laughed softly. "I'll contact you when I have an answer for you."

"Thank you." And she rang off.

Sam took himself outside, as he'd told O'Rourke to do, only to immediately return inside. He'd forgotten how cold it was, and he needed his coat and gloves if he was going to attempt going for a walk.

With his thick coat on, he strode up Wilton Road outside the police station, saying good day to the people he met, busy about their business, even while his mind was focused on the details of all they'd discovered to date. He caught sight of Hamish, sitting on a bench close to the abbey, paper bag in hand.

Sam considered going to join him but decided against it.

Sam turned aside and saw O'Rourke, who was scurrying along the street, a parcel gripped tightly in her left hand, the right on her hat, trying to stop it blowing away, even as her coat whipped her legs. No doubt it was from the butcher's or even a sandwich that she'd purchased from the bakery.

But Sam didn't feel hungry. Instead, with every step he took along Sutton New Road, the murder victims flashed before his eyes. All of them, starting with the familiar staring eyes of Robert but cycling through them all, Anthony, Esme, William, Geoffrey, Deidre, Gerald, Mary and Frederick. The horror of what had happened, because of an unsolved murder on his doorstep, dogging his steps.

He needed to find the link, or he'd be bedevilled by his failure, just as Chief Inspector Fullerton had been before. Sam couldn't allow that to happen.

By the time Sam returned to the station, the sky was starting to darken, the promise of a cold night to come, making his breath cloud before him. It was a relief to make it indoors, and he came with renewed purpose, wincing only slightly at the ache down his back.

O'Rourke had used the other key to gain entry to the back room, and she and Hamish were both engrossed in tasks.

"I've had an idea," Sam said. It wasn't an exciting one, but he hoped it might help them. O'Rourke looked at him with interest.

"We need to get the police artist in here as soon as we can. I want drawings of all of the bodies. For some of them, we only have photos, and for others, we only have drawings, but I'm sure that if we read through the reports, we'll add more details. As we have nothing but images of the bodies to examine, we need to make sure we do it as thoroughly as possible. There might just be something that's been missed."

"It's a bit of a grim task," O'Rourke stated quickly. "I'm not sure the usual artist, Donald, will want to do it."

"I hadn't considered that," Sam admitted, immediately realising his plan wasn't going to work. Donald was skilled at rendering faces, but he didn't like to think about the gritty details.

"I could do it," Hamish offered. "I have a fair hand when I put my mind to it, and I don't mind wading through the gory details with you."

"Really? Aren't you supposed to be on holiday with your sister?"

"Well, yes, I am, but I'm sure my Superintendent would agree to this. He's going to want the case solved as much as we do. Oh, and the physical education teacher was called Captain Stuart McDougall in Inverness."

"Beatrice said the teacher there was either Thomas Roberts or Robert Thomas. She's going to find out from the school. He was in post for years. But, she said that there was often a second teacher. She'll ring when she knows the answer."

"Ah," O'Rourke piped up. "She's already rung. Here," and she stood and handed him a piece of paper with five names on them.

"So, it was Thomas Roberts then," Sam stated, casting his eyes down the other four names. None of them was Stuart McDougall.

"So it's a non-starter," Hamish admitted.

"Maybe not. We just don't know, not yet. I think it's worth pursuing, even as we work on the drawings. We'll ask everywhere else as well. I'll get Williams to make the calls tomorrow because the schools will be shut by now," Sam stated, looking at his watch.

"So, the drawings?" Hamish prompted.

"If you're sure you don't mind," Sam stated. "It might not be pleasant, O'Rourke's right to be cautious."

"Not that I spend my time drawing crime scenes, but I know I can do it. Who shall we start with?"

"Let's start with your victim. You know that case the best, so while you work from the information we have, I can read back through the report, and then we can add the missing details."

"That's fine with me. I'll need some plain paper and some decent pencils," Hamish confirmed. "Oh, and that pie was amazing," he offered. "I'll be going back there tomorrow," he chuckled to himself as he arranged his drawing space in the way he liked it.

Sam was fascinated by people who could draw. He couldn't even make a stick man without it looking wobbly.

Silence filled the room, other than for Hamish's pencils sketching out the body as it had been found. Sam turned to find the victim's name, Esme McDonald, in the case files, and then he kept reading. The case notes read as dry as always. It was always challenging to distil the emotions of a murder to stark facts, and yet, it was a skill that Hamish's father had worked hard to develop. The lack of emotion made it feel like he read about nothing more than a list of military commands.

"April 4th 1919, called to school playing fields behind the old high school. Body discovered at 7.04 am by a dog walker, a Mrs Elsie Stone, and immediately reported to Sergeant Green. Inspector McTavish responded, alongside Inspector Dougall. Suspicion of murder confirmed by Dr Jones, who later diagnosed death by drowning."

Of course, Sam had been told that by Hamish when he'd first called, but now he looked for more facts.

"Victim was wearing a long dark blue skirt, and beneath it, a long red sock, pulled up tight to her knee. She also wore a pale blue shirt. On her feet, she wore black training shoes that showed no scuff marks. The body seemed to have been cleaned, and there was no sign of injury."

"Dr Jones' examination showed that there was dirt beneath the nails on her right hand, while her left hand was tightly clenched. There were no signs of sexual assault, although there were bruises at the top of her arms, suspected to have formed after death when being moved to the place of discovery. A hockey ball was found some distance away. No doubt it had been left behind after a match."

Sam stopped reading at this, his mouth opening in surprise. How had he missed this? How had they missed the connection between the long socks and the clothes worn for playing hockey? He shook his head at the missed opportunity.

"An extensive search of the site also uncovered an abandoned *handkerchief, embroidered with the initials, SM. It was determined that this had been left by a member of the public, perhaps even the physical education teacher from the high school named Capt. Stuart McDougall, although it was kept as evidence."*

Sam sighed again. It seemed to him that too much had been dismissed with little thought. Had they even determined where Stuart McDougall had been while the girl had been missing? He wanted to turn and flick through the interviews that had occurred after, but for now, his focus needed to remain on what had been found at the time. He made a note to check if an alibi had ever been confirmed for Stuart McDougall as he examined the photographs and drawings that accompanied the terse report.

He was surprised to note that the hockey ball's location and that of the handkerchief had been indicated on what seemed to be a plan of the area. It wasn't so much a drawing as a blank sheet of paper with the locations noted on it. He tugged on his lower lip as he gazed at it. After all, it had been a playing field. That wasn't much detail. Not at all.

Still, Sam struggled to determine how the body had been moved there without anyone noticing. It wasn't as though it had been an obscured place. In fact, it seemed to be in the open. Undoubtedly, the murderer must have taken a significant risk to leave the body there. Why not just leave it hidden somewhere? It would have been much less risky.

Perhaps, Sam considered, the murderer had wanted the body to be found? Had he been arrogant enough to think he'd not be caught?

"What do you think?" Hamish roused him from his thoughts, sliding the drawing towards him. All of a sudden, the dry words sprang to life thanks to the drawing. He could even see what Esme had truly looked like, but his eyes alighted on something he'd not seen before.

"What's that?" he asked, pointing at the drawing.

"It's on the photograph, see, it's here," and Hamish riffled through the pages he'd been looking at and then held it up.

"But what is it?" Sam persisted.

"It has initials on it. I'm assuming it's a cufflink or something."

"Can you make out the initials?"

"It looks to me like it says, SM."

"SM again. Surely it can't be," but Sam couldn't shake the feeling that perhaps it was.

"We really need to see if he had an alibi. I'm going to do that now. But the image is fantastic, much clearer than reading the words and looking at the few photographs there are."

"I'm going to continue then and go on to the Weston case. Already we've noticed something we hadn't seen before." Hamish's voice thrummed with excitement, and Sam nodded absent-mindedly, flicking through the case file.

He was convinced it couldn't be so simple, but he needed to check all the same.

The report was reasonably thick and filled with officially filled in forms. It was unfortunate that the black ink on the typed words had begun to fade and that there was a slightly unpleasant damp smell emanating from it as well.

Sam pulled a lamp closer to his head. It was difficult to read the words in the glow from the single overhead bulb, but at least there was a table lamp. With it angled just right, Sam returned to the beginning of the file, carefully reading each and every title before dismissing them as not what he was after, just now. It might be an old file, and it might not be one he was acquainted with, but it felt familiar and ordered, all the same. While they'd not managed to find the perpetrator twenty-four years ago, he couldn't fault the logical way that the Chief Inspector had gone about investigating the murder.

"Ah," Sam didn't even realise he spoke aloud. "Here it is," he continued to talk, despite the fact no one was listening. Hamish was engrossed in the Weston file, his own lamp hanging over the table where he'd pulled a chair so that he could sketch as he went. O'Rourke was equally engrossed in her research.

He read to himself.

"Witness statement from Captain Stuart McDougall of 7 Union

Street, Inverness. Given on 6ᵗʰ April 1919 at 3 pm.

On 2ⁿᵈ April, the witness confirmed his whereabouts at school during the day, and the headteacher confirmed this. After school, he returned immediately home and spent the evening with his wife, Mrs Stuart McDougall. His wife confirmed this.

On 3ʳᵈ April, the witness was again at school, and in the afternoon, attended an after-school football match with his team. He then returned home at 5 pm, and his wife returned at 6 pm.

On 4ᵗʰ April, the witness had yet to arrive at school when the body was discovered, but his wife confirmed he awoke at 7 am and was with her until 8.30 am when news of what had happened was relayed to him."

Sam felt his lips twist in consternation. While he was aware that wives would occasionally give false alibi, he thought she wouldn't have done so for a murder. So, yes, he had an alibi for the days between the victim's disappearance and discovery, the missing person's report had been with the initial report. Esme had been reported missing by her grandmother at 2 pm on the 2ⁿᵈ April. She'd not arrived at school, and her absence had been noted when she'd not returned home for her lunch.

Sam felt that pursuing the matter would be a waste of his time. It just didn't seem to fit.

But, who else was there with the initials SM?

"Have you found any cufflinks in the Weston case?" he called across to Hamish.

Hamish startled at the first words spoken in the room for some time.

"No, no cufflinks, and nothing out of place either. The site seems free from potential evidence."

Sam absorbed the news. It couldn't be that simple; he just knew it.

"Well, I think we should call it a day," he announced. "But we can start again in the morning. But you don't have to if you have plans," he directed this at both of them, aware, after all, that it was a Saturday, but they both shook their heads, even as they stood and stretched out cramped limbs.

"I'll be back for eight am," Sam confirmed. "Just get in when you can, and if you change your mind, that's not a problem."

As he spoke, Sam was pulling his coat on, aware that the room had become steadily cooler throughout the afternoon. Perhaps tomorrow, he'd have to pull one of the portable heaters inside from the main office. His fingers were almost numb.

"Good night," he called to Hamish and O'Rourke. But with every step he took on the way home, he thought of the long-dead children. He needed to find a connection. He needed to solve the conundrum and only then would he feel able to think of anything else.

CHAPTER 9

E very part of him ached. Slumping into his chair, Sam's eyes were arrested by a thin strip of paper on the table, just out of reach of his wife's hand, turned upside down.

His eyes flashed from her shadowed face to the instantly recognisable telegram paper. Sam felt his chest freeze, and he struggled to draw in oxygen. No, he wanted to scream, no, no, no.

"Read it first," her voice tried to tell him something, but Sam couldn't decipher what it was.

Hands shaking, he held the typed paper up to the light, wishing he didn't have to read the words, but knowing he needed to, all the same.

"I regret to inform you that your son John Mason was injured on 3rd January 1944. He will be returned home when his injuries permit travel."

Sam shuddered. Not dead, thank goodness. Not dead.

"But what are his injuries?" he demanded to know. Annie shook her head, as though expecting the question.

"It doesn't say, and there's no point in speculating. Let's be grateful he yet lives." Sam nodded, reaching across to grip her hand. She allowed him to do so, and together they sat in silence. For once, his thoughts were distracted from the case.

Eventually, Annie stood, but he stayed where he was, eyes focused on nothing.

"What are those?" His wife leaned over him as she placed his dinner before him. He barely even noticed.

"Sketches of the victims and how they were found." Sam had

been driven to carry the images home with him. Hamish had drawn all ten now, including the latest reported to Sam in response to the alert; an Ivy Reynolds, found in Exeter in June 1925.

Sam almost dreaded every time he was called to the telephone for fear it would be another unsolved case.

"Well, the artist made them look as though they're merely sleeping. What skill he must have." It seemed Annie was keen to be distracted from their news. He allowed himself to be returned to the here and now.

"Yes, even though the boys and girls all have their eyes closed, they still look more lifelike than any of the photographs that we have from the crimes scenes."

"Can I look at them?" Annie asked, and he relinquished them to her, rubbing tired eyes.

Hamish had returned to Inverness when they'd made no further progress with the idea that it might have been the teachers. Williams had rung schools, from Glasgow to Exeter and all the others in-between, and no two names had ever been the same. Beatrice from the Weston Mercury had called Sam the following day, but the school hadn't kept close records on the substitute teachers who'd helped out the principal physical education teacher. Sam had thanked her.

Hamish was going to try and find out what he could from the locals who remembered the murder in Inverness, but Sam already suspected it wouldn't help. These murders were tied only to the locations because that's where the bodies had been found. The killer, because that's how Sam had to think of him now, had merely wanted to spread his victims around, no doubt in the hope of avoiding detection.

The link still eluded him, and he could feel himself beginning to sink into the same sort of moroseness that had infected Chief Inspector Fullerton. And he didn't want that, yet, the discovery of so many potentially linked cases gnawed at him as soon as he woke in the morning, until he slept at night, and then often in his dreams as well.

He forked his dinner into his mouth, surprised by the delicious taste which forced him from his stupor. Only then did he realise that his wife hadn't joined him. He looked around the small kitchen and even rocked back on his chair, peering into the open door that led into the sitting room. But she wasn't there. Anywhere.

"Annie," he called, even as he chewed.

"Just a moment," was her response, and he detected a flicker of excitement in her voice, even as he startled because she was sitting on the floor in the sitting room, the fire casting her face into shadows and lightness. Still, it was what she was doing that astounded him even more.

"What is it?" he demanded to know, abandoning his dinner, when he appreciated that she held the pencil drawings in one hand.

"Help me," she instructed him, without explanation.

"What are you doing?" He crouched beside her.

"Can't you see? Look," and when he still gazed at her aghast, noting the colour in her cheeks, she picked up the picture showing the Inverness victim, Esme McDonald, his eyes immediately fastening on the cufflink and hockey ball.

Annie held an accompanying image from the Picture Post magazine she was so fond of reading. Sam looked between the two, forehead furrowed before his mouth dropped open in shock at the similarities. The two drawings could almost be identical if not for the hockey stick in the girl's hand on the advert and the small bowl of enticing yellow custard gleaming in the bottom right corner. Then he was beside Annie on the floor, pulling the pile of old Picture Post magazines towards him.

"Really?" he demanded to know, but she was vigorously nodding her head, holding the pencil drawing of the Weston victim, Anthony, against yet another image. Sam noted Anthony's stripy sock, not mentioned on the police report where they'd said he was wearing plain socks, and not one stripy sock, but evident from the images taken by the newspaper photographer.

"It just can't be?" Sam exclaimed, feeling a flutter of excitement in the pit of his stomach. Somehow, and he had no idea how his wife had found the link that had been bedevilling him.

"And this one," she exclaimed, again matching a pencil drawing of the Berwick Upon Tweed image of William Smith to one of her magazine advertisements, showing a young lad as though he were about to bowl a ball in a game of cricket, one arm high in the air, legs split beneath him.

"And here, another one," he pounced on the pair he matched, almost unable to keep his hands from shaking. The Cardiff victim, Gerald Brown, matched the image of a young boy, arms raised, smile on his face, legs far apart, running through a ribbon at the end of a race, wide, white shorts flapping around his skinny legs.

"I just don't understand," he muttered.

"You don't need to understand, not yet," Annie chuckled to him. The room was filled with the crackle of the fire, the smell of the burning wood and coal, with the distinctive scent of the outside that it brought into the house. The only sound was that of the slap of paper against paper, as they both flicked through the magazines, Annie had hoarded looking for the tell-tale bright yellow advertisements for custard.

"Another one," Annie exclaimed, as she showed him an advert of a young girl dancing, wearing a short white tutu, with ballet shoes snaking up her legs, a smile on her face, one leg held behind her, her arms both held before her face. It was Deidre, from Glasgow, who matched the advert.

"And here, as well," Sam cried, holding yet another advert of a young girl crouched low, holding a weight above her head in both hands, arm extended, while her legs were crouched, her bottom nearly touching the ground. It couldn't be more evident that it was young Mary from Watford.

Sam turned to look at the matches they'd made. Of course, not everything was identical. It couldn't be. The advertisements were mostly brightly coloured, offering only a glimpse of a child, male or female, carrying out some sort of physical activity. And yet, the children's poses were just about identical, although they were all very much alive in the drawings for the custard company.

"I don't have all my old copies. I've been using them for vegetable peelings and starting the fire, and all sorts. But the library will have copies," Annie exclaimed with disappointment when they'd spooled through the pages of the final magazine in her collection.

"I'll go first thing in the morning. This. This. I can't. It just doesn't make any sense." Sam couldn't vocalise his thoughts.

"It doesn't, not after all this time, I agree. But, well," and Annie pointed to the magazines she did have which carried an advertisement and for which there was no pencil drawing because there was an advert in every single issue of the Picture Post that Annie did own. "Maybe it means that there are more cases yet."

"Perhaps." Sam picked up one of the magazines, which seemed to mirror the way Anthony McGovern had been discovered and squinted between the advertisement and Hamish's drawing.

"It's just uncanny," he commented.

"It certainly is, but it gives you something to pursue. The artist must know something. They really must."

"Yes, but why only now?" Sam had been looking at the dates of the magazines. None of them was older than 1938.

"I can't answer that," Annie smiled, sitting back and stretching her back, hands on the base of her spine.

"Oh, the dinner," she exclaimed. 'It'll be cold."

"We can warm it in the oven," Sam muttered, moving to pick up another of the magazines.

"I'll do it then," she huffed, but good-naturedly, stooping to plant a kiss on the top of his head as she walked beyond him. He caught her hand.

"Thank you," and he planted a kiss on the inside of her wrist. "Thank you."

"It was easy," she giggled and wandered away from him.

It had been easy. He couldn't deny that. He turned one of the magazines to the front, noting the date. It read 1943, only this year. He picked up another. It read 1943 as well. But the next was

1942, and in fact, a few of them read 1942.

"Come on," Sam's wife called to him.

"Coming," he replied quickly. "I'll just tidy them away."

"Do that in a bit. Come on. I don't want it getting cold again."

He nodded to himself as he staggered to his feet, the old wound choosing that moment to make itself known.

In the morning, he'd be visiting the library on Mason Street and Orphanage Road, leafing through more copies of the Picture Post. And then, well then, he could begin the hunt for the killer, as opposed to the search for more victims.

He would solve this. Sam vowed it there and then.

CHAPTER 10

O'Rourke looked at him in disbelief, her mouth open in shock, while he repeatedly nodded.

"I know it sounds mad, but look, and look." He'd left a message at the station for her to come and join him at the library. The librarian had helped him quickly find all of the recent Picture Posts, and he was busy cross-referencing the ones he'd been able to check last night with the ones the library had. Already, he'd found another mirror image, this one of young Robert.

He'd breathed heavily on finding the familiar face looking at him. The school cap on the advertisement had been different, but the stance, the shorts, the long socks. It had all been far too familiar.

"I don't believe it?" O'Rourke said, her brown eyes wide as she glanced from the drawing to the advertisement, comprehension evident in the resigned set of her downturned lips. Sam was pleased she'd seen the connection as quickly as his wife had.

"Me neither, but it's there. Well, it's there so far. I just need to track down the other three, and then I'm taking this to Smythe."

"But what does it mean?"

"It's too much of a coincidence to ignore. If we find the other three, well, even if we don't, I'm still taking it to Smythe. We'll pursue the lead. We'll certainly find out where the images came from for the advertisements. It'll mean a trip to the Picture Post and probably interviews with their advertising executives." Sam realised he was speaking too fast, but he was excited. He could feel the thrill of the end of the chase coursing through his body. It had been a long time since he'd felt this enthusiastic about something.

"It's just. Well, it's preposterous. Where is the Picture Post based?"

"London, I believe, and I agree with you. But help me. Let's see if it gets more bizarre."

Together they flicked through the pile of weekly issued magazines, hunting down the brightly coloured adverts. They sat opposite one another at the central table in the library, the ornate building at odds with the task at hand. Sam was aware that the bespectacled librarian kept coming to check on him, but other than the two of them, the library was deserted at such an early hour on a Tuesday morning.

Yet, they didn't find another advertisement that mirrored one of the drawings, not throughout the issues for 1943, even though they flicked through all the ones that Annie had been missing from her collection then back to the 1942 issues.

The librarian brought them two mugs of tea, gently steaming, and a plate with four biscuits precisely placed upon it.

"Thank you," Sam acknowledged. "You didn't need to, but I appreciate it, all the same."

She smiled at them. Sam knew Elsie was curious about what they were doing, but he didn't want to tell her too much, and neither would she ask. He'd just informed her it was something to do with a case they were working on when he'd beaten her to the door that morning. Head bowed, hunting for the keys in her bag, she'd startled on looking up to see him blocking her way.

Sam had smiled, hoping he didn't look too crazed, aware his cheeks had been red from trying to run to the library, despite his infirmity, heedless of the icy patches on the pavement and roadway. There'd been few enough people around, the children already in school, only a few parents making their way to the shops or just out for a stroll. It was too bleak to linger.

"Do you have the issues for 1941?" he asked her now, for the dual purpose of having her move away and because he was genuinely curious.

"Yes, I'll get them for you," Elise answered, a slight edge to her voice, as though understanding his intentions. Perhaps she'd hoped that the tea and biscuits would allow her entry into the fervent activity taking place in the middle of her library.

Sam sat back. "This is painful," he admitted, as Elsie turned aside. He rubbed his tired eyes, unaware of just how long he'd been at the task.

"And I can't believe how I've missed all these stories about celebrities. Did you know this about Maureen O'Hara?"

"I didn't, but I also did. My wife tends to tell me what I need to know, and even though I don't think I'm listening, I somehow absorb it."

O'Rourke laughed at his rueful tone.

"Well, you're better informed than I am. But what do you think it all means?" And O'Rourke pointed to the pile of magazines, pages open on the custard adverts.

"I can't say, not until we investigate further."

"But, do you think it could be the artist, who's the murderer?" This, she asked in a whisper, having first peered into the corners of the room to ensure no one could overhear.

"Well, I think it must be something like that. But the timing is decidedly odd."

Elsie returned just as O'Rourke was finishing her tea, and while she glanced between the pair of them, as though realising she'd missed something vital, Elsie widely remained silent. Sam was surprised by her reluctance. He imagined she knew all sorts of things about the local residents. She would probably be an excellent person to speak to if there was ever a severe crime in the vicinity. In fact, she probably knew who the counterfeiter was. He could even inform Jones that he should strike up a conversation with Elsie. She might welcome the company. It must be close to lunchtime, and they were still alone in the vast building.

Evidently, no one else had time to spare for reading, and the building wasn't quite warm enough to entice those who might be running short on coal and wood for the fire.

"I don't seem to have them all, but here's the latter half of the year. It's quite a new publication. Maybe we didn't start taking a copy until it proved so successful. Have you finished with these?" Elsie asked, gesturing to what seemed to be discarded piles of the magazines.

Sam hesitated for a moment but then nodded. It wasn't as if he wouldn't be able to return to the library if it was required, and the adverts in those issues didn't feature any children, such as the ones for which he was thinking. He couldn't think they were relevant.

"Thank you," he muttered, feeling he ought to apologise for the mess but biting his tongue to stop the words from escaping. Elsie offered him a half-hearted smile while O'Rourke pulled one of the new magazines towards her. The sound of pages turning once more filled the air. As Elsie closed the open magazines, O'Rourke flipped them open while Sam nibbled on a biscuit. When O'Rourke exclaimed, Sam knew she'd found another one that matched.

"Here," she said, her cheeks flushed with the joy of discovery as she held out the advertisement and the corresponding drawing that Hamish had produced. It revealed the newest case, Ivy from Exeter, who was pictured riding a horse in the image, face rosy, a black, curved hat on her head, and a selection of coloured rosettes on her riding jacket.

"Keep going," he urged. "Maybe we can find them all."

But it was not to be. By the time they left the library, the sky was darkening towards dusk once more. They'd only found a single other instance of drawing and advert being close enough to match that of the oldest victim, Geoffrey, racing forwards with a rugby ball under his arm, wearing long black shorts and a stripy, black and white top.

Elsie had watched them go with a petulant frown. Sam had wanted to apologise again but hadn't.

"I need to speak to Smythe about all this," Sam stated, his steps clipped as they erupted onto the roadway at the Wilton Road side of the library. Superintendent Smythe was known for leaving early. He'd not realised how much of the day had passed inside while he and O'Rourke had hunted through the seemingly endless pile of magazines. Sam was amazed by how long it had taken to pore through the issues of the Picture Post. At points, it had felt as though there was a different magazine every day, not just every week.

Almost running, his back twinging with the movement, Sam thudded through the door of the police station, startling a woman at the front desk, talking earnestly to Jones. Her head shot upright, grabbing for her bag as though Sam was about to attempt to steal it.

"Excuse me," Sam apologised, removing his peaked hat and bustling his way through to the back offices, O'Rourke following behind. They all but collided with Smythe as he was donning his hat and preparing to hook his coat from the coatrack.

Smythe took one look at them with his intelligent gaze. He carefully placed his hat back on the coat stand, dropping a hand from the coat, before moving behind his desk. His eyes remained on them the entire time.

"Tell me?" he demanded to know, without so much as a greeting. It was evident that Smythe had been aware that he and O'Rourke had been inside the library building all day. Sam admired his resolve not to demand answers sooner.

"I'll show you," and Sam took the magazine he'd been hiding beneath his coat, the first one his wife had found, showing a young girl playing hockey, along with the drawing Hamish had produced of the case he'd known so well.

Sam placed them one beside the other on the desk in front of the superintendent. O'Rourke carried the other drawings and magazines, Elsie having allowed the library issued ones to be removed from her domain, on strict instructions that they were to be returned in the same condition in which they'd left. She'd painstakingly written out the list of issues as soon as Sam had realised he'd need to remove them.

A flicker of consternation touched Smythe's face as he looked aghast, and then it cleared.

"Are there others?" Smythe was quick to decipher the intent. O'Rourke quickly laid out the other eight drawings and advertisements, the one drawing already marking the correct pages.

They covered Smythe's desk, and further as well, O'Rourke forced to place them on the floor because there was nowhere else for them. Smythe examined the items on his desk, his head nodding when he'd satisfied himself of the similarity. Sam held his tongue but then couldn't, not any longer.

"There are nine so far, but my wife, and the local library, don't have all of the editions published to date. There might be others in these missing volumes."

"Yes, yes, I can see why you're so excited," Smythe confirmed, even going so far as to kneel on the wooden floor. "We need to get on to this and quickly. What are you going to do next?"

"I want to visit the magazine headquarters. Search for the final missing image. That would mean a visit to London." Smythe was already nodding.

"Well, if it has to be, then it must be done. Better to have all the evidence than only some of it."

But Sam was thinking.

"Unless, of course, the library in Birmingham might have copies. It would certainly be quicker to get to."

"It would, yes, but if they don't, then it's a day wasted. No, hop on the train and get to the heart of the matter. It'll be best in the long run."

"I'll go tomorrow then and take O'Rourke with me."

"Report to me on Thursday. Let me know how you get on."

And with that, Sam was dismissed. He turned to go, his lips curling at the thought of another train ride.

CHAPTER 11

S am walked through the revolving door; his eyes focused on the building he was entering. He wasn't sure what he'd been expecting, but it wasn't this. Not at all. The rumble of a passing train, almost overhead, made him flinch, the sound far too much like that of the aircraft of the enemy. He tried not to wince as the more comforting smell of the burning coal followed behind.

"Good day," the man behind the high desk spoke immediately on seeing them, startling upright at the sight of two police officers, even if they wore less intimidating hats than the usual curved ones. His accent was smooth, although Sam detected the hint of a London drawl beneath it.

The man was no more than twenty-five, blond hair covering his forehead, although Sam detected a scar running deep beneath the hairline. Evidently another injured soldier, sailor or airman.

"Good day. My name's Chief Inspector Mason. I was hoping to speak to someone about old copies of your magazine, the very first editions, from 1938."

"Ah, you'll need to speak to Harry Underhill about that. If you wait here, I'll go and see if he's available. Where are you from?" And his scared face wrinkled with consternation.

"Erdington, close to Birmingham," Sam clarified when the man didn't recognise the name.

"Right. Just hold on a moment." And he walked from behind his desk and towards a staircase, to the far side of the room.

He and O'Rourke stood in silence. They'd exhausted their conversation during the train journey, choosing a carriage where they were alone and could talk about the case, even as they'd slipped by the ruin of Coventry. Sam hadn't been able to stop himself from staring at the devastated city.

Of course, he'd read about the destructive attacks on the fine city, the fire that had destroyed the ancient cathedral, but it had been quite another thing to see it. Everywhere he'd looked, there'd been broken buildings, and that had just been riding through Coventry on the train. He'd spared a thought to all those who'd died, especially the nine constables from the local police.

Sam had thought the attacks on Erdington had been terrifying enough, but there was little of Coventry that remained standing, even now, over a year since the worse attack.

He returned his thoughts to O'Rourke and his conversation. It had felt like a circular argument, but it had reassured Sam to know she shared his thoughts.

"Right, come this way," the same male voice called from the top of the stairs. "Harry says he can spare you a few minutes."

The cry made Sam jump, and he startled towards the stairs. Behind him, he could hear O'Rourke removing her coat. He thought he should probably have done the same. It was warm inside, very warm, compared to the icy sharpness of the wind gusting down the enclosed streets.

"It's just along here," the voice directed them, Sam's eyes drawn to the framed photographs lining the walls, or rather, the framed covers of the Picture Post, from the first edition onwards. He vaguely recalled seeing some of the later additions, but not these first ones.

"Sorry," he called, on realising he'd come to a stop.

"It's not a problem. It's quite impressive," the receptionist agreed. "Sometimes, I forget how young the publication is. I feel as though this is all I've ever done." There was a pleased resignation to his voice.

With a firm knock, their presence was announced as the heavy wooden door was pushed open. It was a larger door than usual, but once inside, Sam realised why. There was a row of trolleys, all of them just about the same width as the door. He had no idea what they were used for, but clearly, it was important.

"Ah, Chief Inspector Mason, come in, please." The voice that called to him seemed to emanate from far away, and in fact, Sam could see no one, just a collection of large, wooden bookcases, covered in what looked to be small boxes. Just another storeroom. It was beginning to feel as though he could only solve this case when he'd been in the archive of every building in Great Britain.

"I'm here," the disembodied voice called again. "Come to the left-hand side." Sam turned to O'Rourke and quirked an eyebrow at her. She grinned, and he was pleased not to be the only one who found it all a bit strange.

"Ah, there you are," and a thirty-something man knelt before them, his dark hair standing on end. "I've been hunting for a damn photograph that I know is here somewhere, but I'm buggered if I can find it." His voice was filled with resignation, and Sam wanted to laugh at such consternation.

Standing upright, the younger man's eyes swept over O'Rourke, the hint of crimson shading his ears. "Oh, apologies, I thought. Well," and he continued to stutter. "I am sorry," and he swept O'Rourke a small bow. Sam rolled his eyes at the action, but O'Rourke seemed to appreciate it, even though he'd heard her say much worse without considering her audience.

"They told me you were coming up. I'm Harry Underhill. I'm responsible for the archive and what a brute it's already turning out to be. I've set up a good system, but it's not quite infallible." He scratched his head as he spoke, perplexed expression sweeping the room. Sam tried not to wince. While it had the veneer of being organised, he spotted stray photos wedged beneath box lids, while others were peeking from beneath the bottom of the shelving.

"But, I can find the earliest editions, as requested. I've got them over here, on a trolley for you. I don't know how much you need to see."

Sam followed Harry to the far wall, where a sizeable golden lamp hung overhead, casting the trolley into a warm glow. O'Rourke sneezed abruptly, the sound echoing loudly.

"The damn dust, that's the problem with the system," Harry commented, shaking his head while wiping his hands down his jumper. It was not the first time he'd done so; that was patent from the grey patches already stuck to the wool.

"I've told them we need more boxes, sealed boxes, that all the dust will be a problem, but they don't listen, or rather, they don't have the time to listen. It's exhausting for them trying to keep up with all the war news."

Sam fumbled for his handkerchief and handed it to O'Rourke, who just about managed to catch another sneeze. Eyes running, she opened her mouth to speak, only for Harry to continue.

"Don't apologise. I know how it can be. I sneeze all the time when I'm working in the archive. Ah, here we go. The first editions. What's all this about, if you don't mind me asking? We don't normally have the police asking for old editions of the Picture Post, most unusual. Is there a crime in them?" His question ended with a flicker of intrigue in his voice.

"It's to do with an old case. We're chasing up some missing editions that our local library don't have."

"Of course, of course." If Harry was disappointed not to be told more, he didn't show it. Sam had the impression he almost expected to receive no explanation and was just trying on the off-chance.

"Well, I'll leave you to have a look through them. There are some chairs," and Harry peered along the line of trolleys, "over there," he pointed. "If you need them. I'll just go back to looking for that blasted photograph, and you can give me a shout if you have any questions or when you're done."

Without offering anything else, Harry disappeared back along the row of shelves. Sam was already reaching for the top magazine when he heard a soft sigh from O'Rourke. It seemed she'd found young Harry far too appealing.

"He'd drive you mad," Sam offered softly. "Think of the mess in your house. You'd never be able to find anything."

"I might not mind that," O'Rourke stated boldly, no hint of embarrassment on her face, her lips curling up, a throaty chuckle leaving her lips.

"Well, I wish I was allowed such absentmindedness."

"You're a chief inspector. If you couldn't keep a few files in order, I'd be worried," O'Rourke hotly retorted while Sam laughed softly.

"Do we need the chairs?" he asked her.

"No, I've been sitting for hours. I could do with standing for a bit," O'Rourke confirmed. "The walk from the station to here wasn't long enough, even with that blasted cold wind."

"Right then, let's find what we need."

O'Rourke reached for one of the magazines. She placed it on an empty trolley next to the one that held those Harry had pulled aside for them. Sam did the same to the other side, and for a long while, there was just the shush of the magazine pages falling one after another.

As soon as Sam found a custard advert, he lay the magazine down and reached for the next one, only to repeat the same process. To the side of him, O'Rourke mirrored his actions. Sam spared a thought for Harry. Would he be able to sort them back into the proper order? Or would this be it until they employed someone more able to keep order in the archive? He appreciated Elsie's skills then, in Erdington Library. She might have looked a bit put out by their requests, but at least she'd been able to help them quickly and efficiently.

As he picked up the last magazine, Sam felt a flicker of unease. He'd not found what he was looking for, and neither had O'Rourke given any indication that she had. He didn't want this to be a wasted journey. Maybe they should have just gone to Birmingham Library rather than coming all the way to Shoe Lane, London.

"There," Sam broke the silence. "All done, and I found nothing. What about you?"

"Yes, all done, and I found a few, I think, here, I put them to one side."

O'Rourke indicated what she'd found, and Sam turned to examine them.

The first advert was of a boy, on a pair of roller skates, one leg before the other, arms held to either side for balance. The face didn't look familiar at all. The second was of another boy doing the long-jump. This one Sam certainly recognised. This then was the missing victim they'd been told about, Frederick Anderson from Conway. Now they had all ten of the reported cases in editions of the Picture Post, running from 1938 up to the latest edition.

It should probably have pleased him, but it didn't. Here, before him, was the whole sorry mess, laid out, week by week, month by month, year by year, in almost piecemeal detail. He shuddered. Why had no one noticed? Why had these images only appeared now?

"That's Frederick, I'm sure of it," O'Rourke confirmed quietly.

So caught up in his thoughts, Sam didn't realise that he'd rejoined them until Harry spoke.

"Very clever advertising," he offered, pointing to the advert at the top of the pile. It was for custard but wasn't one of the ones that interested them because it showed a much younger child in a high seat, hungrily scooping up custard, rosy-cheeked and filled with life. "They take great pride in being so innovative with their advertising. They spend a huge deal of money on selling their product, even now, during the war. They've taken out a multi-year contract with the advertising department. I know it makes their lives much easier because, with a customer like that, they can plan for the future rather than worry about the revenue falling because of the war effort and everything being so uncertain."

"How much does it cost? To advertise like this?"

"Oh, hundreds of pounds a year. I think they get some sort of discount, but not much. I also know other companies are always trying to poach each other's artists and advertising people. But, really, they've honed their concept now. I can't see why they wouldn't just continue to do the same thing. But, that's why I don't work in advertising."

"The colours are striking," O'Rourke offered, seemingly as an after-thought. Sam knew it was an attempt to keep the conversation with Harry going, see if there was anything further he could offer.

"Yes, they are. And the colours are essential. They draw the eye so that mothers who have only so many coupons in their ration book each year are still determined to give their children a treat of some good old custard. I'm certainly a fan of the stuff, not that I can eat it as often as I'd like. That said, I can't see that it's actually as good for you as these adverts imply. A bowlful of custard doesn't make me want to run around or play football. It makes me want to sit before the fire with a cup of tea." Harry laughed as he spoke, picking up yet another of the magazines and studying the advert inside.

"I do like this series, where the children are playing at being an adult or dressing up, you see, in this one he's pretending to deliver the milk. They make me smile. Is this what you were looking for?" Now Ben's forehead furrowed. "Adverts for custard?"

"Yes, it is," Sam offered, in such a tone that Harry realised he wasn't going to offer anything further.

"Strange," Harry mused. "And not for any other manufacturer, just the custard people. Cor," and here his eyes alight with delight, "I hope you're not about to tell me that they make it with something disgusting, and this is you investigating them. There aren't rats running around the factory or something, are there? Although, no, why would an advert show you that?"

Sam shook his head. He'd have liked to drop the conversation, but it seemed that wasn't possible. Not when Harry was so intrigued.

"No, nothing like that. We just need to look at the adverts and the dates of the adverts. Have you made notes?" He directed this to O'Rourke, who was standing slightly too close to Harry, her hands limp at her side.

"Oh no, not yet," she floundered, reaching into her pocket to remove her notebook and pencil. "I'll get onto it now, though, sorry," she muttered, cheeks reddening at being reminded of the task at hand.

"I've never really understood the power of the advert," Sam mused to Harry as he led him away from O'Rourke without the man seemingly aware.

"Well, I think some people have no interest in being convinced to buy something, but others do. The war has had a huge impact. People are just happy to get hold of anything they can. There's no brand loyalty anymore, well, not according to the advertising department. In our weekly meetings, they're always saying how busy they are. Companies that can afford to advertise are desperate to do so. If you have the stock, you need to make sure people hunger for you. If not, they'll just buy any old thing. I know it's causing plenty of problems. Not that it can be helped, of course."

"You seem very well informed," Sam observed.

"I'd like to work in the advertising department, so I pay attention to the meetings. It would be much more enjoyable than being stuck in here." But before Sam could say more, Harry let out a delighted cry, reaching onto a shelf where a lone photograph lay, face upwards.

"Ha, I knew it was in here, somewhere. Although, well, how did it come to be here?" Sam had no answer for him, and by then, O'Rourke had returned to his side, and they made their farewells.

They'd made some progress, but Sam knew they should have gone straight to the source of the adverts, the custard factory, but still, at least they now had all the information at their fingertips and could justify involving the custard people.

As they stepped outside into the gusting wind, Sam pulled his collar up close to his neck, hand on his hat to prevent it from blowing away.

"I'll find a phone; tell Smythe what we've found."

O'Rourke nodded, and Sam didn't miss that she kept glancing over her shoulder, no doubt hoping to catch sight of Harry again.

Stepping into the first red phone box he found, Sam connected with the exchange office and was quickly put through to Smythe by Williams.

"I'll phone ahead tomorrow, speak to the Managing Director of the custard factory, ensure you have the access that you need."

Sam was nodding as Smythe spoke.

"It's not solved, though," Sam felt compelled to caution, only for Smythe to grunt in agreement.

"No, it's not, but it's a damn sight closer than it ever has been. Well done. Well done. Now, get home safely. We'll reconvene at the station at 8 am sharp. We'll discuss what needs to be done and where we go from here."

CHAPTER 12

Sam was back at the station by 7 am the following morning. He'd barely been able to sleep. He blamed the nap he'd taken on the train journey back to Birmingham and then the cold return journey on the number 64 tram from Steelhouse Lane to Erdington High Street. There'd been the hint of snow in the air, and it had taken him a good hour to warm up before the fire at home. His wife had eventually told him to get out of bed, her tone far from polite, her voice laced with fatigue. He'd been pleased to leave his bed.

Now, he made his way to the back room where all the cases were laid out, startled when he found Smythe already there.

"Couldn't sleep either?" his superior smiled, the rare act startling the last of the fogginess from too little sleep, from Sam's mind.

"No, not at all."

"I've been examining the evidence you collected. It's impressive. I'm still unsure how no one ever made the connection before, but we'll not worry about that. Not now."

"What do you suspect's happened?" Sam had exhausted himself trying to decide what would occur when they spoke with the managing director at the custard factory.

"I can't say for sure, not yet. I hope that we'll find the artist because it has to be the artist, just sat there, and we can arrest him on the spot."

Sam found himself nodding along with this idyllic vision of the future.

"Not that it'll be that easy. I just can't see it, not after all this time. But, well, I remain hopeful. We need to address the difference in time, as well. Why now?"

O'Rourke appeared in the doorway then, bringing with her three mugs of tea and making it clear that they'd all arrived at work well before the 8 am time Smythe had suggested.

"I suggest that instead of telephoning ahead, we just arrive at the factory. I don't want the artist to have any time to make themselves scarce. We'll leave at 8 am and hopefully make it there at about 9 am. It's not that far from here. O'Rourke, you can drive us and also come inside and take notes for the Chief Inspector and I." Smythe looked at the younger woman with encouragement. It would be her first major case. Sam was quietly pleased that Smythe hadn't forgotten about her. After all, she'd been a tremendous help. Really, it was a shame that Hamish had returned to Inverness.

"Thank you, sir," O'Rourke spoke reservedly, but Sam could tell she was excited and pleased to be included.

"Now, I'll do the talking with the managing director, or company owner, whoever happens to be there. We can't just arrest the artist, but we can certainly speak to them and see if we should be. I'll leave that to you, Mason, and O'Rourke. You know the cases better than I do, but I'll observe. We need to do this by the book and make sure that everything is done correctly. We're not going to let a serial murderer escape our clutches again." Smythe fixed Sam with his renowned steely stare, and Sam grunted his agreement as he turned to find the information he wanted to take with him.

Sam had no end of notes written down in his small notebook, but would they be enough?

"I don't want to take the pencil drawings," he confirmed eventually. "But I'll take some of the magazines because I want to make sure we question the correct person. I'm sure they must employ more than one artist. How else would they have so many different adverts? They're not all of children in this age group, some of them are mere babies, and some of them are of random items, such as teddy bears."

Smythe didn't seem to be listening; his attention focused on the large map on the wall, the ten locations pinpointing the potential cases that were linked to the murder of Robert McFarlane.

"Our perpetrator got around a great deal," he mused. "I take it you have the dates and places in your notebook?"

"I do, sir, yes."

"Then I think we're ready. O'Rourke, go and get the car going. It's been a bloody cold night, but at least the snow didn't settle. The car might take some coaxing."

"Sir," and she rushed to leave, taking a swig from her tea mug before setting it on the table closest to the door.

"This could make my career," Smythe mused, his hands one inside the other, thumbs rubbing over one another. Sam couldn't fault him for seeing the opportunities such a discovery would present him with, but they had yet to find the actual murderer.

Sam drank his tea, enjoying the warmth and the sharpness of it. He needed to be alert when they got to the custard factory. Alert and prepared and ready for whatever might happen.

The journey seemed to take no time at all, as O'Rourke drove carefully to Digbeth, wary of places where the road had been diverted because there were still weeping gaps from the air raids, although there had been no actual sighting of an enemy plane since 23rd April that year. Sam, like others, found the waiting terrible. No one could quite believe it was all over, not while the war still raged, and yet, there had been nearly nine months without a single night disturbed by the sirens.

The factory building, when it came into view before them, was imposing. Sam thought he'd read somewhere that rationing had meant the factory simply couldn't produce as much custard powder as expected. But, as he gazed at the tall, imposing four-story building that fronted the acres behind it, he thought it looked busy enough. People were hurrying in and out of the doors.

"Park outside the front door," Smythe instructed O'Rourke, before almost leaping from his seat at the front of the police car to get out first. A sense of anticipation thrummed through them all.

As Sam's feet hit the wide pavement, he looked at the impressive brick building. Was it really possible that the answers were here? It was so close to home it felt wrong, as though it couldn't be quite so simple, and yet he wasn't going to deny what his wife had found and then what he and O'Rourke had gone on to discover.

Smythe strode to the front desk inside the wide doors, every inch the self-important police superintendent, dressed in his full regalia, black shoe heels sharp over the smooth floor. Already, the receptionist had noticed his approach, and she turned almost frightened eyes his way. Her face paled; her red lipstick was nearly so bright as to be blinding. She wore a beige coloured cardigan over a similarly covered dress, a small tie around her neck in a vivid orange colour. It didn't quite match; even Sam could see that.

"Good morning. I'm here to see the managing director, Mr Owl."

"Of, of course. Um," she stuttered, her Black Country accent pronounced, before she recovered her poise. "Sorry, sir, do you have an appointment?" She tried again, her words more assured this time.

"I do not, no, but it is of the utmost importance. A police matter."

"I'll call his receptionist immediately. Please, take a seat," and the young woman indicated a selection of chairs clustered around a small table.

"Very well," Smythe agreed, managing to convey his unhappiness in just those two words.

Not that any of them sat in the offered seats. Instead, Smythe turned and glowered out of the wooden and glass doors facing the road while Sam found himself examining the ceiling high above his head. O'Rourke, in contrast, scooped to pick up a magazine from the table, and Sam noticed with a wry smirk that it was an old and well-thumbed copy of a Picture Post magazine.

"What's the date on it?" he whispered.

"1938." She spoke with obvious relish. Together, they pored over the magazine, looking for the expected advertisement for custard. When they found it, they both sighed, earning them Smythe's regard. It was one of the alternative designs, not of interest to them at all. Not unless their perpetrator had decided that penguins were also of interest to them.

"Good morning," an older woman appeared before them. She oozed efficiency and just had the look about her that meant she must be Mr Owl's personal secretary. She was dressed sensibly, although still with the orange tie around her neck, and warmly, her feet encased in low heeled brown leather shoes.

"Superintendent Smythe," she looked directly at Smythe, with only a flicker of interest. "Mr Owl isn't at the factory today, I'm afraid. He's been called away to business in London. But I will be able to help you if you wish to come to his office. My name is Mrs Lydia Babbington."

Sam felt his shoulders droop a little with disappointment, but Smythe took it in his stride.

"Excellent. I'll follow along," and he indicated she should lead the way.

The first receptionist watched them with an interested gaze but quickly returned to her work when she received a sharp look from Lydia.

The small group was silent as it walked to the spiral staircase and made its way onto the first floor.

"In here, if you please," Lydia held the large wooden door for them, and they streamed into a huge office space, complete with a desk along the far wall. Large windows gave a good amount of natural light but also kept the room too cold for comfort. Sam could appreciate why Lydia was dressed so warmly. A younger woman appeared at the door behind them, carrying a tray on which stood a teapot and four china cups.

"Come, we'll sit inside," Lydia offered, holding open another set of doors that opened into an office that was no smaller than the reception room. Sam noticed the vast mahogany desk and chair behind the desk and the glass decanter set perched on another wooden table, holding a radio and some framed photographs.

The tea was placed on another table, and they found chairs as the younger woman took orders and prepared the required drinks.

Only when the younger woman had departed, closing the door behind her, did Lydia look to the Superintendent with interest.

"It's not very often that we have police attending the factory." Lydia's accent hinted that she was not a local to the area, but Sam couldn't quite place it.

"It's not very often that I need such information," Smythe offered carefully. "Tell me, how long have you worked for your employer?"

"Twenty-five years," Lydia offered quickly and then felt it prudent to offer more. "My husband died during the Great War in 1916, at the Somme. Mr Owl offered me a position as a receptionist, and I've been here ever since, rising through the ranks, so to speak. It was that, or return to Canterbury. I rather liked living here and enjoyed the work."

"Ah, then you are perfectly able to answer my questions." Smythe's words seemed to confuse Lydia, and yet she kept the idea of a smile on her lined face.

"I have some questions regarding the artists employed by Mr Owl, particularly the one who produces the advertisements used in the Picture Post. There's no signature for me to confirm the name, but I can show you the advertisements." Now the smile slipped from Lydia's face, and Sam could see the understandable confusion.

"We employ at least ten people in the advertising department. A Mr Lemmings runs it. I don't know the particulars. Shall I have Mr Lemmings summoned?"

Smythe didn't immediately reply.

"First, would it be possible to perhaps see his employment record, or at least know a little more about him?"

"Well," Lydia looked most ill at ease at the words.

"Can you at least tell me how long he's been with the company?"

"He's only been here a matter of months, no longer than that."

"And before that, he had no connections with the company?"

"No, he used to work for Schweppes. We poached him from them. Mr Owl thought it quite a coup."

"Then, in that case, yes, could you please have Mr Lemmings summoned. He would be an ideal person to speak with." Clearly still perplexed, Lydia paused and then stood, casting a look over her shoulders at them as though unsure what she was doing.

Then she picked up the black telephone receiver on Mr Owl's desk, dialled a few numbers, and waited. It was clear it was an internal call.

"Mr Lemmings. Could you please attend upon me in Mr Owl's office? Yes, immediately." And she rang off, returning the receiver to the cradle. Sam sipped at his tea, appreciating its fresh taste. This tea wasn't stewed beyond reasonable taste.

There was an uncomfortable silence as Lydia returned to her chair and settled herself, one leg folded over the other, cardigan tucked in tightly. She didn't reach for her teacup.

Smythe didn't speak, and as much as Sam wanted to put Lydia at ease, he knew not to. O'Rourke busied herself, drinking yet another cup of tea. It was always better to find something to do with your hands at such times. That way, the temptation to fill such strained silences with meaningless chatter could be avoided.

It felt like only a few minutes passed before a man Sam assumed was Mr Lemmings entered the room. He startled on finding three members of the police waiting for him alongside Lydia, with Mr Owl patently being absent.

"Ah, Mr Lemmings. Please, join us," Lydia stood to allow him room around the table.

"Good morning Mr Lemmings. I'm Superintendent Smythe, and this is Chief Inspector Mason and Constable O'Rourke. We have some questions about the members of your advertising team that we'd appreciate you answering."

The man looked round-eyed at Smythe, and Sam took the time to determine what sort of man Mr Lemmings might well be. He was younger than Sam expected, and he was sure there was a smear of something that looked like charcoal on his long nose. His light hair was already beginning to recede, and he wore glasses perched on the end of his nose. He showed no sign of injury which would excuse him from the duty of fighting for his country, but Sam knew better than to assume he had refused to take up arms. There was always something.

Not all wounds were openly worn.

"Of course, Superintendent Smythe, please ask away, although I'm sure Mrs Babbington has informed you that I've not been in post for very long."

"Of course, I understand that," Smythe assured, even as Sam caught sight of O'Rourke removing her notebook and beginning to make notes.

"Chief Inspector Mason, I believe you might be the best one to begin the questions."

Sam hadn't been expecting that, but all the same, he was ready and began without any preamble. It was better that Mr Lemmings did not know the details.

"The current advertisements, which run in the Picture Post. Could you tell us a little about how they came about and who the designer is?"

A furrow of confusion on Mr Lemmings forehead assured Sam that such a question was the right way to go. It also reassured him that Mr Lemmings had nothing to hide.

"Well, we currently run a rolling stock of four different designers. They each have a theme and work on it, producing new ideas which are discussed and shown to Mr Owl before we decide to run them. Not all of the designs are acceptable, and Mr Owl likes to keep the adverts 'fresh' as he calls it. He doesn't want people turning over the page thinking they've already seen it before."

"But, I digress, I was brought in to oversee a system that had been initiated by the previous head of advertising, or public relations, if you will. He was called Mr Handings and had been in post for the previous decade."

"And the four designers? Have they been employed for the same amount of time?"

Another furrow on his forehead, but this one caused by his contemplation.

"I believe that John, John Morton, has been with the company for many years." Mr Lemmings offered the surname as he realised that O'Rourke was writing down what he said.

"Simon Michaelson and David Davies have been here for about five years, and I brought George with me from Schweppes."

"So the three other men have been here for some time and were more involved in the current advertisements?"

"Yes, I believe it was John and Simon who began the current trend for them, under Mr Handings. They worked on the ideas together, and Mr Owl was most pleased with them. He thinks it's important to have jolly, even fun images, if you will, speaking for the company."

"And could you tell us who does which designs?"

"Well, John is the most unimaginative, he focuses on the images that show custard being eaten with something, so he's responsible for the trifle ones, and also for the pies and fruit, and that sort of thing. He doesn't believe we need the more complex adverts, with people on, but Mr Owl does like them."

"And who does those drawings?"

"Simon. He has a wonderful knack for capturing a moving image, don't you think?" Mr Lemmings glanced at Smythe, and Sam considered just what he was expecting the response to be. Sam hadn't failed to notice that Simon had the initials S and M. He was sure Smythe would have done the same, and O'Rourke would have noticed it as soon as she added the names to her notebook. He was impressed they were all managing to stay calm.

"Indeed. Can you tell me more about Simon?"

"Well," and it seemed that Mr Lemmings was about to flail for an answer.

"Superintendent," Lydia interjected. "These are strange questions. Have the men done something wrong? I think that perhaps I should ask you to return when Mr Owl is here. I certainly didn't anticipate such a line of questioning when I offered to assist you."

Smythe harrumphed and then settled his hands on his thighs.

"I know this approach might seem bizarre, and yes, they are helping us in an on-going enquiry, but I don't believe there's any need for Mr Owl to be here. These are just routine questions, even if they seem strange to you now."

"Well," and Lydia looked far from reassured. "I'll go and find his employee file. I'm sure it'll have the information that you require." She stood and left the room, the door closing softly behind her.

Mr Lemmings glanced at Sam with interest.

"Is it something about the advertising campaigns?" he asked.

"It's a line of enquiry," Sam hedged, realising that Smythe had no intention of offering more information than was necessary.

"Well, I can tell you that Simon is an incredibly talented artist. I keep telling him he should be painting for a living and not putting together advertisements for Mr Owl, but he'll have none of it. And John. Well, John has worked here for so many years I hardly dare comment that his drawings can be subpar and unimaginative. Mr Owl seems to like the designs well enough."

Before he could offer more, Lydia returned, a single sheet of paper in her hands.

"Here," and she passed it to Sam. He scanned it, noting the pertinent details, date of birth, full name, place of birth and where he lived before giving it to first Smythe and then O'Rourke. Sam wasn't interested in Simon's design credentials, although he did seem skilled in his chosen profession. He'd worked for Dolcis and Shell before coming to the custard factory. Perhaps, as Harry Underhill had said the day before, the world of advertising was genuinely cut-throat and relatively small.

"Would it be possible to meet him?"

An unspoken question passed between Lydia and Mr Lemmings, but really, they couldn't refuse.

"I'll go and retrieve him."

"Please don't tell him the police are here," Smythe stated smoothly.

"Of course," Mr Lemmings agreed, but he also offered them a parting glance before he left the room. Lydia followed him out, leaving them alone.

"Well, it can't be him," Sam stated with frustration.

"No, it clearly can't."

The fact had them all reconsidering their assumptions. From the single piece of paper Lydia had presented to them, it was clear Simon was far too young, born after the first murders had taken place.

"Damn and blast," Smythe complained, standing to pace from one side of the office to the other.

"I just felt sure," the superintendent muttered to himself.

"Yet, there must be some connection," O'Rourke commented, and Sam stared at her in surprise.

"It can be no coincidence. The similarity is there. We can't just give up because this one fact has stumped us."

Sam grunted his agreement, and even Smythe stopped his frustrated pacing.

"You're right, O'Rourke. You are. Yes, let's see what sort of character this Simon possesses. There has to be something there. I'm sure of it."

When the door opened again, the young man following behind Mr Lemmings, Sam felt more composed. He just needed to determine the right questions to ask. He wasn't going to leave without learning all he could about the designer whose drawings seemed so similar to the dead children's poses.

Simon looked at the people waiting for him with alarm, and Sam detected a flicker of unease in his eyes. It immediately aroused his suspicions. Yet, he couldn't deny that most people would be surprised to walk into a room with three members of the police waiting for them, especially if they could read the stripes on their arms and know that both a superintendent and a chief inspector were part of the party.

"Hello," Smythe took command of the situation.

"My name is Superintendent Smythe, and this is Chief Inspector Mason and Constable O'Rourke. We just have a few questions with which we hope you can help us. Please, take a seat."

Simon, his hazel eyes wide with indecision, looked from Mr Lemmings to Smythe, unsure what to do. Sam detected that the man had clearly arrived in clean clothes that morning but that already the cuffs on his white shirt showed faint black marks, perhaps of charcoal, and there was a bright pink stain running over his knee. His shoes were also splattered with specks of paint.

"Please, take a seat," Smythe repeated, and Simon did so, slinking into the seat vacated by Lydia. The fact Lydia hadn't returned made Sam suspicious that she might be trying to contact Mr Owl.

"Shall I stay or leave?" Mr Lemmings asked his question directed to his subordinate.

"I think you should stay," Simon exhaled, his words light and breathy. Sam noted that his face was flushed behind his neatly trimmed beard and moustache, and he felt a flicker of sympathy. He'd thought it was just a typical day in the office.

"Very well," Smythe confirmed, inviting Mr Lemmings to sit once more.

"This must all seem quite peculiar to you, but we're hoping you might be able to tell us something about your designs, as they've appeared in the Picture Post. Could you tell us how you chose those particular images?" As Smythe spoke, he looked to O'Rourke, and she quickly pulled two of the magazines from the file she'd laid on the table and placed them before Simon.

His eyes flickered to the two images, the one of a footballer, the ball high in the air, the other of a hockey player, the small ball just out of reach of the hockey stick. The confusion on his face was genuine. Sam already realised that Simon wasn't going to be able to help them, far from it.

"Well," and Simon paused, running his hand through his hair. Sam noticed that it shook and that it left behind white marks. Whatever the designer had been doing before summoned to Mr Owl's office involved a lot of paint or chalk.

"Well," and he swallowed and then met Smythe's keen gaze evenly and began to speak, his words measured and reasoned. "Mr Owl decided he wanted the custard to be shown as healthy and able to help the young people achieve their best, even while there's a war being fought. I decided that the best way to do that was through a series of sketches showing young people succeeding in feats of physical activity. I, well, I made a list of possible sports and then started to draw in shapes and faces. Mr Owl likes the children we use to be smiling and happy."

"That one," and he pointed to the footballer. "I found an image in the archive and used it as a basis. Over the years, Mr Owl has employed some amazing artists. And for the hockey player, well, again, there was an image of the girl in the archive. I can show you if you want to see?" This he offered hopefully, even though Mr Lemmings looked less than pleased at the revelation.

"Come now, Simon, you're telling me this is just a copy of an earlier advertisement?" The news was unwelcome to Mr Lemmings.

"No, no, not at all. I did look through previous campaigns, but I found a huge collection of unused images as well. Don't you know about them?" Simon looked as surprised by the possibility, as Mr Lemmings looked unhappy with the realisation that the images weren't all Simon's work.

For a minute, it appeared the two of them were about to have a raging argument, but then Mr Lemmings recovered himself with some effort.

"Does that answer your question for you?" Lemmings pointed the remark to Smythe.

"Not at all. We would need to see the archive as well, find out more information about the original artist." But Mr Lemmings was shaking his head.

"I wouldn't be allowed to do that, not without permission

from Mr Owl, and no matter how urgent it might be for you to find out the answers to these bizarre questions. Surely there must be something more crucial for you to be investigating. If it's a matter of copyright infringement, then it hardly seems to need the three of you to interrogate one man."

"It really is pressing, and I can inform you, the matter is nothing to do with copyright infringement."

"All the same, it's Mr Owl who will make the decision, not me." Lemmings was determined not to assist them further.

Smythe sighed, quite dramatically, but then stood, all the same.

"Very well. I'll arrange to return when Mr Owl is available and have a discussion with him. In the meantime, we thank you for your assistance. Please don't mention our conversation to anyone for the foreseeable future. It could compromise a significant investigation."

Simon nodded, a look of relief on his face, even as Mr Lemmings twisted his mouth in dismay.

"Good day," Smythe finished, and he stalked from the room. Sam lingered, watching the interplay between the two men, aware that Smythe would be speaking to Lydia to arrange an appointment to return.

It was becoming stranger and stranger, and it had already been an incredibly perplexing and complicated case. And it was far from solved yet.

CHAPTER 13

"**W**ell," it was Smythe who broke the silence between them as they entered the car. "That was not at all what I'd expected." Sam didn't feel he needed to respond to such an obvious statement.

"It can't have been that Simon fellow. He wasn't even born back in 1919."

"No, it's inexplicable."

"It's frustrating that Mr Lemmings wouldn't give us access to this 'archive' about which Simon spoke. Is it possible he's merely been copying something that the real murderer drew? And if he has, then why would the drawings be at the custard factory?"

These were all excellent questions, and yet Sam still had no answer for them.

"Lydia has made an appointment for Friday. It's bloody inconvenient," Smythe mused to himself. At the same time, O'Rourke carefully pulled the car into the small flow of traffic, mainly consisting of buses and trams, and began reversing their earlier journey.

"Is there any way of finding out who they've previously employed?" Sam eventually asked.

"Well, I asked Lydia about that, but she was not forthcoming. It seems that Mrs Babbington and Mr Lemmings have decided they've been as helpful as it's possible to be without involving their managing director."

It was discouraging. Sam had believed they'd been close to finally solving the cases. He knew he'd cautioned himself, but all the same, he felt deflated to be returning to Erdington none the wiser. O'Rourke was silent at the front of the car, hands tightly holding the large steering wheel, and he realised that she must be feeling the same.

What did it all mean?

"We'll just have to wait and see what we discover when we manage to speak to Mr Owl." Sam tried to infuse his warmth with conviction, but one look from Smythe told him he'd failed and failed miserably.

What none of them was expecting was the arrival of Mr Owl himself at the police station the following morning at 11 am. Heavy rain thudded against the roof, and Sam had decided he wasn't leaving the station that day, even if the air raid siren did make one of its now sporadic calls to take shelter.

"The Superintendent wants you," Williams announced to Sam when he entered the back room, and instinctively, O'Rourke stood as well. Sam had no reason to tell her to stay behind. On entering the office, he only just managed not to show his shock.

"Ah, Chief Inspector Mason, this is Mr Owl," Smythe wasted no time in making the introductions, a glint of something that looked like triumph in his eyes, although his tone was modulated.

Although it wasn't that easy to tell, Mr Owl was a man of middling years, perhaps older than Mason. He made a note that he'd ask O'Rourke later on. Mr Owl had a full head of black hair, shimmering with oil, and which Sam hazarded half a hope, wasn't entirely his natural colour. But for all that, he was a pleasant enough looking man, fierce blue eyes watching from beneath furrowed black eyebrows. He was neither fat nor slim, and Sam realised that, whatever his age, he'd not succumbed to the temptation of indulging in excess bowlfuls of sweet custard.

"Good day, Mr Owl," Sam extended his hand to the man, and the handshake was firm and perfunctory.

"I thought it better to get this matter dealt with sooner rather than later. I'm afraid you quite put the wind-up Mr Lemmings and Mrs Babbington. I would have been content if they'd handed you this portfolio."

Sam looked at the large black case that even now rested against the chair leg that Mr Owl sat within.

"It's been part of our stock of drawings for some time, I think about seven years. And what I can tell you is that I bought it at auction. There was just something about the way the artist had drawn the young people that appealed to me. I'd thought we might use it when I was considering changing the packaging for the blancmange, but I changed my mind. I hadn't even made the connection that Simon was basing his advertisements on these older drawings."

"Can you tell us the name of the artist?" Smythe asked, but Mr Owl was already shaking his head.

"No, I'm afraid I can't. It was an auction house in London. I can't remember which one. I'll have the details somewhere. I've asked Mrs Babbington to hunt down the receipt for you. I'll have her send it to you if she manages to track it down. I confess, I can't even remember why I attended the auction in person, but it certainly wasn't to buy drawings. I imagine the artist's estate was being sold off to pay taxes or some such. It's often that way. These relatively unknown artists. Their equipment is worth more than their life's work. A shame, really." Mr Owl had a slightly loud voice, as though perhaps his hearing might have been damaged by gunshot or cannon during the Great War.

"But you can keep them. I have no more use for them, and Simon assures me he's already devised the entire campaign, and so I have no need for them. I hope they help you answer your questions. I'd be grateful if you could keep my company's good name out of any reporting you do. The situation at the moment is perilous enough, what with people having to use their ration coupons to purchase our custard and blancmange. The business will surely fail if there's any hint of a scandal."

"Now, I bid you a good day, and if you do have further questions, please telephone me immediately. Mrs Babbington has strict instructions to track me down, wherever I am, and I'll do what I can to help you."

At that, Mr Owl stood, dipped his head, and made for the door. O'Rourke held it open for him and then rushed to see him out to the front of the station. Sam caught sight of a goggling Jones at his desk and realised he probably had the same expression on his face.

"Well," Smythe glanced from the portfolio to Sam, "let's get these in the backroom and see what we've uncovered now."

Sam hardly needed telling twice. He bent and took hold of the black portfolio, threading one arm one way around the case and the other on the far side so that he could clasp his hands beneath it.

"It's quite heavy," he commented, standing and feeling his back twinge again. He'd regret his eagerness. He should have waited for O'Rourke or summoned Williams.

He didn't expect Smythe to follow him to the centre of their investigation in the back room, but neither was it a great surprise when he did.

By the time he'd worked the strap loose, O'Rourke had returned as well, and it was her gasp of horror that rang through the room as they all glanced at the first drawing.

It was far more graphic than the resultant advertisements that Simon had created. There was no denying that the picture was of the Inverness victim, Esme, or that it was also the basis for the advertisement for custard from which his wife had made the connection.

"Bloody hell," Sam expelled his pent-up breath, turning to check that O'Rourke was okay before turning to the next image. It wasn't like Smythe to be sensitive to such niceties, but it was a disturbing sight. It made a mockery of Mr Owl's sentiment that the children looked so alive in the artist's drawings.

The next image was definitely of the McGovern boy.

"Well, we've found our offender," Smythe acknowledged, but even he sounded shocked by what they were seeing.

"Now we just need to decipher who they actually were."

Sam nodded, words beyond him, as he turned to the next

drawing and the next after that.

It was impossible to deny the meticulous attention to detail, and Sam shuddered. He couldn't understand why Owl had purchased the collection. It was far too evident to him that the drawings had been sketched once the victims were already dead. They were almost lifeless. Neither could he understand how Simon could have found inspiration from them. They were far too morbid.

But of course, Sam reasoned, they'd lacked the knowledge that the drawings had been done of children who'd had their lives taken from them by the artist.

"Goodness me," O'Rourke eventually exclaimed, her voice reflecting the shock. "These are so graphic."

"Yes, they are," Sam agreed. Like Sam and O'Rourke, Smythe was turning through the portfolio, looking at each drawing, and then slowly shaking his head. It was a great deal to absorb.

"What worries me is that some of these drawings are not amongst our current roster of victims."

"No." Smythe's voice was thick, and he paused, coughed and then began again. "No, they're not. I think there are three we've never seen before; there's another football one, a netball one and I think, a rowing one. But we can only work with what we have. If we find the identity of this person, then we can go from there."

But Sam already knew it was going to be difficult. He'd searched on the first drawing for some sort of artist's mark, but there was nothing, well, there was, but it was merely two initials, S and M, two tiny letters in the shadows beneath the corpse. He considered that's what had drawn Simon to the images in the first place; some sort of connection, even as tenuous as it had been, between his initials and that of the original artist.

Sam found the same on the second and the third, and then he pointed it out to the others.

"Some of them don't have it," O'Rourke confirmed from those drawings she'd been examining.

"And some of them do, and I think the style is similar enough that this SM must have drawn them all. I imagine that's how the auction house sold the drawings."

"SM could be anyone?" Sam tugged at his hair in frustration.

"It could be, yes, but the net is certainly closing," Smythe commented, his fierce eyes directed at Sam. "We can't give up now, not when we're so close to solving this. We'll wait for the details from Mrs Babbington."

"Yes, we could do that," O'Rourke agreed, "or we could just take them to Sotheby's. If their art expert is the same person, they would be able to look up the details anyway."

"Why Sotheby's?" Smythe asked.

O'Rourke grinned.

"A man like Mr Owl isn't going to just walk into any old auction house. I'm sure of it. So, it can only be Sotheby's or that other, oh, I've forgotten the name, which is why I said Sotheby's."

"Christie's," Smythe offered. "Then I'm going to send you both to London tomorrow, on the early train. I'll call ahead and have an appointment set up at Sotheby's." Smythe's decision brokered no argument.

Sam groaned at the prospect of another train journey and then brightened.

"We need only take some of the portfolio with us, surely?"

"Yes, just three, they're damn heavy. I can't have you walking around London with all of our evidence. I'll leave it to you as to which ones you take, but I suggest the ones for which we can't yet account." Smythe turned away as he spoke, his gaze resting on the map of Great Britain once more.

"What a bloody mess," he harrumphed and only then left the room.

CHAPTER 14

O'Rourke walked beside him as they exited the train. Sam was not enamoured of the hustle and bustle of London, but he'd managed to overlook the fact that the war still raged. As such, he found the place to be quieter than expected, and as they made their way towards Mayfair, it grew quieter still.

He'd instructed O'Rourke not to wear her police uniform, unlike when they'd visited the Picture Post head office, and so both of them merely looked as though they wore their best clothes, as they came closer and closer to the affluent area in which they'd find Sotheby's.

Smythe hadn't been able to arrange an appointment the day before. The telephone line had been busy all day, causing the Superintendent to curse in frustration before instructing them to make the journey anyway. Auction, or no auction, Smythe had informed them that there was police work to be done, and it was going to get done.

Sam appreciated his superior's support, but it made him apprehensive as they paused before the auction house's large double doors. He hoped Smythe had since managed to make an appointment for them, but if not, he was going to have to offer a great deal of explanation before he managed to speak to the person they were after.

"Well, let's get it done," and he walked forwards and held the door open for O'Rourke.

Inside the door, plush carpets stretched out all around, and a beautiful receptionist, with her hair styled in the latest fashions wearing bright red lipstick, walked directly towards them.

"Can I help you?" She had a pleasant voice, for all she sounded as though she'd been raised at Buckingham Palace. Sam detected iron behind it. She was used to keeping out the riff-raff.

"Good day. I'm Chief Inspector Mason," at his words, her smile faltered just a little.

"You are the people Superintendent Smythe from Erdington police station telephoned about?"

"Ah, he managed to get through, did he? It was impossible yesterday."

"We had a large auction taking place. I'm afraid that all three phone lines were busy all day long. But, we're expecting you, and I've informed our modern art expert that you require some time with him. Now, if you'll come this way, I'll get you set up in an area where you're unlikely to be disturbed."

"Thank you," Sam responded quickly.

He went to follow the receptionist, only to realise that O'Rourke wasn't beside him. He turned and found her, mouth agape, staring at part of the display in the foyer.

"Look at that," she gasped, pointing.

"Yes, it's a piece of needlepoint showing Louis XIV of France," the receptionist trilled. "It's been sold, but we're displaying it for the time being. Please, don't breathe on it incorrectly." Her words snapped with irritation.

"Breathe on it wrong?" O'Rourke mused while Sam shrugged. It was a strange thing to say, but perhaps it made sense to the receptionist.

"It sold for two hundred thousand pounds," the receptionist offered, holding open an opulent door for them, which disappointingly opened onto a room that wouldn't have looked out of place in the dour police station in Erdington. "I really wish they'd keep it behind a screen, but you know, they say they know best. Now, can I get you tea, coffee? Biscuits, and I'll inform Mr Rain at the same time."

Sam asked for tea and biscuits, as did O'Rourke, and then they settled themselves in the chairs waiting for Mr Rain to appear.

It was an odd room, a lone green-leafed plant inhabiting one of the corners. But there were no windows, and it felt cool, too cold as they'd been on a train for close to three hours and had then walked from Euston to Mayfair while the wind had whipped their coats and hats. The train had been delayed, first of all by a signalling problem, and then because they'd had to wait for a freight train laden with coal to pass them.

There was a low table and also a high table, and they sat around it, choosing an end each, with the slimmed-down portfolio between them. Sam stifled a yawn. It had been an early start, and he'd not thought to sleep on the train journey, even though he probably should have done. O'Rourke had buried herself in an Agatha Christie book for the length of the train ride, and he'd had little to do but consider what they knew so far. The solution felt tantalisingly close but also very far away.

"Here you go," the receptionist returned before Mr Rain arrived, and the purpose of the lower table became abundantly clear as she placed the tea tray there.

"It's better to keep fluid away from canvas," she offered, with half a smile. "He won't be more than five minutes," she assured them and then left again.

O'Rourke looked at the teacups, but Sam leapt to his feet first and expertly made the tea before offering a biscuit to her. Perhaps they should have found somewhere to eat breakfast first, but Sam had wanted to get to Sotheby's, just in case Smythe hadn't been able to speak to anyone yet. He would have been frustrated if they'd eaten and then been sent away to wait for an hour or two. How then could they have filled their time?

"Oh," and the receptionist popped her head back through the door, startling Sam. "If the air raid sirens do go off, we've converted the basement to a shelter, not that it's happened for many months now, but it's best to know. Just come into the hall, and you'll see us all making our way downstairs. Not that I think it'll happen, not today, and I always get a feel for these things."

As she went to close the door, Sam heard muted conversation and then someone he assumed to be Mr Rain entered the room.

He was a man of perhaps sixty or so, a full head of hair turned to silver, and with wide crinkles around his eyes that denoted a man who liked to laugh and smile a great deal. His clothes were excellent but dated. Sam knew the type well.

"Good day, Chief Inspector Mason and Constable O'Rourke. I'm Mr Rain, head of art acquisitions at Sotheby's. I understand you need my assistance with something."

"Yes, please. We believe these images might have come from a portfolio you sold about seven years ago to a Mr Owl. We hoped you might be able to tell us about the artist."

"Well, I'm not sure I remember a Mr Owl, but I have no memory for people and names, only drawings and paintings."

O'Rourke opened the catch on the portfolio, and the first of the images could be seen, the one that showed the young girl playing netball, the ball in mid-air, after she'd thrown it. Sam watched Mr Rain, and he knew that the man remembered the drawings with just a swift glance.

"Please, close the portfolio. There's no need to show me more. I remember it well enough."

O'Rourke was clearly startled by the words, but hastened to seal the drawing away, while Mr Rain sank into an empty chair, his excellent humour evaporated on seeing the canvas.

"The portfolio always made me feel quite strange, but we were asked to sell them at auction, and I'm not really allowed to veto these things unless there's a very good reason why we can't profit from such a sale. In the end, I believe the whole lot went for a much lower sum than expected but to be honest. I was surprised it sold at all. Those paintings always looked 'wrong' to me, too posed, too artificial. It was as though the children were unmoving, even while they were shown in motion."

Sam considered telling Mr Rain more but decided against it for the time being.

"And where did they come from?"

"I would need to find the bill of sale. I believe the artist was a Samuel Wickinson or a Middlewick; there was a wick in there. Something like that. It was his effects, I'm sure of it. I believe it came with all of his drawing supplies, sold on as an 'artist's studio.' But there were some strange things in the collection. If I remember it correctly, there was an entire case containing false eyeballs, all different colours, made of glass or some such. And some other items as well. No doubt they were used so that he could draw them. There were at least three different mannequins. You know, wooden bodies, the sort an artist can use to copy the poses. They were made of different woods and varied in size. One could almost be thought of as childlike, the limbs and head so small. I found it most odd, and I didn't sleep well for an entire week. I was pleased when the stuff sold."

"Please don't tell me I was right to be suspicious of the items. I said it at the time, but the Manager was adamant there was nothing wrong with it all. 'Odd,' he called it, but not 'illegal.' Oh, do tell me. I should certainly like to tell the old boy that he was wrong."

"Well, Mr Rain, these do form part of an on-going investigation. I really can't tell you too much, not at this stage, but I can confirm that you were right to be wary of the items."

"Hah, I knew it. Now, if you'll excuse me, I'll hunt out the records and see if there's more that I can tell you. I'll have some more tea and biscuits brought for you." And the man stood, and then shuddered, all the way from the top of his head, down to his feet, as though a swan fluffing out its plumage. "I knew it," he muttered, opening and then closing the door behind him.

O'Rourke looked at Sam with an arched eyebrow, a half-smile on her face.

"Someone is going to enjoy informing their manager of this."

"He certainly is, and I don't blame him. How terrible will they feel when they realise they auctioned the effects of a serial killer? That would make me tremble as well."

Mr Rain appeared a few minutes later on the heels of the fresh pot of tea delivered by the receptionist.

"I remember now," his face was flushed, and in his wake trailed another man. Sam knew without the introduction that he'd prove to be the very man who'd insisted on auctioning off the items. "I spoke with Mr Spinkle, and he reminded me that I had to go to the artist's house. In fact, we both went and performed an appraisal before we decided whether to include the items or not."

"Hello," Mr Spinkle commented, reaching out to shake the hand of Sam and O'Rourke, while the tea tray was carefully placed on the table. "I'm Mr Rain's manager. I've come to see what all this is about, and of course, to help, if I can." The offer of assistance was made somewhat half-heartedly in a light baritone. Sam understood the motivations for what they were. Mr Spinkle wanted to protect his employer and be helpful, but the desire to protect overrode all else.

"These images have come to our attention as potentially relevant to a large case we're currently working on. It's a historic case, I can tell you that, and as such, we need to know as much as we can about the artist."

Mr Spinkle sobered immediately. It was as though he'd reasoned everything out for himself.

"Well, you wouldn't be here for any sort of minor offence, so I'll tell you all I can, and so will Mr Rain. I assure you that Mr Rain was most unhappy about including the items in an auction, I'm sure he'd told you that, but it's not our place to turn down perfectly good items just because of a belief that there was something not quite right with them. But, I confess it was an odd occasion."

On seeing Mr Spinkle joining the party, the receptionist quickly returned with an additional cup for tea and more biscuits. Mr Spinkle eyed the plate of thick shortcrust biscuits with appreciation but continued to talk. O'Rourke was less constrained, but Sam couldn't get to them without reaching over the teapot. He didn't want to distract Mr Spinkle, so he held back a craving for one.

"Now, it was a property close to Cambridge. It was a pleasant enough little cottage, almost charming, to be honest. The gardens were somewhat of a mess, and the windows needed a good clean and the woodwork, repainting, but that was where the pleasantness ended. Inside, there was hardly any natural light, which I found extraordinary for an artist. There was a strange smell in the air. It made me think of too much dust and badly cooked meals. It was before the beginning of the war, so it wasn't as though there was rationing to blame for the poor meals being prepared."

"It was the artist's niece, I believe, or perhaps a niece through marriage, who'd asked us to appraise the contents of the property. I could see why because there were some quite pleasant pieces of sculpture, some marbles, and some stone, and some wonderful watercolours, but it was the contents of the artist's studio that she was determined we should auction."

"Here, I must digress, the studio wasn't actually a part of the house, but rather a separate building, at the top of the garden. I can't believe that the woman had been fully inside because there were some truly frightening sights lurking in boxes and cupboards, but on the surface, it did appear to be a well-stocked studio. It offered some interesting paintings, as well as pencil drawings. The man had clearly been skilled, although he'd remained unknown throughout his life."

"I was convinced there would be a market for the landscape paintings. There was a delightful one of Inverness Castle. Oh, and one of Loch Ness that featured Urquhart Castle from a few years ago. I recognised it straight away from a trip I'd taken between the wars. There were other landscapes as well, a few seascapes, one of Cambridge Castle, local, you see, oh and Cardiff Castle as well, although it took us a while to place a name to that one. Ah, there were other identifiable locations as well, Conway Castle featuring the walls, an abbey church I didn't recognise. I was happy to list all those. There's always a market for such."

"But by then, Mr Rain had begun to search in boxes and crates, and what he found in them upset me greatly. There were some strange items in bottles. They were clearly feet and hands, in formaldehyde, and where they came from, I just don't know. And this really put the wind up me, a small wooden box, a bit like a cigar case, that contained nothing but odd socks."

"What was so strange about them?" Sam asked, leaning for-wards.

"Well, they all looked as though they'd been worn and had been removed carefully and rolled up, you know, the tops rolled into the bottom of the sock. They were stripy, all of them, and I confess, I just didn't expect to find them in the ownership of a grown man. More likely to find them in the lost property box of a grammar school than in a little studio like that."

"And what did you do with them?" Sam had moved his hands beneath the table. He didn't want either of the gentlemen to see how desperately this news thrilled him. He could imagine the socks had come from only one place, or rather, ten such places.

"I don't recall. We only arranged to remove a crate full of sup-plies and another crate with paintings and drawings. The rest we left behind. It really wasn't for us."

"And do you have the address?"

"Yes, I found the bill of sale. Here," and Mr Spinkle handed over a small wad of papers, held together with paperclips. Sam imagined they'd just been removed from an old filing cabinet, and indeed, the documents smelled of old dust, and he tried not to sneeze although O'Rourke did, an embarrassed expression on her face.

He quickly scanned the inventory, having noted the address and name of the vendor.

"You didn't manage to sell a great deal of it then?"

"No, we didn't, sadly."

"And what happens to the unsold items."

"Well, that was strange as well. Normally we arrange to ship them back to the vendor, but we were unable to contact them on this occasion. We sent a cheque in the post for the items that did sell, minus our expenses, of course, and although the cheque cleared a few days later, we never heard from the niece again. In fact, we still have the items, all packaged up and ready to go."

Sam was on his feet before Mr Spinkle had finished speaking.

"Yes, yes," Mr Spinkle held up a hand. "I'll show them to you. If it helps, we can ship the crate to your police station. But first, well, can you tell us more about your investigation. I should like to report to my superior if we are about to become embroiled in a scandal once more. It's not unheard of, unfortunately. There are some strange characters out there, and people do like to profit from forged art and overvalued books."

Sam nodded and slowly returned to his seat as Mr Spinkle reached for one of the pieces of shortbread and bit into it with obvious relish.

"What I am about to tell you is highly confidential, but of course, you can inform your superior. We're investigating what might be a series of murders that took place between 1919 and 1933, all over Great Britain."

Mr Spinkle's enthusiastic chewing stopped almost immediately, his eyes widening in horror.

"Murders. Oh my. We've had fraud and counterfeiting, but a murder. Oh my. I wish I'd listened to you, Mr Rain." This he directed to the other man, who was holding his teacup in a tense hand. Sam worried that he might even crack the delicate blue cup if he wasn't careful.

"You took me into the home of a murderer?" the accusation in Mr Rain's words was easy to hear.

"Do you know anything about the man, other than the niece?"

"Nothing, other than his name. The niece knew nothing about him either. It had been quite a surprise for her when the letter had arrived through the door telling her of her husband's inheritance."

"I believe we'll visit the property as well, see if we can track down the niece. But now, could you show me the crate you still have."

"Of course," it was Mr Rain who stood and made his way to the door. Mr Spinkle was still absentmindedly chewing on his shortbread and shaking his head from side to side. No doubt, he was considering the problematic conversations he needed to have once the police had left.

"Come this way. You can leave the portfolio there. No one will use the room, and I think Mr Spinkle might still be sitting there, anyway." Surprisingly, there was sympathy in Mr Rain's voice.

O'Rourke followed Sam from the room, and he could feel the tension in her clipped strides.

They'd thought they were close to answers when they'd visited the custard factory, only to be disappointed. Now Sam felt the familiar thrill of finding the answer, even if the man, Samuel Wick-something, or something-Wick had died some time ago.

Mr Rain led them through a small door and then into a large room, lavishly carpeted and with a small black dais at the front of it. Sam realised it must be the auction room itself, although there were no chairs to be seen. No doubt they were folded away when not in use. From there, they were taken through a set of double doors and then along an echoing corridor before entering a vast space, so gargantuan it felt as though they were in a cathedral.

"This is where we receive and send out all the items. Most of the items are with us for only a short amount of time. But some linger." As he spoke, Mr Rain walked through a busy area filled with open crates and reams of tissue paper and straw, where a handful of men and women, wearing long brown coats, were carefully checking off items before packaging them. "It's busy, the day after an auction. But alas, we didn't sell as much as we would have liked. Difficult times."

Sam made eye contact with one or two of the staff but hurried to keep up with Mr Rain. The man had a long stride, and O'Rourke was almost running to keep up. He turned to her, considering asking Mr Rain to slow down, but she shook her head. "I'll keep up," she exhaled. "Or I'll catch up if I do get lost."

As they strode further and further away from the hub of activity, the light grew dimmer and the shadows longer. Sam appreciated that it wasn't worth lighting the entire expanse if it wasn't going to be used.

Eventually, Mr Rain pulled to the wall and flicked several switches so that light bulbs noisily flickered to life.

"Ah, nearly there," Mr Rain assured. "Some of these items have been here for longer than fifty years. We really should dispose of them, but, well, they're historical artefacts, and while we don't own them, someone out there does. And we have the room, after all. Every so often, someone does appear with a long-lost bill of sale and claim their goods. I only wish it could happen to me. I'd appreciate suddenly finding I owned an expensive painting or sculpture. I'm sure everyone would," he mused. And then came to a stop.

"Here, it's down this row," Mr Rain muttered, all joviality gone from his voice. "I hope you won't object if I make myself scarce when you open the crate."

"Not at all. And you've already made it clear that it might be unsettling. I'll remember that before I search the contents."

"Yes, I would if I were you. Every so often, I have a recurring nightmare about that house."

As Mr Rain spoke, he was scanning the boxes and crates that lined the row. Some were placed on top of others, and Sam could see no order to it, but Mr Rain seemed to know what he was doing.

"This one," he finally announced when they were about half-way down the row. "It stands alone. I'm not surprised. I imagine that the stores-people instinctively know to stay away from it. Now, will you be able to find your way back if I leave you alone?"

"Yes, and if we do get lost, I'll call out to the employees in the packaging department."

"Very good. I'll leave you to explore while I return to Mr Spinkle. I believe he may be quite worried about his coming dis-cussion with the managing director. I don't envy him. Not at all. Here you go. You might need these."

"My thanks for your assistance," Sam acknowledged, but his eyes were on the crate, the knife and scissors that he'd been handed just waiting to be used. He could see a paper label with the intended address on it, but there was another piece of paper, dirty now and crusted with dust, which explained that the crate hadn't been collected and should be placed in the 'long-term storage' area.

Sam hesitated for just a second and then stepped close enough to open the wooden lid on the crate. It hadn't been nailed down, and that surprised him, but then, he didn't work in the auction trade. Perhaps it was just the way things were done.

"Help me," he asked O'Rourke when the lid was far heavier than he'd been expecting, and she'd caught up to him. Between them, they managed to move it to rest against the side of the crate, and then Sam peered over the side, hesitant, despite the fact he knew nothing too horrific would greet him.

He sensed O'Rourke beside him, doing the same, and then he laughed at himself.

"It's just a layer of paper and straw packaging. Not what I was expecting."

It made it difficult to see what was actually in the crate.

"We'll have to remove it all," O'Rourke offered, stepping back and looking around. "I'll find something to put it in, a box or something." Sam shared her worry about making a mess in the pristine storeroom. Yes, it might be dusty, and yes, things might have been stacked haphazardly, but Sam could sense there was order here. Someone had taken the time to lay the place out to a specific plan, and he wasn't about to disturb it.

"Here," O'Rourke returned with an empty steel waste bin, and between them, they moved aside the protective layer of straw and paper. Not that it revealed a great deal.

"Everything's wrapped," Sam huffed, reaching in to grab a flat parcel and handing it to O'Rourke.

There wasn't a huge amount inside the crate, and most of it was stacked close to the bottom. He pulled out a rounded shape and quickly removed the paper covering.

"A statue," Sam complained, re-covering the statue of a naked woman in white stone, placing it on the floor away from his feet. He then pulled a more rectangular shape from the crate and carefully unwrapped it.

"Another statue," he commented once more, although this time he squinted at the shape. It was of a female figure, although lacking a defined face or hands, as though it had never been finished. It made him grimace. Not to his taste at all.

Only then did he realise that O'Rourke hadn't spoken or discarded her parcel. She'd slumped to the floor and was slowly leafing through what could only be an artist's sketchbook.

"What's that?" he asked, but she didn't respond, and so he moved to stand behind her, looking down as she turned page after page. It was a large sketchbook, A3 in size.

The first image was of a leg, including the foot and ankle. It was expertly drawn, almost life-like, and clearly with only a few sketches of a pencil. The second was of an arm and hand. Again, life-like, although missing any defining features. He was just about to dismiss it as little more than a sketchbook when O'Rourke turned another page, and the face of Anthony McGovern stared at him.

"My God," he exclaimed.

"It's not the only one. There's quite a few that I recognised in here. I started from the back by mistake."

"So he had, what, a practise sketchbook?"

"Yes, but, well, Anthony is smiling, and Robert seems to be laughing, and well, there's one of Esme crying. I think the children were alive when he did these."

Sam's blood ran cold at the words.

"I always just assumed he killed them straight away," he admitted.

"I think we all did, but perhaps not."

Sam shook his head, a lump in his throat, making it difficult to speak.

"We'll need to take that back with us. It's important evidence. I'll see if there's any more."

He turned aside from the sketchbook, only to swivel once more and gently prise it from O'Rourke's fingers, to place it on the ground to the side of them both.

"Enough of that," he said softly. "Even hardened police officers will struggle to look at those smiling and distressed children." He noticed the tears quietly streaming down her shadowed cheeks, and he felt compelled to lay a comforting hand on her shoulder.

"I won't say you shouldn't look, and I won't dare say it's because you're a woman. But I will say that those images disturb me, greatly. We can't un-see what we've seen, but we can try not to dwell on it, even while we use the knowledge to solve this terrible series of crimes."

"Of course, Chief Inspector," but her voice was thick with sorrow. If there was time for a cup of tea, it was now, but there was the rest of the crate to search first. Sam appreciated that if he walked away from this task, he'd struggle to return to it.

Resolutely, he searched for more of the sketchbooks and pulled not one but three likely looking parcels from the depths of the crate. He opened them to assure himself that they contained images of his victims and set them aside. He wasn't about to sift through them now. That would be done back at the station.

Sam also ran his hands over the odd shapes that remained but quickly realised they were all statues as well. Sam carefully unwrapped one of them, but it was merely another naked torso, this time, a male one. It seemed the artist had enjoyed surrounding himself with the human form.

Other than the three new sketchbooks, and another five statues, there was little worth in the crate aside from an artist's paraphernalia of blank canvasses, easel, brushes, and a multi-layered box that contained paints and brushes.

Carefully, he returned the packaging materials to the crate, and with the aid of O'Rourke, who still looked drained from her initial discovery, managed to replace the lid.

"Now for a nice cup of tea," he promised O'Rourke, as they walked in silence back through the stockroom. He noticed the packers' interested faces but shook his head slightly, stopping them from asking questions. He felt weighed down with the new knowledge he carried. There was a relief in knowing the case would be solved. Still, there was also the dawning realisation that for all these years he'd hoped Anthony hadn't suffered or been aware of what was happening to him, he no longer carried that assertion, and they'd have to share it with the family who still lived.

CHAPTER 15

S mythe met them at Birmingham New Street railway station with the police car which he'd evidently driven there, himself.

"I need to see what you've found," Smythe offered, but there was an intensity to the gaze that made Sam appreciate that his Superintendent was not quite the non-nonsense fellow he always appeared.

Darkness had long fallen, and Sam felt as though the day had lasted for twice as long as usual. Every part of him ached, not just his back. His head was pounding; probably from all the tea he'd consumed. O'Rourke had spoken little, but she'd offered a few small smiles when he'd tried to speak with her. He wasn't going to treat her with kid-gloves. No, she was a police constable who, like him, had discovered something unsettling about human nature that day.

They'd both recover, but he doubted that would start until they'd been able to draw a definitive end to all of the cases they knew about, perhaps even discovering more along the way.

Sam had telephoned Smythe from Sotheby's to inform him of their findings. Smythe had been his usual taciturn self, promising to send a car to collect them from the 3 pm train rather than make them take the tram back to Erdington because they now carried the four heavy sketchbooks as well as the portfolio from Mr Owl. Sam hadn't expected Smythe to drive the car himself.

"I've informed the Chief Superintendent of your discoveries. He's going to inspect everything tomorrow morning, and then we'll determine how we move from here. If the man is dead, as seems to be the case, it'll be both a blessing for the families and a disappointment. But, we need to ensure everything is proved, incontrovertibly. We need to be able to tie all the cases together and discover if there are others. It'll be a huge task, but for now, we need to acknowledge how difficult the case has been and how unsettling it all is."

It was a long speech for the Superintendent, and the words were a comfort, although Sam struggled to find a way of responding.

"To the station," Smythe quickly stated, as though he'd not expected a response, and O'Rourke settled in the car beside him. It was an unusual arrangement. Normally, she'd be the one driving. Between them, the four sketchbooks and the portfolio seemed to occupy a considerable amount of space. They were as silent as the rest of them, but they promised answers and horrors that Sam had never expected to see in all his years with the police force.

There was little traffic on the road. It had been a bitterly cold day, and of course, there was little petrol to spare with all the rationing, even for the police cars, ambulances, and fire engines.

Sam hefted the sketchbooks as soon as they arrived outside the station and strode through to the back room without pausing to speak to anyone. Luckily, Jones had finished for the day, but Sam also carried the conviction that Smythe had warned the rest of his police officers about the burden of their task.

With the overhead lights on, Sam went to unwrap the sketchbooks. Mr Spinkle had eagerly agreed that they could take the sketchbooks without even looking at them. Sam had insisted on leaving a receipt with him. He didn't want there to be any problems with the evidence later on. Especially as Smythe had since heard from Mr Owl's secretary, and she'd confirmed that it had been Sotheby's auction house who'd sold the portfolio. And that was as it should be. Everything needs to tie together.

"You can just leave them there," Smythe instructed when he entered the room, O'Rourke behind him. "I'll look through them now. What I need from you both is an idea of who the drawings represent."

"I think when you see them that there'll be no doubt in your mind," O'Rourke stated, her voice wobbling a little.

"Perhaps," Smythe stated, and Sam watched him carefully, noticing how the man seemed to reconsider his suggestion, only to open the first sketchbook and visibly shudder. It gave him some small comfort to know that he'd not overreacted.

"I think we have Anthony, Robert and Esme in the first book, as well as some unknowns. I've not looked in any detail at the other books."

"We'll do that now then," and Smythe pulled one of the other books toward him. He opened the first page with hesitation, and Sam wasn't surprised.

"I don't know who the girl is," Sam commented quickly. On the second page, he gasped with recognition.

"That's the Berwick Upon Tweed boy, William."

"And that's Geoffrey," O'Rourke confirmed."

"And that's Deirdre." Sam could hear the fatigue in his voice. Smythe closed the sketchbook with a resounding thud.

"And in this one?" he asked.

"That's Frederick on page one," O'Rourke confirmed.

"And Mary and Gerald," Sam confirmed.

Smythe's movements were slower now, the tension clear to see on his face.

"And finally."

"Well, that's Ivy, but I don't recognise the other male," Sam confirmed. Smythe closed the sketchbook, which was empty after those two drawings. He turned to gaze at Sam. O'Rourke had taken a seat, her hands clasped tightly to the surface of the table, as though she needed to hold on to keep upright.

"What I want to know, if possible, is if we have the first victim, what was his name, I forget?"

"Geoffrey," O'Rourke quickly provided, her eyes scanning the map before them, and to which Smythe had his back turned.

"So we do have him, then?

"Yes, Geoffrey is in the second book we looked at."

Smythe fixed him with a firm stare, no doubt hearing the exhaustion in Sam's voice and noting that O'Rourke was struggling as well.

"You've both done more than enough. That's why I'm here. I'm thinking of bringing in some specialists in the area, but I've discovered that there is no specialist for such a crime. The Chief Superintendent's told me to do whatever needs to be done and to ensure you keep fit and well, both of you."

At that moment, the door opened, and young Roger appeared with a tray of tea and a cheerful grin. The lad had only just joined the police. He was filled with enthusiasm for even the most mundane of tasks, even at this time of night. Just looking at him made Sam feel old. He'd known his father, his grandfather as well. It didn't seem right that Roger should be old enough for a proper job.

"Here you go, guv," and he slid the tea tray down onto the table nearest the door. He sought out O'Rourke, and after grinning widely at her, so much that Sam suspected all of his white, gleaming teeth were visible, he left the room. Sam couldn't help but smile. He remembered being that young, but he didn't remember being quite so carefree. It was a knack he didn't think he'd ever possessed.

After a few minutes of flicking through the pages, Smythe spoke.

"These are most disturbing," he confirmed, coughing to clear the thickness of his throat. "I think I need a cup of tea," and he closed the sketchbook and moved to pick up one of the mugs. Roger had chosen the thick, heavy mugs, and Sam could see the mud of the tea, so strong he knew he might regret the taste, even as he spooned three sugars into the swirling mixture.

Smythe slurped his tea, turning to peer at the map on the wall.

"The railways or the roads," he offered, startling Sam.

"Pardon?"

"He made use of the railways or the roads. I'll be curious to know what he used. I'm leaning towards the railways. Everywhere he went was on the main train line. If he'd come into Birmingham from Cambridge, he would have been able to reach every destination without too much trouble."

"Well, we might determine that when we visit the property," a task that Sam was not looking forward to, not at all, especially having seen the impact it had had on the men from Sotheby's.

"Yes, we need to find all the answers, all of them." And Sam detected the menace in Smythe's voice. It was clear even he wouldn't be happy until they'd resolved all of their lingering questions.

CHAPTER 16

"The first task of the day must be to check that this fellow is actually dead. I've placed a call to the Registrar General in London. I've given them the date of death, his name, and his address, as we now have it. They said they'd get on to it, but I'm not sure how quickly they'll be able to track down the record, what with everything going on right now. And, if it was all those years ago, they've probably archived the things." Sam had barely walked through the door of the station, and he still wore his coat. Glancing at Smythe in surprise, he noted the telephone receiver in his hand.

"Now, I'm going to contact the Chief Superintendent and invite him to see the evidence. I want him to see what we have before we involve the Cambridge police. When O'Rourke arrives, you two need to have a good sort through, make everything as obvious as possible. Those drawings, the details of the deaths, and of course, the adverts that tie the drawings to the children, and vice versa, the invoice from Owl and Sotheby's. Make sure it's all nice and tight, easy to decipher."

Sam opened his mouth to decry the necessity, only for Smythe to start speaking into the receiver.

"Chief Superintendent, it's Smythe here. Erdington, sir." Exasperation rippled through his good cheer. "The old case from 1923. This could be it. The breakthrough we need, but I need you to see it all first."

A pause, while Smythe energetically nodded his head, and Sam slowly backed into the main office door, keen to be away from the bright-eyed and keyed-up superintendent. It was clearly going to be another long day.

At the last possible moment, before he disappeared inside, O'Rourke swung open the front door, bringing with her a blast of cold air, her face bright with exertion. Her chin immediately bobbed upwards as she caught sight of Smythe, eyes wide, and only then Sam. He beckoned her through quickly, and she skipped across the tiled area while Smythe continued to speak to the Chief Superintendent.

"What's that about?" she asked as soon as they were ensconced in the back room.

"The Chief Superintendent, and he's been on the phone to the Registrar General already this morning. He wants to check our murderer is really dead. I hadn't considered that, I must admit."

"What time did he get here?" she arched an eyebrow as she spoke in a voice that was little more than a whisper.

"Goodness only knows. He's zealous. I can't deny it."

"What do you suggest then? We really can't get much more obvious than it already is," and she indicated the tables filled with information, the map on the wall in front of them, with the pertinent facts on white pieces of card.

"We'll put together a one-page summary for each case and then place it next to the drawing and the advert. I know we know it all, but it makes sense. We want this to be as clear as possible. And, we'll do it in chronological order. No point starting at the end, or even with Robert, not when we know so many went before him."

She grimaced at the tedious task allotted to them, and he chuckled softly.

"It'll keep us in the warm all day," he consoled. "I hear there's been a case of grave robbing in the cemetery, or perhaps not robbing, but a disturbance, shall we say. Someone else will get to spend the day canvassing those who live close by to see if they can find the scoundrel who did that to the war graves."

"And speaking to the vicar. You know how he can talk?" Sam nodded, pleased to see that O'Rourke was prepared to play along.

He imagined that if she was like him, the only focus was on getting to Cambridge. But there was much to do before that.

"If this goes well, I'm going to ask if we can summon Hamish back to Erdington. Without his help, we wouldn't be where we are. I think he should see all this, see what his drawings revealed to us."

O'Rourke laughed as he spoke, turning to hang her coat over the back of a chair, removing her hat with a sign of relish.

"At some point, you'll have to take the acclaim for this. It was you who pursued the case. It was you who gathered together all the right information to bring an end to it."

Sam grunted at her words, and her laughter pealed around the room, but she held her tongue.

"Okay, so first of all, there's the 1918 case, Geoffrey."

"Yes, I've got the file here," O'Rourke called to him, standing before the table filled with the information they'd obtained from Cambridge thanks to the assistance of Chief Inspector Willows (retired). Sam shook his head. Even now, he considered whether the Cambridge force would have made any sort of connection between Geoffrey and the other murders. He doubted it.

"What was his full name again? These surnames bedevil me." Sam had a plain sheet of paper before him, with the name Geoffrey written at the top.

"Geoffrey Swinton, date of birth 1st July 1900."

Sam's head swivelled up at that, his hand faltering.

"And he died on the 1st July?"

"He did, yes. Poor soul." Sam hadn't made the connection before. He swallowed away another swathe of grief.

"Poor parents, and his poor uncle as well."

"He was found at the playing fields that belonged to the Higher Grade School, just off Queen Edith's Way."

"What was he wearing?"

"Um, well, he was beneath the rugby posts. Let me see." Sam waited. He couldn't remember either but was sure it would be detailed in the notes.

"Here it is. It lists his clothes. He had on rugby boots, long black shorts, a white and red striped jersey, and socks. Well, one sock. Just the one. It was black and white, striped."

"Did they find anything else with the body?"

"Just the rugby ball, which they said belonged to his uncle."

"Hum, and was there any other connection to his uncle?"

"Only that he was the last to see him alive."

"But the cause of death was drowning?"

"It was, yes. They say that the uncle killed him in the river and dragged the body to the sports field, hoping no one would realise he'd been drowned. Also, I don't know if you read this part; the uncle would inherit the estate if his nephew died. So, they had him with a decent motive as well."

"All the same, shoddy police work to have a man hang for a crime he didn't commit." Wisely, O'Rourke held her tongue, even as Sam flicked a glance at her, and appreciated that she was studying the file Cambridge had sent to them. No doubt, she wanted to see if there was anything else.

"You know how we have those initials found in Inverness, on a cufflink?" she eventually asked.

"What about them?"

"Well, what do you make of this?" and O'Rourke passed a photograph to him. "Look, there?" and Sam did as he was bid.

"What's that?"

"It looks like a tie pin to me, and see, faintly, you can make out the initials S and M on it."

"Blasted thing. How did they not realise that was there?"

"Well," and again, she had her nose in the file. "It looks to me as though they did but dismissed it. They took it away with the body but never thought to find out to who it belonged."

"It seems to me that should have been followed up and quickly. I wonder if that's why he moved so far away for the next victim, Cambridge and then all the way to Inverness."

"Seems highly possible. I imagine, when he realised the tie pin had been lost, he must have worried he'd be caught, and pretty quickly. Maybe it made him more cautious?"

"Or more arrogant," Sam mused unhappily, considering all

the murders he'd committed since.

"Just think of all those lives that could have been saved," O'Rourke stated unhappily.

"So, we have Hamish's drawing and the advert for the rugby player. Just look at how similar it is. Yes, the face has been altered, made to look younger, no doubt to fit with the other drawings, but even the missing sock is the same."

"We do, yes. Here you are," O'Rourke stated as she passed both items to him. She was shaking her head with unhappiness. Sam thought how easy it was to bring everything together, now they knew the answers.

"What shall we do about the art in the sketchbook?"

"We'll number the books and the pages, and then they can refer to them. I don't want to take the sketchbooks apart."

"Right, I'll do that."

"Make them book A, B, C and D. So, he was in Book B on page 4. We can put the images from the loose portfolio next to the corresponding advert and Hamish's drawings. We can't make it much more obvious than that."

O'Rourke chuckled at his dark tone.

"I take it you don't think much of the Chief Superintendent."

"I don't know the man," Sam felt compelled to qualify.

"But you've heard stories about him?"

"I have, yes. They're not very kind about him. I should probably wait until I meet him before I make a decision."

"Perhaps, but knowing what you do, we should ensure we make these connections patently obvious."

"Yes, it'll be worth it to get his agreement and support. So, who was the second victim?"

"The second is Esme McDonald, in Inverness, the one Hamish informed us about." O'Rourke squinted at the map as she spoke. Sam stood and moved to the table, holding all the details.

"Date of birth, 12th December 1911. Date of death, or rather, her body was found on April 4th 1919, at a school again, this time the Inverness Royal, on Crown Road. A hockey ball was found close by, as was a set of cufflinks and a handkerchief with the initials S.M on them. They thought it was a teacher to start with, but again, no one was ever arrested for the murder. They did get the cause of the death correct, drowning." Sam reeled off the facts. Esme's case was almost as familiar to him as that of Robert's. O'Rourke quickly wrote down his words.

"No arrests. It seems they were too busy trying to contain the problems caused by the American soldiers attacking the police that evening. Poor Esme."

"And here, this is the image that Hamish drew, and there's an image of her, crying in sketchbook A on page five, and then this, the advertisement. At least she's smiling in it," Sam spoke aloud.

"Chronologically, it's Robert next," Sam stated when O'Rourke had finished with her notes on Esme.

"Robert McFarlane, date of birth, 7th of August 1916. Date of death, 30th September 1923, cause of death was drowning, and he was found in the church hall on High Street. Never really any suspects."

Sam nodded along with her words. He was sorting through the advertisements, looking for the correct one.

There it was, the advertisement with a smiling boy playing cricket, bat high in the air, hat jauntily on his head. Quickly, he found the image from Sketchbook A on page four, once more noticing the similarities. Then he hunted out Hamish's drawing as well.

"You know," he'd not realised that O'Rourke was behind him. "If you didn't know better, you could almost accuse Hamish of being the one who produced the drawings." A startled gasp escaped Sam and O'Rourke nodded knowingly.

"I'm just playing devil's advocate," she reassured hurriedly, realising how much she'd surprised him.

"Yes, but you do have a point. Maybe we shouldn't show Hamish's drawings alongside the ones we've discovered from Sotheby's and the custard company."

"I really don't think the Chief Superintendent will accuse Hamish. Not with all this other evidence. And of course, Hamish has never had his drawings turned into advertisements for the custard company."

"No, no, you're right. I'm just seeing problems where there aren't any," Sam offered hastily.

"You're probably right to be cautious," O'Rourke mollified, and Sam knew he was looking for problems where there weren't any. Not really.

Mason shook himself, wanting to dispel the worry.

"Ivy Reynolds is next. Date of birth 17th March 1918. She was found on 29th June 1925 in the sports ground that belonged to St Luke's College off Magdalen Road at 6.30 am. It was ruled death by misadventure. There was never any mention of drowning. But, well, the file was the smallest of them all. You get the impression that no one cared that much. She wasn't from the most affluent area of town. Posing her as though she was riding a horse was a mockery. Poor girl. Poor family."

O'Rourke wrote as he spoke. Sam found Hamish's drawing and then the matching advertisement in the 18th November 1939 edition of the Picture Post.

"She's in Sketchbook D, on page 1," Sam continued. All of the cases upset him, but there was something about Ivy's that enraged him. So little care for her and her family. It shocked him to think that the local police had been so callous. The fact that there were no paper cuttings from the local newspaper made him realise it might not just have been the police who hadn't thought it worth investigating properly.

"And so to Anthony McGovern," O'Rourke recited the details quickly. Anthony's file was familiar to them both by now.

"Born 18th May 1919, body found on the 6th October 1926, in the Women's Institute's gardens on Walliscote Road. The coroner ruled it as an unlawful death, a drowning, again. He was only wearing one stripy sock when he was found."

"The sketch is in book A, on the third page, and," Sam paused. "Here's the advertisement, from the 30th September 1939 edition and Hamish's drawing." He gazed at the image from the sketchbook. They'd not had police photographs to look at, only the ones from Cyril Rothbottom at the Weston Mercury. Seeing the drawing brought Anthony to life. It was unsettling to real-ise just how talented the murderer had been. Had it been easy for him to kill these children, or had it been a compulsion that tormented him? The desire for such answers plagued Sam. It pushed him even though the case was, to all intents and pur-poses, solved.

"The next one was quick, after Anthony," O'Rourke mused. Sam's head snapped up to the map, and he eyed the date.

"Only four months later. That's not like him. Usually, the gaps are for years, not months."

O'Rourke nodded unhappily.

"It makes me worry that there are other cases we don't know about, even now, after all, we have two unknown images in the sketchbooks that we have, one in sketchbook B and one in D."

"Hum," Sam mused. "It does beg the question as to why. But we'll never know. Not now."

O'Rourke's hooded eyes returned to her note-taking while Sam read from the report.

"Born on 25th December 1919. Body found on the 2nd February 1927. Poor family," he couldn't help but add. "Every Christmas Day since then must have been torture for them."

O'Rourke's silence filled the room, and Sam had to clear his throat before he could continue.

"Gerald Brown's body was found beneath a layer of snow. He'd been missing for nearly a week. They only found him when the thaw started. This time they ruled it as death by misadventure. They assumed he'd been caught out in the snow and plunging temperatures and not managed to make it home. Especially as he was only wearing shorts and a shirt."

"Again, no crime photographs because the doctor decided he died from hypothermia. But here's the advertisement, and Hamish has produced this image from the notes taken by the police sergeant who was called to the scene, a Davydd Davies. The chief inspector was down with influenza at the time, or so it says. It was Inspector Davies who contacted us. Said he couldn't miss the similarity now he'd been alerted to the other deaths."

Sam kept his tone light. After all, who was he to criticise another? Even so, it would be a heavy burden for Davies when the truth was known.

"It seems to me that it's another one where our killer got away with it because the investigation was lacklustre, to say the least," O'Rourke grumbled, although Sam didn't miss the sorrow in her sharp words.

"The drawing is in Book C, on page five."

O'Rourke sighed heavily. "It doesn't get any easier, does it?"

"No, it doesn't. We have to take solace in knowing he's dead and gone, and no one else will die at his hands."

"Perhaps, but if there are more cases that come to light, it'll still feel as though he's out there, enjoying himself if that's why he did it." She shivered as she spoke. Sam swallowed heavily. O'Rourke made an excellent point.

"Mary Thompson was found in Watford on 15th November 1928 by her older sister, Polly. She was born on 3rd May 1920, so one of the older children. Unfortunately, Polly ran to her mother on finding her sister unresponsive. Her mother then rushed to help Mary. They thought she might still be alive. She'd only been missing since the day before. The body was entirely disturbed by the time the police were involved. All the same, the report states that Polly had commented her sister was in a strange crouched position, both arms above her head."

"Hamish produced a drawing that we matched to this advert of a girl weightlifting on 11th October 1941, and again, to sketchbook C, page three. It's a bit of a stretch to make the connection with the details after the police were involved, but the fact that she only wore one sock makes it a certainty, in my mind, at least."

"What was the coroner's verdict?"

"Death by misadventure. They didn't even do an autopsy. The body was unmarked. It had been a cold night."

"Only the third female victim," Sam mused.

"Yes, for this occasion and the choice of weightlifting, it would have been perfectly acceptable if he'd decided to pursue only males," but there was no real bite to O'Rourke's words.

"It was a risk, going to London," Sam ruminated.

"Yes, and no. The greater risk was going to Watford. It's far less built up there."

"You would have thought someone might have noticed."

"Apparently not. It's as though he was always hidden. Not once has he even appeared as a suspect. Family members, or people close to the victims, but not strangers."

Sam held his tongue. It was good that he and O'Rourke had the same opinion about the murders. But then, hindsight was a wonderful thing.

"And so to Glasgow. Deidre McGregor, date of birth, 6th August 1922, was found on Glasgow Green, close to Montieth Row, on 14th September 1929. The cause of death was determined to be drowning. While it made sense that she'd drowned, the river was close by; no one could decipher how the body had made its way away from the river or even why it hadn't been found sooner. It was hardly hidden from view."

"There was a year-long investigation into what had happened. The city's parents were in an uproar, but again, they found no answers, and eventually, only the father was asking for answers. And he died five years later, and since then, it seems that no one has even picked up the case file, not until one of Deidre's friends, who happens to be in the police force now, read your alert."

"Deidre was found with one leg extended far behind her, one arm far in front, and her head slightly tilted. The police photographs make it seem as though she's dancing. Hamish drew her as well. She's in Book B, on page seven."

Sam paused and glanced at O'Rourke.

"Are you thinking the same thing as me?"

"Perhaps," there was hesitation in her voice, so he took pity on her.

"The victims are spread across these books, in no discernible order. It must mean that these aren't the only drawings he made of them. He must have continued to draw and copy from his original drawings, and we've not found those yet."

O'Rourke gasped at the announcement, her face pale.

"That's a terrible thought. But," and O'Rourke paused. "It makes sense, I suppose. Unfortunately."

"Do you want to take a break?" Sam asked because she did look quite unwell.

"No, no, it's fine. I just. Well, do you think we'll find the original drawings?"

"I would hope so. If they were also dated, as I know some artists date their work, it would seal the case even more."

"I suppose I've just become so used to thinking of them in the adverts, smiling and playing, that I don't want to consider how frightened they must have been. Or how twisted the artist truly was."

"I agree. When we go to Cambridge, we're going to need to be prepared for it all to be so much worse than everything we've already seen."

Sam still considered calling an end to their morbid quest through the murdered children, but they were so nearly finished that he decided against it. Better to have the task completed than have to return to it later that day.

"Frederick Anderson was found on 23rd January 1930, by Conway Castle, opposite the railway line. He was found by a police sergeant called out to a disturbance at the castle. What he found was more horrifying than he could have hoped. Frederick hadn't even been reported missing. His family believed him asleep upstairs. They had quite the shock when the police knocked at their home."

O'Rourke scribbled away as Sam spoke.

"His date of birth was 17th April 1922. The cause of death was never fully determined. Some said that he must have fallen from the castle ramparts, but there were no marks on the body, and once more, he was placed strangely. The doctor determined that it must have been a head wound. The police sergeant said it could only have just happened because he was still warm to the touch even though it was freezing. It seems the fact he was wearing only his school uniform and no coat raised no alarm bells."

"Again, Hamish's drawing makes sense of it all, legs wide apart, arms flung back behind him. It's so obvious that he's been posed as though performing a long jump. I just can't ignore it."

"So, another one where there was no suspicion of foul play."

"Yes. At least they did take photographs, and even in those, you can see that his lips are blue. Even I know he was drowned, and I'm no doctor." Sam spoke with fury, and O'Rourke wisely held her silence. He breathed deeply, fought for calm, and then offered half a smile.

"Sorry, it seems this is unsettling both of us. Anyway. Hamish drew him, and here's the advert as well, from 13th January 1940. And his image was in Book C, page 1."

O'Rourke wrote as he spoke while Sam once more felt his eyes drawn to the map.

"I can't believe he got away with it, not somewhere like Conway. It's so small," O'Rourke spoke conversationally.

"It does seem to me as though sometimes the risk of getting caught was more than half of the appeal."

"So, you're saying that just killing the children and drawing them wasn't enough?"

"Absolutely. Or maybe, he tried to stop but couldn't and became more and more reckless in the hope that he might be caught. It's impossible to tell without being able to speak to him."

O'Rourke considered his words, her eyes flashing from the map to the notes she was making.

"Come on, let's finish off. I need a cup of tea and something to take my mind from all this."

"Well, our last victim, that we know off, was William Smith, date of birth, 5th April 1924. He was discovered on 15th January 1933. He was found on the cricket pitch off Pier Road in Berwick upon Tweed. It was ruled as death by misadventure. Hamish has drawn the lad. He has his legs wide apart, one arm in the air. I would say he was throwing the cricket ball."

"Bowling," O'Rourke mused. Sam smiled at the correction.

"Yes, bowling. The wrong time of year to be playing cricket, if you ask me." And she raised her head from the pile of papers and grinned at him.

"His drawing is in book B on page two."

"Are we going to say anything about the other two images and not knowing who they are?"

"I don't think we need to draw attention to the fact that there are even more unsolved cases out there. I think that'll be obvious enough. Or at least, I hope it is."

"Then, we'll just lay out all the items, and we can leave it for the Chief Superintendent to draw his own conclusion."

"Yes, I think we need some fresh air and to be away from all this, for now, at least."

"Thank you," O'Rourke's words were soft, and she kept her eyes focused on her feet.

"I should be thanking you. You've supported me through all these terrible stories of lives cut short. No matter how much I wanted to solve the case, it never wanted to be in such a way."

O'Rourke met his eyes then.

"I know, Chief, but, well, at least now, a lot of people will be able to grieve properly. Everyone needs answers, even to the most horrific of questions."

With that, she stood and turned to the door.

"I'm going to sit in the sun for a bit with a mug of tea."

"I'll be along in a few minutes, and then I'm locking the door, and neither of us is allowed back in, not until we need to show off our house of horrors."

Sam stood and placed the final magazine image next to Hamish's drawing. He cocked his head to one side, appreciating just how good an artist Hamish was all over again.

Without those drawings, his wife would never have made the connection to the custard adverts. And then all these cases would still be unsolved. It was all such happenstance, but however it had happened, he was pleased that he'd been there to witness it all."

CHAPTER 17

They arrived in a convoy. Smythe had deemed it worthless to simply go by train to Cambridge. He'd decided that whatever they found there, whatever it might be, would be brought to Erdington police station. The back room was no longer the preserve of Sam and O'Rourke. Now there was a steady stream of men and a few women who'd been sent there by the Chief Superintendent. Everything was to be categorised in a certain way. There was to be order from the chaos of the lost lives. The work that Sam and O'Rourke had completed had been deemed 'adequate.' Sam had tried not to take offence. After all, whether it was 'adequate' or not, it had still solved ten murder cases.

"Nearly there," O'Rourke spoke, her words jolting Sam from his deep thoughts. He came to and stared out of the windows, mud-encrusted by now. It had rained heavily for at least half of the distance, but now it was just brown and black mud as far as the eye could see. He was glad he'd brought his wellingtons with him. It had been Annie's suggestion, and one he'd thought was a bit over the top, but he'd thank her now.

"We'll be met by the Chief Inspector from Cambridge, along with his team of officers. We'll be going through everything carefully." It was Hamish who spoke, his Scottish accent a counter-part to their duller ones.

"Yes, if there's any of it still there. His niece, if that's who it is, might have emptied the place." O'Rourke had become increasingly despondent on the journey.

"She might yes, or it might be abandoned. No one has been to see because Smythe didn't want to give away what we're about."

"Smythe, he surprises me," O'Rourke admitted, her voice hesitant to make the admission.

"He's surprised me too. I just thought he was a pencil pusher, but evidently not."

"I almost expected him to come with us," Hamish laughed as he spoke from his place in the rear of the police car. He didn't seem at all concerned that some might assume he was the one under arrest.

"I think he would have done if Superintendent Hosean had decided to get involved," Sam stated quickly.

"Here we are," and the police truck they'd brought along for the occasion rumbled to a stop in front of a picturesque cottage, close to the road, but up a slight hill. Trees shielded the property, and Sam felt a shiver of apprehension down his spine. What would they find, if anything, hidden away inside the house?

"It looks empty," O'Rourke commented, opening the door and jumping down, only to land with a soft squelch. "Be careful," she called next. "There's mud up to your blinking elbows down here." She sounded like a city person, her distaste evident to hear.

Sam nodded, swallowed down his unease, and joined her while Hamish had to struggle through the row of front seats to exit the truck. Sam could hear the other vehicles pulling up behind them, twisting their way along the country road, which seemed as deserted as the house. They were hardly quiet.

He looked at the property. Perhaps, on a day less grim than this one, it might have looked inviting. But the looming grey clouds, and his knowledge of the person who'd once lived there, drove away any enjoyment he might have taken in the small rock garden snaking to the front door and the clean, white net curtains hanging in the bay windows.

"Do we go in?" O'Rourke asked. Hamish seemed content to wait for someone to tell him what to do.

"No, we have to wait for the others," Sam stated, peering along the road, in the direction from which he thought the Cambridge lot might appear. In the distance, the land gently undulated before falling flat. He could see a river, murky with the mud that must have poured into it from the torrential downpour. "It makes little sense. I mean, if there's anyone inside, they'll have seen all the cars pull up. They'll know something is going on, but we have to work together with the locals on this one."

O'Rourke sighed softly, and Sam shared her frustration, even though he didn't speak. Hamish didn't have quite the same restraint.

"It's always the same. You solve the case, and some other bigwig wants to take all the glory."

Sam agreed with him. What, after all, had been the point in ensuring they arrived at exactly noon if Hosean and the Cambridge officers weren't going to appear then?

By now, more of their fellow officers had joined them, six altogether. They were officially under the command of Smythe, but their loyalty was to the Chief Superintendent, and Sam had his reservations about them and their motivations. Yet, if he was honest with himself, he wasn't in this for the glory. No, he wanted to solve it and absolve Fullerton from his failure, even if the man had been dead these last few years.

"Do they still observe local mean time in Cambridge?" Chief Inspector Roberts from the Birmingham station tried to joke, but there was an intensity to his words that assured Sam he was just as annoyed with the late arrival as he was.

"Aye, it's thirteen minutes behind in Inverness," Hamish stated, and O'Rourke smiled. Sam was pleased the other man had been allowed to come with them. Otherwise, it might have been far too gloomy a proposition

"All that bloody arguing about time and they're not even here," Roberts continued, only for an aggrieved, female voice to penetrate their conversation.

"Here, what are you doing on the road? There'll be an accident." Sam turned surprised eyes on the woman, making her way down the steep drive. She was about thirty years old, Sam decided, not unattractive, for all she was tightly wrapped in a drab brown cardigan, hair beneath a grey coloured scarf, but with a look about her, that brokered no arguments.

"Good day," he stepped to intercept her. "My name's Chief Inspector Mason. My officers and I are on official police business."

"That's as maybe," she stated, her fierce grey eyes peering along the road, "but you'll cause an accident, mark my words."

"Mrs ?" Sam left the question hanging.

"Mrs Middlewick," she quickly replied, her lips tightly pursed as she crouched beneath a mackintosh she'd thrown over her shoulders, the glimmering sky promising more rain yet.

"Is this your home?" he asked, indicating the house.

"Yes, it is. Why?"

"Would you mind if I came inside and spoke to you?" he diverted her. He didn't want to have this conversation on the road, and certainly not when other, curious eyes were starting to appear from the line of cottages that hugged the road nearby. One young lad had even scampered onto his bicycle, so he could peddle quickly to determine the cause of the commotion. Damn the bloody Cambridge branch. Why couldn't they have arrived on time?

Sam noticed with relief that Hamish turned to divert the bicycle rider. He could hear the lilting tones of the Scots man as he spoke to the boy.

"What is all this about?" Mrs Middlewick demanded to know, but Sam, with O'Rourke at his side, began to walk towards the open front door, offering her nothing but the option to follow them.

"If you would?" he stated, and Mrs Middlewick was swept along with them, Roberts behind them all. Hamish and some of Roberts' people staying to divert the curious.

Mrs Middlewick stepped inside the open doorway, turning to glare once more at the line of police cars headed by the lorry O'Rourke had driven, her face a mask of unease. Sam hesitated, finding he had to force himself to cross the threshold of the home that had sheltered a fugitive from justice for so many years. It hardly mattered that the killer was dead.

But, he needn't have feared. He could tell straight away that Mrs Middlewick had altered the house beyond anything Mr Rain from Sotheby's had described. It was light and airy, a cheery fire warming the front room. It seemed they'd disturbed Mrs Middlewick at her lunch because a sandwich, made with thick-cut bread, sat waiting on a side table, a cup and saucer gently steaming, a book left open on the table close to the window. No doubt she'd been reading it when they'd arrived.

"Mrs Middlewick, I'd advise you to take a seat. What I'm about to tell you may disturb you."

Again, the hesitation, but she quickly sank into her chair, hands on her knees, as she sat slightly forward, coat discarded although her shoes remained in place.

"I'm investigating a series of unsolved crimes which have taken me from Erdington to Sotheby's in London, and from there, to here. It concerns,"

But before he could finish his sentence, she spoke, her voice cold and filled with fury.

"My husband's uncle."

"Yes, it does." Sam felt his forehead furrow. Could it be possible that Mrs Middlewick knew of her uncle by marriage's depravations? Certainly, he'd expected her to faint away at the thought of being associated with some horrific crimes, and if not, then to argue vehemently.

"Very well. You'll want his studio, at the top of the garden, and not the house. I've left the studio as I found it. I've been waiting for you to come ever since I saw the items in there. I had my husband contact the local police with my concerns, but of course, they ignored them."

Sam felt his eyes bulge at the admission.

"I was sure that some of the items he had must have been illegal, no doubt from smuggling or some such. When the police refused to act, I had Sotheby's come and value them. It was a disappointing return on the sales, but at least it removed the items from my proximity. All those naked statues he liked to collect and then draw. A strange man, not that I ever met him, I've only been able to make my decisions based on what he left behind after his death. I wish he'd had the time to get rid of some of the more unsettling items before his death. It was hardly a surprise for him. The doctor warned him he had only months to live."

"Then I apologise for the extended delay in responding to your report. I can assure you, we'll now conduct a thorough search of the studio, and I apologise for any inconvenience caused."

"Just be careful where your vehicles are parked," Mrs Middlewick worried; her concern more about that than what the police had come to find. "I've witnessed two terrible accidents in my few years here. Motorcars are dangerous when driven too fast along country lanes designed for horses and carts and not roaring engines." She finished on an exclamation of horror. Sam could only imagine what drove her fears. He worried enough about cyclists and buses on the main road in Erdington. Here it would be even worse.

Mrs Middlewick settled back in her chair, moving to resume eating her sandwich, and Sam stood and looked out of the window. He could see that the Cambridge lot were finally starting to arrive, Hamish speaking with them.

"Please, if you have any questions, ask to speak to me, Chief Inspector Mason, or my constable, O'Rourke, here, or Hamish, the Scottish one."

"Very well." Only she stood again and moved her hand along the high stone mantlepiece. "You'll need these to get inside. No one's been in there for seven years. I dread to think what it'll be like."

"Thank you," as he gripped the copper coloured key, Sam felt the tremor in her hand, and he offered a smile. This wasn't her fault, not at all, and yet, she would have to live with the stigma of the revelations when they came. He felt a moment of remorse for her. When casting dispersion, people often forgot that the family weren't responsible for the actions of the individual.

The neighbours were already curious enough. What they'd be

like when everything was revealed, he could only imagine.

"What's all this?" A gruff voice greeted Sam's return to the outside world, the clouds hanging ever lower. It was going to rain, and then the mud would get stickier and sticker.

"Chief Inspector Hosean?" he responded with as much politeness as his anger allowed him.

"Yes."

"You're late," Sam said nothing else but began to walk around the house, heading towards the squat wooden building at the top of the garden. It was a steep climb, and by the time he arrived, he could feel his old wound aching. He realised that he wouldn't be able to do much, if any, of the carrying, not and be able to walk easily.

Sam hoped that the Cambridge Chief Inspector followed him, but he wasn't about to check, his eyes focused on the building he could see beneath the reaching growths and blossoming fruit trees that stood starkly in the brown gloom. The years of neglect were easy to see. The brown creosote had started to peel back, revealing the grey of old wood beneath it. It was quite well hidden, and Sam appreciated that Mrs Middlewick had managed to mostly forget about its existence in the last seven years, until now.

He took the key and tried to insert it into the chunky padlock that sealed it. Only it was so rusted, he almost couldn't force the key into the mechanism. For a moment, he struggled with it, cursing himself for not thinking to bring some oil to ease the movement, and then the key snapped.

"Bugger."

"Here," and Roberts stepped forward, making use of a huge pair of clippers to snap the lock free.

"Thank you," Sam muttered, once more pausing to ensure he was ready for whatever they might find inside.

He pulled on the door, and for a moment, he thought nothing would happen. Only then it gave with a shrill shriek of outrage. The smell hit him first, the unmistakable scent of heat and damp and trapped air. Mrs Middlewick was surely right to say that no one had been inside for seven years.

The curtains had been closed, and only a thin beam of daylight slipped in between the gap between them, a second flood of muted light from the open door.

Sam flicked his torch on, and O'Rourke promptly sneezed.

O'Rourke's torch joined his, and standing in the doorway, they both flashed the beams over the space before them. Nothing untoward jumped out at them, and Sam shook himself and stepped inside, taking a careful path to open the distant curtains wider. Then he turned, curious to see what was there, and was startled by a loud gasp from O'Rourke and Hamish both.

His eyes flashed to O'Rourke's and then to what had attracted the attention of his constable and Hamish.

In front of them, illuminated by the weak sunlight, was a considerable canvas placed on the wall. It had to be almost life-size, if not bigger, the frame, golden and flashy. The eyes peering from the massive artwork left Sam in no doubt if he'd had any, that they were in the correct place. Anthony McGovern stared down at them, or rather, laughed at them, his young face flung back, exposing his neck, caught in mid-flight as he chased a black and white striped ball in front of him, the image so realistic, it could have been a colour photograph.

Sam coughed, cleared the sudden thickness that settled in his throat, the sorrow at the knowledge of what had befallen Anthony weighing him once more. Hamish's eyes didn't leave the painting. Sam thought he was probably deciding how good an artist the killer had been. Only then did Sam give Roberts and Hosean an indication that they could continue their work.

"We need to find out all we can about him," Sam muttered to O'Rourke and Hamish. O'Rourke nodded distractedly, whereas Hamish was still gazing at the painting, one hand almost reaching out to touch it, only to hover there, as though he couldn't bring himself to disturb the dust on the frame.

"We do, yes, but what will we do with that?" Hamish asked, but Sam had turned aside. He couldn't bear to look at it. So much life, stolen from Anthony, all so a man could take pleasure in it. It sickened him.

It felt as though a flood of police officers rushed through the door behind them. Sam was buffeted from side to side and watched with a strange detachment. Twenty years of his life had been spent trying to track down the murderer of Robert McFarlane, and yet he still felt unsettled. He might have answers, but they weren't the ones he wanted, not yet. Knowing who had done it was different to understanding the why of it all.

Sam walked through the studio, trying to get a feel for the man, little more than a name, trying to understand what had driven him to commit such terrible acts of cruelty.

"I think you should see this," O'Rourke spoke softly at Sam's ear, directing him to a far corner of the studio. It was as though Sam had walked into the storage area in Sotheby's once more. The wooden crates on show were smaller, as they lined the far side of the studio, covered, most of the time, by great swathes of heavy fabric, but they had the address labels pasted onto them, the writing in bold ink, and Sam swallowed his unease.

"What are they?" he asked, but O'Rourke remained quiet, deciding, instead, to show him. Sam turned to look for Hamish, but he hadn't moved from his position close to the door.

Sam was right to fear as he peered into the three crates that O'Rourke and Roberts had already opened.

"He sent these items to himself?" Sam shook his head, unease making him wish he had some water to drink.

"That's what it looks like," Roberts stated flatly. Sam admired the man for being able to keep his tone so neutral.

"There are more than ten of them," Sam winced as his voice squeaked.

"Yes, there are. The three we've opened are the more recent ones, from 1931, 1932 and 1933. They all seem to contain the same items, a large white towel, gloves, a set of dark clothes, no doubt worn whilst the murder was taking place, and this," Roberts held out a half-used bottle of bubble bath.

"So we're finding out how he did it, then?" Sam spoke because he needed to do something normal to restore his composure.

"Yes, he was clearly very organised and had a set way of committing his crimes."

"He took a risk in sending these to his home, though."

"Yes, but it was probably all part of the thrill for him. To see if he could get away with it and then see if he could continue to get away with it. All these years, just waiting to be discovered, should someone come into his shed."

"Yet, they've not been opened before now, not as far as I can tell," Hamish commented. He'd finally arrived beside them and had been there long enough to understand the object of their conversation.

"Maybe he was ensuring he left nothing behind to identify him," O'Rourke mused.

"That as well," Roberts nodded in agreement. His eyes were shadowed, although his voice remained even. When Sam had first met him, he'd not thought Roberts understood his need to solve the murders. Now, he realised that the man had the same desire, and more, it wasn't due to a personal connection with those killed, but rather a craving to ensure justice was done, no matter what.

"Sir," a strained voice broke the silence.

"What is it?" Roberts spoke with his subordinate.

"We found these," the officer held up a black leather book, his head turning to take in the fact that there were others on a bookcase in the far corner.

"What are they?" Roberts demanded to know.

"They're his diaries. They show his movements. He kept meticulous records."

Sam took hold of the book, surprised by its heft, only to realise it was the knowledge inside that weighed him and not the book at all.

"It's for 1923," Sam commented, opening the book and flipping through the pages.

He came to September and slowed his perusal. The killer's hand was firm, and Sam startled when he was only on 5th September, and he realised the killer was already in Erdington.

More slowly, he paged forward. The records were detailed, but of course, they made no mention of Robert McFarlane, but rather only of someone's movements, evidently Robert's. On the 25th of September, the entry simply read, 'I have chosen.' For the next five days, there was nothing written, until on 30th September it simply said. 'It has been done.'

Sam wanted nothing more than to fling the diary to one side, but it was far too valuable. While it didn't mention Robert by name, it showed that the killer had been in Erdington on the required date. Especially as on the 1st October, the entry stated, 'returned home. Work to do.'

"They go all the way back to 1913," Roberts' man continued.

"1913?"

"Yes, and they stop after 1933."

"A twenty-year period," it felt too long, far too long for Samuel Middlewick to have gotten away with murder.

"Box them up and have them shipped with everything else. But make sure they're easy to find. The diary entries will need to be cross-referenced with the dates we already have," Roberts gave the order, but Sam agreed. "And make sure there's one for every year. I don't want to have one missing."

"Sir," the constable moved to perform the task, picking up one of the empty boxes that had been brought for such a need. Sam turned once more. Everywhere he looked in this terrible room, there was something that tied the artist to the murders of the children, from the crates to the drawings and paintings on the wall. Hamish had wandered away, and now he peered carefully at every mounted image he saw.

Sam wasn't surprised that Mr Rain had felt uneasy with the task given to him. A pity he'd not been firmer in his desire to have nothing to do with the sale of the goods.

"But why did he even start?" Sam was desperate to know. What, after all, had driven the killer to take such terrible actions?

"I think Mrs Middlewick can help with that." Sam realised then that Roberts had left the studio, and conversational voices could be heard from outside.

"Here, Mrs Middlewick has made us tea," Roberts offered as Sam stepped to join them. It was a relief to be out of the shed, and he'd only been in there for a few moments. Roberts had half a smile on his face as he sipped at a delicate white china cup, birds in flight covering it. "And I've been asking her about her uncle by marriage."

The woman attempted to smile, but it was clear she was upset by what was happening as she hunkered inside her coat, sensible wellingtons on her feet. Sam grimaced at the dankness, but at least the rain had stopped.

"I never knew him, you must know that, but my husband did tell me about him, for all he only met him once or twice when he was growing up. There was a family rift or something. Samuel Middlewick refused to have a great deal to do with his parents or with his brother. I got the impression he was quite a bitter man. It was a huge surprise when we inherited this house. It's nothing like where my husband grew up. This is much finer and in a beautiful location. I could never have expected to live somewhere like this. It is beautiful."

"What did he tell you?" Sam tried not to rush the words, but he was desperate to understand.

"He said his uncle had a commission, in 1912, a profitable one, where he was paid enough money never to have to work again. It pleased him. He'd been a book-keeper before but hadn't enjoyed the work. He'd wanted to be an artist, but his father wouldn't allow it. He said all men needed a 'proper' profession."

She paused, forehead wrinkling.

"From then on he, I understand, or rather my husband did, that his uncle painted and drew and travelled around Great Britain a great deal, but never saw his father again, and his brother, my husband's father, only once a year. Samuel made it a point to bring the most expensive gifts he could, much to his brother's chagrin. My husband loved it, of course. He wouldn't have owned the things he did if it hadn't been for his uncle." Her words revealed unease.

"He bought this property with his windfall. I always thought it strange that he had so much money and purchased somewhere so small and out of the way. He could have lived in London, easily, perhaps with all the other artists, but no, he settled here, away from everything and everyone. He didn't even have a car."

"Do you know what the commission was for?"

"I don't, and neither does my husband, I'm sure of it. My husband said he never spoke about it other than in a vague way. A rich family, well, a very rich family. I believe he might have been forced to sign something that promised he would never speak of it again."

"And he died in 1933?"

"No, in 1936, early that year. We received the letter in November, I believe. It took the solicitor a long time to find my husband. We were living in Inverness then, with my family. Tell me, what did Samuel do."

Sam paused, his eyes flicking to Roberts before he decided how to answer.

"I'm afraid your husband's uncle was a murderer. He killed at least ten people, spread out over many years, all over the mainland of Great Britain."

Her hand fluttered at her throat, face draining of all colour, and yet Mrs Middlewick stayed standing.

"And you can definitely prove all this?" Sam admired her presence of mind to ask such a question.

"We will, in good time, and we're nearly there now, for a number of the murders. Tell me, do your husband's parents still live? Or does he have any other aunts or uncles?" But Mrs Middlewick was already shaking her head.

"No, there were only ever the two brothers, and my father in law died during the Great War. There's no one left for you to speak to about Samuel, I'm afraid."

"It's lucky that he kept such detailed records then."

"Yes, it is," but her eyes were on the boxes being taken from the studio, a look of dismay on her face.

"My husband will be most upset," she breathed.

"And where is your husband, if you don't mind me asking."

"He's fighting for our country. I understand that he's currently based in Italy."

"And do you have someone who could come and stay with you?"

"No, I'll be fine. I've been alone for much of the last five years." Her voice was strong, yet she wavered all the same on the 'five years.' Sam nodded at her, his eyes filled with sympathy. She wasn't saying something, but he believed it was about her husband and not the murderer. Sam felt she deserved privacy and decided not to pry.

"We'll warn you before we make any sort of public statement about your husband's uncle. It might be that you need to move away for a while if only to avoid the press and people being curious about it all."

"No, I'll remain here. I have nowhere else to go." Her tone was so bereft that Sam had to look away. She'd mentioned family in Inverness, but it seemed they were no longer living if her reaction was to be believed, and certainly, she didn't share Hamish's accent.

So much grief and sorrow. While he tried to drive some of it away for the family of those who'd been murdered, all he was doing was placing it on the shoulders of another.

It settled uneasily on him. Mrs Middlewick had done nothing wrong other than inherit a house. She'd even tried to involve the police in the past, and they'd ignored her concerns.

"Thank you for the tea," he stated quickly, placing the cup and saucer back onto the tray that Mrs Middlewick still held, albeit slightly limply in her hand.

Returning inside, he walked to Hamish's side. He and O'Rourke were carefully taking frames from the wall, talking to one another as they went. O'Rourke had found herself a clipboard and made a note of the items being packed into the crate.

"They're all different sizes," she was musing.

"Aye, that they are. But I recognise some of the children, all the same."

"Should we list who the drawings or paintings show, or just list them as portraits?"

"Put the name in brackets, or list it as unknown," Sam commanded. "It'll aid us if we know who we have and who we don't."

She nodded quickly, her unhappiness evident, although Hamish was doing his best to chatter on about nothing.

"Mason," Hosean's voice was rigid as he hailed him.

"Is she sticking to the story that she knew nothing about all this?" Mason didn't appreciate the tone in his voice.

"She is yes. And adamant that she alerted your police force about all this in 1936."

"Well, well," and his entire body puffed up at the criticism. "If she did, it can't have been made very clear what it was all about. Otherwise, we'd have hot-footed it over here."

"And what would you have done with all the diaries and artwork?"

"We'd have investigated, of course, solved all these crimes before you did." But Hosean's voice was quickly losing its certainty. Sam almost felt pity for the other police officer, but then he happened to gaze at the shiny boots he wore, still shining despite the mud outside. Sam's boots were more brown than black. Perhaps, he thought, knowing it was unkind, but enjoying it all the same, if Hosean worried less about his shoes, he might have discovered all this many years ago.

CHAPTER 18

"So it's confirmed. We can substantiate that he killed at least nine of our victims?" Smythe was presiding over a meeting in the backroom in Erdington, and it was full to bursting in there with the men under Roberts as well as someone who'd been sent from Cambridge to ensure everything went smoothly. Sam was pleased it wasn't Hosean. He'd had quite enough of the man's incompetence.

Sam was standing close to Smythe, Roberts there as well, Hamish and O'Rourke. She'd been promoted to sergeant in light of what they'd found, and she deserved it.

"Yes, nine of them, we're still waiting for confirmation for the ninth. They're very reluctant to admit a mistake was made with Geoffrey Swinton." Smythe's lips tightened at the explanation, and Sam effected not to look at the Cambridge chief inspector. He wouldn't be the only one. In fact, Jones was glaring at the man. Sam almost liked him at that moment.

"Then, I believe it's time we made a public announcement. It'll be good for morale." Sam held his tongue. It was a strange way to raise morale by announcing that they'd caught a murderer who'd been killing small children for fifteen years, and who'd died seven years ago.

"Before we do so, we'll ensure the families are notified of the developments, and Mrs Middlewick as well, Mr Owl and Sotheby's too. I know we don't know the motivations, but we'll have to be content with what we do know."

Sam had insisted on making the connections himself, between the diary entries and the crates of possessions. It had been one of the most draining experiences he'd ever endured, but the answers he'd been hoping for still eluded him, and no doubt always would.

"I'll speak with Rebecca McFarlane," Sam stated quickly. He didn't want Smythe to do so. He had known Rebecca for years. Smythe hadn't.

He took O'Rourke with him when he went to Bracken Road and knocked on the smart new brown door. This area had escaped the bombings, but other places hadn't been so lucky.

"Good day," he smiled as Rebecca answered the door. She was wearing a pretty dress, in a sensible blue shade, with an apron tied over it and a dusting of flour on her nose. "I was hoping you might have time to talk to me. But you probably don't want to do it here."

"Of course, of course," she repeated, already untying her apron and reaching behind the door for her coat. There was an eagerness in her fingers, even as she fumbled with the key in the lock, and Sam could hear her trying to calm her breathing.

In silence, the three of them walked along the pavement, watching the trams and buses as they made their way along Tyburn Road. Sam winced at yet another near-miss between a cyclist and a bus, but his eyes were taken with the view of the Dunlop Rubber factory far in the distance. It was impossible to miss its vastness. It was impossible to ignore the fact that it was a clear target for the German fighter planes.

"Do you have some news?" Rebecca eventually asked, sitting on a handy garden wall still under construction.

"I do, yes. I don't know how you'll feel about it. But, I'll tell you what we know, and you must tell me if I need to stop."

She nodded, hands folded one over the other on the top of crossed legs.

"Thanks to you bringing me the details from Weston, I was able to find a direct link between the boy killed there, Anthony McGovern, was his name, and your brother."

"It was the same person?" The words were a gasp of horror.

"It was yes, but there's much more, and it's not easy listening. Anthony and Robert weren't the only victims. We've uncovered evidence of ten children who were all killed by the same person, a man."

"Ten children?" Her voice trailed away, her eyes seeming to focus on the past and not the present.

"Yes, ten of them, and we think more, but we can confirm ten, for now. They took place from 1919 to 1933, and the man responsible is now dead. He was an artist, and his name was Samuel Middlewick."

The look of relief on Rebecca's face at the news assured him that not knowing had nibbled at her, just as much as it had him. Silence fell between the three of them, Sam's thoughts on what he'd seen in the past few months.

"So, this Samuel Middlewick killed ten young boys?" Rebecca broke the silence.

"He didn't only kill boys. There were some girls as well." O'Rourke spoke for the first time. Rebecca was nodding, even as her lower lip trembled at the revelation.

"So, it's all over?"

"Yes, it's finally all over. But, I warn you, the newspapers will make a great deal of the discovery. You might find your brother's name spoken about by people who never knew him. And the connection. Well, it was a strange one?"

"You said the man was an artist?"

"He was, yes."

"Tell me." Rebecca's voice had stabilised, and when she asked the question, Sam knew it was time to tell her everything. He told her about the drawings and the custard adverts, and she nodded, eyes shadowed.

"Thank you," Rebecca stood abruptly. "I think I'll go home now, but thank you. I just can't thank you enough." And Rebecca's rigid back walked firmly away from them. Sam watched her, only turning aside when he saw her slump, shoulders shaking, against another wall further away.

"Should we go after her?" O'Rourke queried, worry in her

voice.

"No, she's a strong young woman. If she'd wanted us to sympathise with her, she'd have stayed." And together, he and O'Rourke made their way back to the station. Cambridge was going to inform Mrs Middlewick, and Smythe had spoken to the managing director at Sotheby's and Mr Owl.

Of course, Smythe presided over the press conference called to inform the public and the press later that day. He was dressed smartly, his boots polished, his ceremonial uniform exuding authority.

Not that a huge amount of journalists attended, but The Times sent a local reporter, so too had the Birmingham Mail. Sam stood beside Smythe, wincing as flashbulbs went off, pleased that Smythe was the one making the announcement.

"I've gathered you together today," Smythe began. If he was dismayed by the small number of attendees, he didn't let it show. "To inform you that the mystery of who took young Robert McFarlane's life on 30th September 1923 has been solved."

Sam watched consternation on the faces of the reporters. A further woman had slunk through the doors and made herself comfortable in one of the chairs available. The two men both shared a look of consternation. They were young, and no doubt, neither knew anything about the case, but the woman did. That was clear from the way she sat forward and frantically reached for her notebook.

"The perpetrator was responsible for more than Robert McFarlane's murder. In fact, he was active throughout the years from 1919 to 1933, and we can confirm he killed ten children in total. Geoffrey Swinton from Cambridge in 1918, Esme McDonald from Inverness in 1919, Robert McFarlane from Erdington in 1923, Ivy Reynolds from Exeter in 1925, Anthony McGovern from Weston Super Mare in 1926, Gerald Brown from Cardiff in 1927, Mary Thompson from Watford in 1928, Deidre McGregor from Glasgow in 1929, Frederick Anderson from Conway in 1930 and William Smith from Berwick upon Tweed in 1933. We've produced some information sheets for you," Smythe paused to inform them, a gleam in his eye. "There is rather a lot to take in. We also believe that there were other victims in the intervening years. Anyone with information should please contact the station."

The woman continued to scribble frantically, whereas the two male reporters looked stunned by what they were being told.

"The man responsible, Samuel Middlewick has been dead since 1936. So it pleases me to let parents know that they need no longer fear for their children's lives from that quarter."

Before Smythe could continue, the woman reporter stood.

"How did you make the connections?"

"Ah, now here, I have the endeavours of Constable Hamish Dougall from Inverness and my Chief Inspector Mason and Constable O'Rourke to thank for their hard work. Using old case files, they were able to make the connection between the victims and a series of high-profile advertisements run in recent years. This led us, in a circuitous route, and one which I must stress, assigned no blame to the company involved, to the artist, who had drawn images of the victims."

Sam kept a bland face. He knew that Smythe was being prevailed upon to keep the custard factory out of the limelight, but he really didn't think it would take a great deal of effort to determine to which company Smythe referred. It wouldn't take a genius to make the connection. And when those at the Picture Post heard the announcement, Sam didn't think they'd be shy in sharing the information.

As such, the following day, he wasn't surprised to read 'The Custard Corpses,' even on the front page of the ordinarily reasonable, The Times, with a woman's name as the reporter. It seemed she'd managed to beat her male counterparts to the scoop and had made her case to The Times. He appreciated that Mr Owl would be most displeased about his company being involved in something so scandalous.

"More post for you," Jones' voice reflected his frustration that Mason was suddenly so well-known and so well revered. Sam took the offered packet of envelopes with a heavy sigh. It had been the same for the last few days. He didn't have the time to open every one of the letters, and yet Smythe had made it clear he was to do so. And to be honest, there was a flicker of interest, as well. So much of the case had fallen into place from chance finds and stray pieces of information that Sam knew he couldn't afford to overlook anything, no matter how trivial it might appear.

He grabbed his cup of tea and settled in the only clear corner in the case room. For a second, he glanced at the walls and the charts, every one of them covered in details, facts and information. Just looking at what they'd accomplished so far filled him with pride. Fullerton, if he were alive to walk into the room right this minute, would be shocked. He'd always thought Sam was shoddy at keeping notes and that the idea of order was alien to him. How times had changed.

Sam thought to count the envelopes but thought better of it. Jones, he noted, had already been forced to apply a stamp to the envelopes. It simply said, 'Received', with the date underneath it. There were times that Sam loved the tedious task of stamping the post each morning, but he was sure it accounted for Jones' puckered face. He was not the sort of man to enjoy the monotony that order encouraged.

The king's face stared at Sam from the selection of stamps, depending on the size of the envelope and how far it had travelled. These cases had brought him information from all over Great Britain.

The first letter was little more than a thank you from someone he'd never met or even knew but who'd known Esme McDonald. The words were scrawled over the thin notepaper, and yet Sam felt a lump in his throat as he read.

"Dear Chief Inspector Mason. I am writing to thank you for allowing me to rest easy knowing that I've not lived all my life knowing someone who killed young Esme. She was my friend, but I remember her more for the fear and nightmares I endured after her death. Thank you from the bottom of my heart."

There was that as well. All of these cases, all of them, had created a ripple effect. Children had heard of their friend's murder or even their enemy's murder, perhaps worried for their own safety, but more than that, spent a lifetime reminiscing about someone who'd not lived long enough.

It was the same with the men who'd fought in the Great War. It would be the same for the men and women who fought in this current war and for those who lost their lives in the bloody bombings that had taken place in London, Birmingham, Coventry and other built-up areas rich with industry. Even Weston hadn't been left unscathed from enemy bombs.

Many lives were lost, and so many others left to ponder just what they would have become if they'd lived longer.

He placed the letter back into the envelope, moving it to one side, and picked up the second. His hand pulled out the paper and then furrowed with consternation.

This envelope didn't contain a letter, but rather a copy of one of the custard adverts, with the word 'murderer' written across it in thick, red pen. He shook his head. Why were people wasting their time sending such bits and pieces? He knew all this.

O'Rourke glanced at him from her place to the other side of the room.

"More crackpots?" she asked. Aside from the letters of thanks, there'd also been a wave of letters where others had claimed responsibility for the killings. Sam had no idea why people would do such a thing. When the first such letter had arrived, he'd almost run, sweating, to Smythe's side, only for Smythe to nod, intelligent eyes keen.

"It's to be expected, Mason. I've been warned this sort of thing would happen. For now, keep a close track of them. If you see any pattern, we might need to do something about it, but it'll stop soon enough. Some people just like the thrill of causing uncertainty and chaos. It disgusts me."

"Not really, just this," and he held the advert to her.

O'Rourke's eyes widened in shock as she read the words and then shook her head, long braids flying with the movement.

"I just don't understand it," she offered.

"Neither do I. Such a waste of a good stamp," Sam smiled but didn't feel the joy in his eyes. It was wearisome.

He reached for another envelope, this one larger than the other. He felt a momentary flash of worry as he opened the large, padded envelope.

A slim notebook fell from it. He picked up the package again, checking it was addressed to him, and then opened the notebook. It looked like a diary but was nothing of the sort. Instead, he gazed at pages and pages of thick black lettering, the same words repeated over and over again.

"It was me." He thought that was all it contained, but he came upon what seemed to be a letter close to the back. Sam began to read.

"Chief Inspector Mason, you're wrong. You're so very wrong. You've got the wrong person, the wrong man, the wrong everything. You've made connections where there are none. You've found patterns where none exist. You're a fool, and you'll be made an even bigger fool when someone realises what you've done. I know it was you. You're the murderer. You killed all those children. If you hadn't, how could you know all the details? You're a sick, sick man, and I'm going to make sure that everyone knows it was you. You evil man. Evil, evil man."

"Well," Sam looked up from the notebook, shaking his head and passing it to O'Rourke.

"Take a look at that."

She read quickly, shocked eyes meeting his.

"Oh my God," she gasped. "I can't believe it. How do these people get such ideas?"

"I've no idea. It's worrying, that's for sure."

"Look," O'Rourke had gone to the very back of the notebook. "The damn fool's left their name and address in it."

"Really?" Sam hadn't noticed. "Then I think we might need to send someone round to have a word with them about wasting police time." O'Rourke grinned.

"I'll go and call the local police for," and she peered at the writing, "Kent," and tell them to go and have a little chat with them."

"Thank you," and Sam moved to the next envelope. So far this morning, he'd found nothing of interest. Not yet. But there was always time.

The next letter was thin and small, and he anticipated yet another missive thanking him for finding the killer, or even another letter from someone who'd been affected by the killings. And that was what he found—almost.

"Chief Inspector Mason," the writing was crabbed and hard to read. *"I am aware that you're being lauded in the local paper, in the national newspapers, and even on the radio, but you shouldn't be pleased with yourself. How can anyone be happy with themselves when it's taken over two decades to solve a crime, and so many children were cruelly murdered by that, by that man. You should be ashamed of yourself. It should have been solved immediately. It seems that the clues were there all the time. It merely needed someone with a modicum of wit and intelligence to piece those parts of the puzzle together. It was evidently, not you.*

I saw your picture in the newspaper. You don't look like a clever man. In fact, you look like someone who can't even tie their own shoelaces. And, more, why aren't you fighting in the war, beside men who are more intelligent than you? You claim the spoils for deciphering a series of crimes that should never have lain unsolved for so long, and all the time, you shirk your responsibility to your country's freedom."

Sam sighed heavily. This wasn't the first such letter of criticism he'd received either. He found it frustrating. He'd not done it for the glory or the honour. He'd solved the case because, finally, pieces of the puzzle had begun to make sense. Damn these fools who didn't realise that.

But the letter continued.

"I have looked at the information made available to the press. How anyone could have missed such obvious connections is beyond me, it speaks only of incompetence. I'm disgusted with the whole thing and will be writing to my local MP about the state of our police force and the wasting of our taxes."

Sam didn't even bother to read the name of the person who'd sent the letter. They weren't worth his time and consideration.

"These came for you, Mason," Jones' shouldered his way through the door once more, of all things, a hamper of fruit held before him.

"What?" Sam didn't know how to respond to that.

"There's a card inside. It came in a very shiny delivery van."

"Thank you." He stood to investigate the arrangement while Jones shook his head and left the room.

Sam hadn't seen this much fruit since before the war. Where had they even managed to source it? Not that he wanted to question that too much. No, he wanted to eat it. Still, he reached for the white card nestled inside the fruit hamper and carefully opened the thick envelope.

"Chief Inspector Mason," was scrawled on the outside.

"Please accept this small show of appreciation for solving the murder of my sister so many years ago. It's a stain on my childhood, and one that I'm now pleased to see is finally resolved. My mother also wishes to express her appreciation, although my father sadly died without knowing the truth. The sick and twisted mind of the killer clearly knew no bounds, and I'll never find it in my heart to forgive him, even if it is the Christian ideal, but I thank you, and wanted you to know that no matter the passage of time, what you have done still feels important and immediate to my mother and me."

"Yours Mary McGregor."

Sam nodded as he finished reading the note. He didn't need the attendant gift. He didn't even need the long note. But the knowledge that he'd managed to find peace for yet another of the affected families did buoy him, especially after the strange letters he'd received that morning.

"Where on earth did they find those bananas from?" O'Rourke exclaimed, entering the room with a grin on her face.

"The Kent Superintendent I spoke to was furious," she continued, without pausing for a breath. "He's almost on his way already. He says Bob Davies is nothing but a 'bloody pain in the arse,' and he'll give him 'what's for.'"

"Help yourself," Sam offered, already biting into a bright green apple, and savouring the crispness of it.

"Who's it from?"

Sam explained while O'Rourke determined what she wanted. Her hand kept snatching from one piece of fruit to another. Sam would have laughed if he hadn't played the same game only moments before.

"Wow, I'd never made the connection," O'Rourke's eye widened in surprise. "She's a very famous actress, you know. In fact," and here she stilled, a realisation just hitting her as she swallowed thickly. "Oh my goodness," and she turned aside, reaching for one of the stray copies of Picture Post that littered the room. Sam had no idea what she was about to say, and he was stunned when she flicked through a few of the magazines and then presented it to him.

"We can never tell her," he exclaimed and hoped she'd never find out because there, next to an image of her smiling, healthy face, was the same advert based on her sister's lifeless body.

"Chief Inspector Mason," Jones appeared once more in the doorway, half an eye to the fruit basket. "There's someone here to speak to you."

"I'm coming," Sam stood. "Help yourself," he encouraged the other man. He wasn't petty enough to hoard their unexpected windfall to himself.

"I'll introduce you first and then come back," Jones almost smiled. They snaked between the desks and to the front desk, where Sam could see a woman's back.

"This is Mrs Esme Warburton," Jones introduced them. "She wants to speak with you about the Middlewick cases."

"Good day," Sam peered at the woman. She could be no more than thirty or thirty-five, her auburn hair swept up beneath a black hat, her brown eyes fierce and worried all at the same time. Jones had been reading the Times newspaper report about solving the crimes, and her eyes kept flicking to it.

"I would like to speak to you about the Middlewick cases,

please." Her voice was firm but rigid, and Sam took note that she refused to call them by the name the press had adopted. It gave him some hope that this might be someone who held pertinent information.

"Of course," Sam agreed. "Do you want to come through, or would you rather speak outside?" He offered the second because she was peering uneasily into the gloom of the back offices and then back through the door as though regretting the decision to come inside.

"Outside, please."

"I'll just get my coat," Sam stated, making his way into the main office to retrieve it. He caught O'Rourke's quizzical eye and just shrugged his shoulders. Sam had no idea what the woman wanted. He thought it could perhaps be to discuss another case, but he wasn't all that convinced by that idea. Sam decided this was something else, something else entirely.

"Shall we," and he held the door open for Mrs Warburton, but she shied away from him stepping through the gap, and he felt his forehead furrow.

"There's a pond we can walk to, with frogs and lily pads. Shall we go that way?"

"Yes," was the almost sullen reply.

For all her intention had been to speak with him, not one word passed her lips as they journeyed towards Rookery Park, along Sutton New Road. It was not so much bustling, as slightly busy. People were clustered together, no doubt discussing the details from the newspaper. A few even met Sam's eyes, offering him their respect. It felt strange. He'd walked amongst these people for years and yet never felt as though they saw him as anything more than a man who spent his time digging into people's private lives. It all felt quite different now.

Even his wife had popped into the station that morning, a smile on her face for his achievements. She'd been invited out to morning tea with the ladies from the Women's Institute. She was not at all fazed by the knowledge that the invitation had only been made because they wanted to hear all the gory details of the murders her husband had finally solved.

Sam held his tongue, aware Mrs Warburton would speak when she felt able. His eyes roved around him, noting the buses trundling along the road. It was the time of day when, if you were lucky, you could hop from the open-topped Midland Red to the white and dark-blue festooned Birmingham line, the buses distinctive because they were entirely enclosed. Provided everything ran like clock-work. He noted the flushed face of a young boy on the top of the Midland Red, a harassed and cold-looking woman sat next to him, and he allowed a soft smile. It never grew old, sitting on the top deck, even in weather such as this. He hoped they had a warm fire waiting for them at home.

"Here it is," he broke the silence, directing Mrs Warburton across the road and first onto Church Road and then into the Rookery. The blossom was just appearing on the boughs of the trees inside the park. He had fond memories of the ponds within Rookery, of the frogs and lily-pads. It had been about all a boy could have hoped to see when he was much younger.

Their footsteps sounded loudly on the paving slabs, and still, Mrs Warburton didn't speak, not until they were beside the pond, peering into the green depths, did she say anything.

"I should have been one of the victims," her words startled him, and yet somehow, he'd been expecting to hear them ever since he'd laid eyes on her. After all, she was about the age the earliest victims would have been had they lived.

"Mr Middlewick, he came for me, only I managed to escape. I've tried not to think about it all these years, believing it was a one-off, knowing that no one would believe me. If I'd known. If only I'd known," and a sob escaped her mouth, her hand shooting up to cover it. Sam appreciated then that her taciturn stance was just an attempt to hold onto her emotions.

"You couldn't have known," Sam tried to console, even while appreciating she wouldn't heed his words.

"It was 1916. I was sixteen years old," this startled Sam. Mrs Warburton was older than he'd realised. "I lived in Ely, not far from Cambridge, an easy journey by train. I used to play lacrosse for the local team. I was quite good at it," a soft smile touched her tear-stained face as she spoke. "My family didn't really approve of it. They never came to watch the matches, no matter how many times I won."

"Mr Middlewick came to a few games. I noticed him on the sidelines, and so did the other girls, but no one knew who he was. We all thought he must be there with one of the opposition team players, but clearly not."

"Well, one day, I'd taken a proper whack from the ball, and it caused me to trip over my own feet. I had to limp home alone as I lived on the other side of town to everyone else. No one had a car, and no one offered to help me. I confess I was feeling quite sorry for myself when Mr Middlewick introduced himself to me and extended to me his help."

"I was wary but also upset that I'd been abandoned. I don't think the coach even realised how badly I'd hurt myself. I did turn him down, though, and told him I would be alright on my own. It was June, the day was bright, but not too hot, and even if I had to limp the whole two miles, I knew I'd get there before darkness fell."

"But, he must have followed me. I was so tired, I stopped under a tree for a rest, and I must have fallen asleep. When I woke up, I wasn't under the tree anymore, and my head hurt, and I couldn't work out where I was or anything, and then Mr Middlewick spoke. He was wearing a brown apron, and we seemed to be in a bathroom because his voice echoed as though from tiles. He was sitting on a chair, a sketchbook open before him, and he kept looking at me appraisingly and then adding to his drawing."

"I was frightened and scared and tried to stand up and run away. Mr Middlewick laughed and told me not to worry. Everything would be alright. Once he'd finished his drawing, he'd see me home. He sounded so worried, so filled with concern. Yet I didn't believe a single word he said. I noticed then that there was a wooden tub in the corner, gently steaming with hot water and a pile of white towels. It was terrifying." Here she paused, a sob escaping her mouth as she relieved those memories. Sam's stomach had turned hard at her words. He couldn't quite believe that there was someone still alive who might be able to describe the experience the other children had endured.

"I'd been lying on a rug on the floor, all of my sporting clothes still on, including my muddy lacrosse boots, but the bath gave me pause for thought, as did the strange taste in my mouth. It felt like I'd been to the dentist."

"Mr Middlewick asked me to talk about myself, to stay in the position I'd woken up in, all splayed out, arms and legs to either side of my body, but I couldn't do it. I clutched my legs tight to my body and refused to look at him. He carried on as though it wasn't important at all. Eventually, I conquered my terror and tried to speak to him, asking him what he was doing, but he didn't answer any of my questions. I grew cross. I turned aside, only for a moment, and next thing, he'd moved so quickly and put something over my mouth and nose. I must have fallen asleep again."

"When I woke up next time, I was being lowered into the steaming water, and all my clothes were off. I was horrified, and I fought him. I kicked him and thrust my elbows into his face, into his eyes and then his nose. Although he held me tight, he had to let go eventually because his blood was everywhere from where I'd hit his nose. He hadn't tied me up, so I could keep attacking him. He couldn't keep hold of both of my arms and legs at the same time. He screamed at me, and I reached for the bubble bath bottle and squirted into his eyes. Then I grabbed for my clothes and rushed to the door while I tried to pull on my clothes. I was torn between being seen naked and getting away, stupid, I know."

"I caught sight of him. He writhed on the floor in agony, clawing at his eyes where I'd squirted the bubble bath into them. I stopped and watched him, trying to decide what I could do to him, but I just wanted to escape. Still, before I ran out of the door, I grabbed his sketchbook where he'd left it to the side."

"Here, I've kept it all these years," and Mrs Warburton pulled a familiar-looking black book from her large handbag.

"Please, don't look at it here. Please. And I never want to see it again, either. I don't know why I've kept it all these years, hidden away. Perhaps I hoped it might come in handy." She half-sobbed as she spoke, only to finally look at him.

"And you know, no one at my home even noticed I was late or that I was covered in bruises, my clothes all in disarray."

"And so you kept quiet about it?" He could understand why she'd been so concerned.

"I did, yes. Even with the sketchbook, I was worried people would say it was my fault."

"But it was never your fault," Sam offered softly.

"Thank you. I know that now. But it's taken me a long time to forgive myself."

"I, I wish I'd told someone, then all these other children would have lived."

"There's no guarantee of that. Even now, it's taken all this time for people to realise the connections."

"You're kind to say so, but I know that I should have persisted."

"That way lies madness," Sam offered, wanting to reach out and lay his hand on her arm, but knowing better, after her reaction to him holding the door open earlier. "My old Chief Inspector was bedevilled by the local case. It ruined his life. I think you've suffered enough," Sam stated flatly. He couldn't imagine her guilt but knew he needed to do something to make her forget about it.

"It has certainly affected many decisions I've made in my life, but at least I've had that life to live."

"Did he speak to you about why he was doing it?"

She shook her head.

"He wouldn't answer my questions, so no, he didn't. But there's a picture in there that I think might answer your questions. It's even more disturbing than the drawings he did of me, but please, don't look at it here."

"I won't," Sam assured, although he could feel curiosity gnawing at him. "Tell me, how can I get in touch with you if I had the need."

A flicker of unease on her face, but she straightened her shoulders firmly.

"I live in Tamworth now, so not far from here, Castle View, you can find me there, and now, I really must go. I've left my husband, but I must return to him. He's been invalided out of the navy."

"Thank you," Sam called to her retreating back, but she gave no indication that his words had been heard, her shoulders rigid, her steps sharp.

He stumbled to a bench beside the pond, checking to make sure no one could see what he was doing, and then he opened the sketchbook.

It was identical to the ones they'd uncovered at Sotheby's; only the first page didn't have the face of a smiling child on it, but rather the face of a child with staring eyes and no hint of movement. He swallowed thickly and turned to the next page.

This image contained three children, all of them prone and clearly placed in such a way. Their unseeing eyes seemed to mock him. It was evident the children were dead, all of them.

He tried to determine their ages, perhaps ranging from a seven-year-old up to a seventeen-year-old. They wore similar clothes, a rugby jersey perhaps, the striped colours picked out in two red and yellow shades.

They were one next to another, but there were spaces between them, as though they played different positions in the rugby match. The older child was posed so that he might have been throwing the rugby ball that hovered on the ground beneath him. The youngest child had legs splayed as though running hard, one arm behind their body, the other across it, arched at the elbow as though running. And the final child, aged in the middle of the other two, had arms outstretched as though to catch the ball in the air.

Sam swallowed thickly, immediately thinking that this was another crime scene they'd yet to find or one that hadn't yet made it into their investigation.

Only then, he looked down, noting the date on the picture: 1912 and a name. And the name horrified him and made sense of so much else.

He slammed the sketchbook shut, not looking any further, and hastened back to the police station as fast as his old injury would allow.

The horror of the Fitzpatrick murders had rocked British society for the whole of the year in 1912. And this whole sequence of murders could be traced back to that eventful year. Sam felt sickened even as the realisation that he finally had all of his answers started to percolate his thinking.

Lord Fitzpatrick had killed his children, pretended they'd died of natural causes and created ructions by having a portrait of the dead children produced. It had been hung in the dining room of his house, where all could see and where he could gloat over the crime he'd gotten away with, even while accepting the sympathy of those who'd seen the drawing.

Or at least, he'd thought himself above suspicion. Fitzpatrick hadn't factored in the quizzical nature of the local chief inspector who'd risked his job and his life to bring the lord to justice, the painting of the dead children arousing his suspicions.

Lord Fitzpatrick had swung for his crimes when the coroner had been asked to re-examine the bodies. Great Britain had believed that had been the end of it, but all this time, Mr Middlewick had been re-enacting the very same crime, only with the added atrocity of drawing those children both while they were alive and when he'd murdered them as well.

The answers, now Sam had them, were even more unsettling.

CHAPTER 19

S am took himself back to the station. He needed to show Smythe what more he'd discovered. He huddled deep inside his coat, not meeting the eyes of anyone he met. The day had turned chilly, a sharp wind threatening to drag his cap from his head, and he no longer welcomed the glances people shot his way. His desire for answers had brought him this terrible truth.

He felt both burdened and also free.

All these years, he'd felt the weight of Fullerton's grief at the unsolved case, but, while it had been theirs to solve, it had never been theirs to prevent. The knowledge that such an outrage had occurred under their stewardship had been painful. Sam now realised that he'd carried it with him. Everything, no matter what it was, had been tempered with the feeling of failure.

Now all that was gone.

"Mason?"

Smythe had been in jovial form ever since the story had been plastered across the newspapers and even reported on the radio. He'd taken telephone calls from more than just the police commissioner, but the local minister for parliament, and some even suggested they might receive congratulations from the king.

While Smythe took pains to admit he'd not solved the crimes, Sam knew that wasn't how the rest of his fellow superintendents saw it. To them, it had been solved under his auspices, and that was what mattered. He could revel in concluding something that any of them could have done had they been proactive enough.

"I had a visitor," Sam began when being told to enter Smythe's office with a cheery 'come in'. "I think we've found our first case and also some answers about the killer's motivation."

"I don't believe I truly care about the motivation, just that the case is solved."

"All the same," and Sam slid the sketchbook onto the desk in front of Smythe.

"What's this?"

"Just look," Sam offered, taking a seat and settling to watch his superior's response.

He wasn't to be disappointed.

What began as a desultory skim through yet another sketchbook, head shaking from side to side, quickly became a slow and deliberate examination of the images.

"This just can't be?" Smythe questioned, but Sam heard the resignation and acceptance in his voice, all the same.

Sam remained silent. He knew the impact the knowledge would have on Smythe. After all, it had been Smythe who'd told Sam all about the case when he'd not long become their superintendent. All those years ago, just before the beginning of the Great War, when the country had still been recovering from the shock of the sinking of the Titanic, there'd been another scandal to draw everyone's attention, threatening to force an even larger rift between the different levels of society.

Smythe, a young man at the time, had cut his teeth on the case. He'd been insistent that Lord Fitzpatrick wasn't to be trusted, that there was something else going on, that nothing had been as it had been presented.

Smythe had earned his first promotion from his tenacious resolve to bring Lord Fitzpatrick to justice. The case had made Smythe's career. But Lord Fitzpatrick had murdered only his three children, and in not even considering who the artist had been, who'd brought those dead children to life, Smythe had allowed, alongside his superiors, an even greater menace to go free. In fact, Sam believed the painting had been dismissed as no doubt executed by the disgraced lord, anyway.

Smythe sighed heavily, closing the sketchbook tightly, hands resting on the cover.

"I would never have even considered," he admitted.

"Me neither," Sam agreed, but it left them with a problem, a huge problem that needed solving.

"I'll take this to the Commissioner," Smythe expelled. "It's for me to take responsibility."

"No," Sam stated flatly. "No, I don't think it is. We solved these cases together. That's all that matters."

Smythe's anguished eyes flashed to meet Sam's.

"Why?"

"You didn't make a killer. None of the investigating officers did."

"Perhaps," Smythe stated, but the flicker of hope gave away his need to hear those words.

"The perpetrator of the Middlewick Killings, the Custard Corpses as the papers have taken to calling them, has been identified. The man is dead. The families will, at last, have peace. I won't have that taken from them, not now." So speaking, Sam stood, leaving the sketchbook on the desk. Smythe glanced at it and then at Sam.

"Put it with the archive," he stated flatly. "One day, it might be needed, but that day isn't today."

Sam inclined his head, scooping up the sketchbook as he went. Quickly, he strode to the back room, empty now, apart from an extensive collection of brown boxes, just waiting to go into storage.

Removing the lid from the first box, dated 1919, he slid the sketchbook between the back cover and the sketchbook that was already there. Resolutely, he replaced the lid and allowed his eyes to travel over the remaining boxes. O'Rourke hadn't yet added them all to the archive in the basement, but by tomorrow the room would be devoid of them all, the case solved, and then there'd be nothing else for it.

A new case would beckon, and Sam found the idea appealing.

He'd spent enough of his life trying to solve the riddle of Robert's murder. Now, he could finally move on to something else.

On his way home, Sam stopped beside the graveyard and then decided to walk inside. Fullerton's gravestone was plain and unremarkable, and yet bright flowers graced it. Sam smiled. He knew who brought the flowers, his wife.

Sam settled a hand on the gravestone, feeling the cool of the stone.

"We did it, sir," he found himself saying. "We solved the case of Robert McFarlane. The boy can rest in peace now, and so can you."

He heard gentle laughter then and turned to meet Rebecca's eyes from the other side of the metal fence that enclosed the graveyard.

"I thought I'd find you here," she called softly. "I hope you told the old boy not to worry anymore."

"I have," Sam called, striding closer to the low fence so that he didn't need to shout across the silent place; so that the dead could rest in peace.

"Thank you," Rebecca offered.

"For what, doing my job?"

"For never giving up. That meant a great deal to me through all the years of not knowing."

"A pity it took so long," Sam offered sadly.

"I don't know. I think it might make it easier for me. Robert's killer is dead. I can't hate him or anguish about whether I want him to hang or not. It brings me a sense of well-being. I can get on with my life without ever having to worry that his killer might strike again. Every day, for as long as I can remember, I've scoured the newspaper pages and listened to the news on the radio. Not for the horrors of war, or what Hitler might be up to now, or the Japanese, but rather for the story that he'd taken another life, stolen the future from another family."

Sam nodded. He understood what she was saying.

"Now, he's gone, dead these last eight years, and welcome to it. Hopefully, he's been burning in Hell all that time." Rebecca softly laughed as she spoke, her eyes distant, as though seeing the very sight she mentioned before her. "And at the same time, my mother, and my father, have long been reunited with Robert, and wherever they are, they're happy, together."

Sam found his lips quivering at her words, remorse driving at his resolve never to show his emotion.

"And now, what does the future hold for you?" Rebecca asked Sam, her eyes back on the here and now.

"Back to the usual grime of being a police inspector during a war."

"And your son? He's well?"

"Yes," Sam admitted. "He's healing from his wounds and should be able to return home soon, and then, no more war for him. Not with such an injury. But, men can live with his wounds. It could have been much worse. I count it as a blessing."

"And will he be following in your footsteps?"

"Oh, never that. He has his ambitions set on a far more exciting career than just being a police inspector."

"Then he has my warm wishes," Rebecca insisted. "We all deserve some peace."

"That we do," Sam muttered, but she was turning aside, and Sam watched her wave to a man, further down the road.

"I must go," Rebecca trilled, excitement warbling through her voice.

"Good luck," Sam offered.

"We make our own luck," Rebecca replied. "Remember that," and she was gone.

Sam turned once more to Fullerton's grave, unsurprised to find his wife waiting for him, a glimmer in her eyes, and someone else he wasn't expecting to see. Not yet.

His son stared at him, a hint of defiance on his face, which quickly softened. Sam stared at the handsome man, noting his navy uniform, the long, dark coat that fell beyond his knees, and the hint of metal that glimmered beneath it. He'd fought in a war. He was no longer a child, although he would always be Sam's son.

"Come here," Sam found he could hardly speak, as he rushed to throw his arms around John, mindful of the reddened patches of skin and his half-missing ear on the right side of his face.

For a second, John was rigid under such a sign of affection, and then he melted into Sam. Sam laughed and found tears in his eyes.

"Look at you," he said, standing back but not letting go of him. "Just look how smart you look."

"Well, if you avoid the disfiguring burns," his son tried to joke, although it sounded flat and filled with pain, his voice ragged.

"I'll never ignore them," Sam stated softly. "They're as much a part of you now as my dodgy leg and back are me, but it doesn't change who we are. You will realise that," Sam offered firmly.

He caught sight of his wife's reddened eyes and thought he'd probably said the wrong thing.

"Thank you," John choked, gripping Sam's forearm tightly. "I needed to hear that, and I also wanted to thank you. What happened to Robert has tormented me all these years. You've found the answers I needed. You're ensured I don't have to feel afraid anymore of the same thing happening to me, even though that sounds selfish."

"I think a lot of people will say the same," Sam confirmed, still refusing to let go of his son.

"Well, Sam and John Mason, it seems to me that you might both be wanting an ale in the pub, and then perhaps, something warm and inviting for your tea at home. It's about all the celebrating we can do."

"And that's just fine with me," Sam was quick to respond as he went to his wife's side, dragging John with him. Sam looped his arm so that she could thread her hand between it and his coat.

"I think we've done more than enough police work for the foreseeable."

"Yes, here's hoping there are no other twenty-year-old crimes for you to solve," but Annie laughed as she spoke. "Or rather for me to solve, using those terrible magazines that I read."

Sam arched an eyebrow at her.

"I have a mind to make you some custard," she winked at him, and Sam chuckled while John laughed.

"I don't know if I'll ever eat the stuff again," he complained.

"Oh, you will," she assured him. "No matter what, custard will always be custard."

THANK YOU FOR READING
THE CUSTARD CORPSES. IF
YOU ENJOYED IT, PLEASE
CONSIDER LEAVING A
REVIEW. THANK YOU
IN ADVANCE.

HISTORICAL NOTES

A quick look on the internet assured me that there were female police officers in the 1940s, although not many of them. The number increased from 300 to 385 throughout the war years of 1939-1945, even though police work was deemed a 'man's job.' They might have been outnumbered by the 60,000 men but they were definitely represented. (Source http://www.open.ac.uk/Arts/history-from-police-archives/PolCit/polww2.html).

The Picture Post magazine was a photojournalist magazine that first appeared in 1938 and was issued weekly until 1957. It has been archived and can be accessed here, https://www.gale.com/intl/c/picture-post-historical-archive, although I note it is only available for institutions. You can also find issues for sale on eBay. It's stuffed with photographs, and adverts of the day, and so to the Birds Custard adverts that form the basis for the story. (Wikipedia)

Birds Custard was first formulated in 1837, and the company seems to have gone from strength to strength. They were, according to Wikipedia, one of the first companies to invest in bright and colourful advertising, and indeed, it is just that. I have seen a long series of adverts that they ran, not only in the Picture Post, and they all benefit from a firm design brief, bright colours, happy children, lots of custard. They used the phrase 'every little helps' in much of their advertising. I wanted to bring the adverts to the attention of people who might never have seen them, and also try my hand at writing something a bit more 'modern,' even if the story runs from the 1920s to the 1940s. It is still strange to have characters get into cars and onto buses and trains. I'm just used to writing about horses.

If you would like to see more of these advertising images, then I would recommend googling them and looking on images. They are wonderful to behold. My cover image, brilliantly designed by Flintlock Covers, is a homage to their works of art.

The factory building owned by Birds in Birmingham is still in existence, and has been converted into office space. Again, you can see what it looks like by searching on the internet.

I decided on the main location of this novel, Erdington, because it was where my old granny grew up, and I have vague memories of what it was like, 'back in the day.' It was, it transpires, quite a good choice, and I was quite astounded to discover, that in 1066 Erdington was one of Earl Morcar's possessions (this will amuse fans of my Earls of Mercia series).

Erdington was the first suburb of Birmingham to be bombed during the Blitz. An unhappy coincidence, but one I wove into the story, none the less. I was surprised to discover that Weston had also been bombed, and would thank my Dad for reminding me that the trains from Birmingham travel through Coventry, so I could also mention the destruction that took place there.

It's quite amazing what you find when you look on the internet. I had initially planned for the Inverness murder to take place in May 1919, but when looking for details of local events and the name of the local newspaper, I stumbled on a news report concerning a fight in the town centre between Americans and the police, and felt it was just too good to miss out, and so shifted the murder forward by a month.

I've attempted to name roads and institutions as they would have been at the correct time period. Any mistakes are mine, and I apologise. This book was written during Lockdown 2020/21 and so I couldn't travel anywhere to check and relied on memory, and the experiences of those who had visited places in the past. I am grateful to many websites for hosting old maps which allowed me to look at places as they were in the 1920s, 1930s and 1940s.

Sotheby's really did build a bomb shelter during the Second World War, but apparently, people were not keen to leave the auction room in case they missed out on their bargain.

This story is entirely fictional, bringing together a number of historical resources I have to hand – old maps of the UK showing train routes, the Picture Post magazines, as well as a weird imagination. I hope it doesn't put you off your custard!

MEET THE AUTHOR

I 'm an author of fantasy (viking age/dragon themed) and historical fiction (Early English, Vikings and the British Isles as a whole before the Norman Conquest), and now a mystery set in the 1940s, born in the old Mercian kingdom at some point since AD1066. I write A LOT. You've been warned!

Find me at mjporterauthor.com, mjporterauthor.blog and @coloursofunison on twitter. I have a newsletter, which can be joined via my website.

Books by M J Porter (in chronological order)

Gods and Kings Series (seventh century Britain)
Pagan Warrior (audio book coming soon)
Pagan King
Warrior King

The Ninth Century
The Last King (audio book now available)
The Last Warrior (audio book coming soon)
The Last Horse
The Last Enemy
The Last Sword
The Last Shield (coming soon)

The Tenth Century
The Lady of Mercia's Daughter
A Conspiracy of Kings (the sequel to The Lady of Mercia's Daughter)

Kingmaker
The King's Daughter

Chronicles of the English (tenth century Britain)
Brunanburh
Of Kings and Half-Kings
The Second English King

The Mercian Brexit (can be read as a prequel to The First Queen of England)

The First Queen of England (The story of Lady Elfrida) (tenth century England)
The First Queen of England Part 2
The First Queen of England Part 3

The King's Mother (The continuing story of Lady Elfrida)
The Queen Dowager
Once A Queen

The Earls of Mercia
The Earl of Mercia's Father
The Danish King's Enemy
Swein: The Danish King (side story)
Northman Part 1
Northman Part 2
Cnut: The Conqueror (full length side story)
Wulfstan: An Anglo-Saxon Thegn (side story)
The King's Earl
The Earl of Mercia
The English Earl
The Earl's King
Viking King
The English King

Lady Estrid (a novel of eleventh century Denmark)

Fantasy

<u>The Dragon of Unison</u>
Hidden Dragon
Dragon Gone
Dragon Alone
Dragon Ally
Dragon Lost
Dragon Bond

Throne of Ash (coming soon)

<u>As JE Porter</u>
The Innkeeper

<u>Mystery</u>
The Custard Corpses

ACKNOWLEDGEMENT

I would like to thank my father for sharing his memories of Erdington with me, and for adding the sort of little details that make a book feel so authentic. And equally, for giving me the inspiration to write this book in the first place – it's amazing what can happen when presented with some period advertising!

I would also like to thank my team of beta readers, CS, CH, ST, AM and EP. You all help me in so many ways, and I'm grateful for your candour and support.

I would also like to thank my cover artist – Flintlock Covers – for bringing the cover to life in just the way I wanted.

And my readers and followers – thank you for encouraging me and being there on a day to day basis.